"Jean Pierre Michel wanted everything. Cars, clocks, cloaks, pianos, horses, houses, racing yachts, swimming pools, aeroplanes. To money itself he was indifferent; he spent no Scrooge-like hours stacking up coins, and he gave away prodigious amounts to hospitals and universities. There was one thing Jean Pierre Michel desired that could not be purchased in a shop. It was not entirely triggered by the pumice moon, yet the pumice moon had helped him to articulate it. Jean Pierre Michel wanted the moon, but, more than the moon, he wanted a son...."

Also by Michael Golding

Simple Prayers

BENJAMIN'S GIFT

BENJAMIN'S GIFT

MICHAEL GOLDING

WARNER BOOKS

A Time Warner Company

This book is a work of fiction. Names, characters, places and incidents are either the product of the author's imagination or are used fictitiously, and any resemblance to actual persons, living or dead, events, or locales is entirely coincidental.

Copyright © 1999 by Michael Golding
All rights reserved.

Warner Books, Inc., 1271 Avenue of the Americas, New York, NY 10020
Visit our Web site at www.twbookmark.com

Ⓦ A Time Warner Company

Printed in The United States of America
Originally published in hardcover by Warner Books, Inc.
First Trade Printing: April 2000

10 9 8 7 6 5 4 3 2 1

The Library of Congress has cataloged the hardcover edition as follows:

Golding, Michael.
  Benjamin's gift / Michael Golding.
    p.   cm.
  ISBN 0-446-52110-8
  I. Title.
  PS3557.O3644B4   1999
  813'.54—dc21   98-50917
                                                        CIP

ISBN 0-446-67571-7 (pbk.)

Book design by Giorgetta Bell McRee
Cover design by Honi Werner

ATTENTION: SCHOOLS AND CORPORATIONS
WARNER books are available at quantity discounts with bulk purchase for educational, business, or sales promotional use. For information, please write to: SPECIAL SALES DEPARTMENT, WARNER BOOKS, 1271 AVENUE OF THE AMERICAS, NEW YORK, NY 10020

For Joshua,
whose gift is love

Acknowledgments

There are many people who have helped to make this book possible. I would like to express my gratitude to Jamie Raab, my editor, whose warmth and encouragement provide a beacon by which to write; to Mary Evans, my agent, whose humor and intelligence always challenge and inspire me; to the wonderful people at Warner Books, for their unwavering support; to Mari Reeves, whose friendship has made so many things possible; to Nancy Huston, who showed me new possibilities; to my teachers and fellow writers at UCI, who helped me to go beyond myself; to my friends, for their laughter and patience; to my parents, for their love; and to Robert Burton, for the inestimable gift of his teaching.

Although it would be impossible to list all of the volumes that have yielded inspiration and information for *Benjamin's Gift*, I would like to give particular thanks to *Only Yesterday* by Frederick Lewis Allen, *The Decorative Twenties* by Martin Battersby, *We Remember the Holocaust* by

David A. Adler, *Jazz Masters of the '40's* by Ira Gitler, *The Golden Age of Television: Notes from the Survivors* by Max Wilk, *Out of Their Minds* by Dennis Shasha and Cathy Lazere, *Timelines of the 20th Century* by David Brownstone and Irene Franck, and *The Theory of Celestial Influence* and *The Theory of Eternal Life* by Rodney Collin.

You knock at the door of reality,
Shake your thought-wings, loosen
Your shoulders,

        and open . . .

      —Rumi
       The Gift of Water

Contents

1 / The Shape of a Miracle

2 / (How He Did It)

3 / A New Home

4 / School Days

5 / A Grand Tour

6 / The Ghost of Hamlet's Dad

7 / An Affair to Remember

8 / Chernovsky's Total History of the World

9 / The Tenor's Daughter

10 / Repercussions

11 / The Family Guildenstern

12 / An Upside-Down World

13 / The Shadow of an Eclipse

14 / (How He Did It This Time)

15 / Ghosts

16 / Whoopee

17 / A Farewell to Clam Sauce

18 / The Power of Bop

19 / Snow Falling Up

20 / The Black-and-White Blues

21 / Home Before Midnight

22 / Time Folds

23 / Time Retracts

24 / The Theater of the Gods

25 / The Spirit in the Machine
(How He Did It the Last Time)

26 / The Odds Is Gone

27 / Time Flies

BENJAMIN'S GIFT

1/The Shape of a Miracle

a pumice moon

N OCTOBER 31, 1929, Jean Pierre Michel Chernovsky sat in his Carrara marble bathtub in his twenty-seven-room Fifth Avenue mansion and stared at the putty-colored, porous sphere that floated in the violet water. Approximately the size of a small grapefruit, it was carved to resemble the elusive fellow who peered down from the night sky over Manhattan. The pumice moon was not the only object to adorn Jean Pierre Michel's bath; on the broad ledge that surrounded the tub sat a red-and-gold Japanese eggshell-lacquer dragon, a hexagonal fired-clay bowl inscribed in Sanskrit, and a miniature Egyptian chrysoprase-and-moonstone funerary urn. The pumice moon, however, was the only thing that interested Jean Pierre Michel at the moment. It had been given to him the night before by one of the chief attractions of the Lieberman Follies, one Clarisse Mimsette O'Connor. She'd presented it to him in bed after hav-

ing discovered, the night before that, that after having made love to her four times, at the age of seventy-one, Jean Pierre Michel was still erect. Clarisse Mimsette O'Connor had been too exhausted for a fifth round (she had, after all, performed three solo numbers in that evening's Follies, including an elaborate and somewhat embarrassing routine with an ostrich), but she'd spent the following afternoon, between the matinee and evening performances, in search of an appropriate gift to express her gratitude. When she'd found the pumice moon she was delighted: as far as she could tell, the only thing that Jean Pierre Michel did not possess was the moon.

Jean Pierre Michel wanted everything. Cars, clocks, cloaks, pianos, horses, houses, racing yachts, swimming pools, aeroplanes. To money itself he was indifferent; he spent no Scrooge-like hours stacking up coins, and he gave away prodigious amounts to hospitals and universities and arts foundations. All that mattered was that he had enough left over to buy beautiful things. Beauty was like a drug to Jean Pierre Michel; it filled him with such intense pleasure, he became near catatonic. An Aschermann lamp or a Matisse nude simply froze him in place, and a woman—well, just thinking about Clarisse Mimsette O'Connor set his septuagenarian body on fire.

Jean Pierre Michel slid down beneath the water and laid his head back into the smooth cavity that had been carved, at the apex of the tub, to fit the exact dimensions of his cranium. As he glanced down at his body, it looked distorted beneath the water, yet even from that skewed perspective it held no surprises for him. When dressed in a waistcoat and a silk cravat, Jean Pierre Michel could easily pass for a man in his late fifties. Without his clothes, however, he was every bit his age, and he could almost chart the decay on a daily basis. It was strange to be old, like suddenly finding yourself driving a car that was desperately in need of a paint job. Only the infallibility of his sexual drive kept him from junking the entire thing; with an engine so insistent, he could accept the brutal decline of the outer shell.

Having settled beneath the water, Jean Pierre Michel looked about the room. It was lavish by any standards, with eighteen-karat-gold fixtures and carved onyx sinks and rose quartz sconces upon the walls. No matter how magnificent his surroundings, however, he could never forget that he had not always lived in such splendor. Jean Pierre Michel had been born in 1858 in the small town of Lud, North Dakota. As far as anyone could tell, his mother and father were the only Jews ever to have lived in Lud, and how they had gotten there was something of a mystery. Yes, Jews wander; in the middle of the nineteenth century, however, they rarely wandered to places where pig farming was the chief means of earning a living. Isaac Aaron and Alma Esther Rosenberg Chernovsky had nevertheless managed it and once there had set up a small general store, stocked with the basic necessities of the North Dakota life (plus a few oddities, like Isaac Aaron's mother's cheese piroshkis), and had proceeded to live quite nicely. Alma Esther was a delicate girl, with frail, slender limbs and that pale, almost translucent skin that reveals the fine tracery of the veinwork beneath. It was from her that Jean Pierre Michel got his air of nobility, as well as his somewhat unorthodox name. After a lifetime of Rosenberg, Chernovsky was little relief to Alma Esther. She therefore chose to give her firstborn son (her only son, for birth, with her tiny body, was a trauma she would never allow herself to repeat) a set of fluid French *prénoms* to balance it out. Isaac Aaron thought that it was ridiculous to give French names to a Russian-German–North Dakotian Jew, but he soon discovered that they suited his son: there was something strangely refined about Jean Pierre Michel, though it was coupled with a vigor that prevented him from seeming effete.

Jean Pierre Michel's affection for beautiful things was apparent from the start: before he could even walk he began rearranging the decorative objects in his mother's salon. When he was old enough to do chores, he hired himself out to the neighboring farms in return for whatever caught his eye: a pair of old stirrups, a milking pail, a piece of bubbled glass. He would carry these things back to his room and study them for hours — holding them gently up to the light, running his fingers across their rough or smooth surfaces. There was a secret inside the beauty of these treasures; there was a reason that they gave him the feeling they did, though he did not know what it was.

As childhood gave way to adolescence and adolescence to manhood, Jean Pierre Michel found his life taking on the shape and specificity of one of his gathered objects. After selling enough bromide and licorice root to gather independent means, Isaac Aaron and Alma Esther decided to move on from Lud: first to Spokane, Washington, then to Baton Rouge, Philadelphia, Phoenix, and New York. Try as he might, Jean Pierre Michel could never get either of his parents to explain their crisscross journeying. Alma Esther suggested that they were exploring the parameters of a new diaspora; Isaac Aaron suggested that Jean Pierre Michel stop asking so many questions and learn to leave his suitcases partially packed. Because each city was so far from the one that preceded it, Jean Pierre Michel was forced to assemble a new collection in each new place he went, thus experiencing respective seasons with objects of the Pacific Northwest, the South during its reconstruction, the City of the Founding Fathers, the Seenaw and Moojalook Indian tribes, and, finally, whatever his heart desired. Manhattan was a dream city to Jean Pierre Michel, a place that contained the sort of diversity and energy for which he had spent his entire life developing an appetite. When Isaac Aaron and Alma Esther announced that they were pushing on for Europe, Jean Pierre Michel took a large chunk of his personal savings and bought them a steamer trunk. He was staying put.

For the next fifteen years, from the late 1870s to the mid-1890s, Jean Pierre Michel lived the exuberant life of the New York intellectual, holding down a wide variety of menial jobs while pursuing the erudition of his soul. It was a glory time in America: the Civil War was receding into the past, the second hundred years were just beginning. It was a time of hope, of the advent of iron and steel, of the promise of a new tomorrow. And Jean Pierre Michel was content just to sit at the table and be a part of the discussion. Until one day—June 16, 1895, to be exact—he decided that it was time to become rich. It was actually a decision: he woke at dawn, and by the time he had finished his morning coffee he had determined that he would become a millionaire before he reached his fortieth birthday. Perhaps it was his version of awakening in a dark wood, or perhaps it was the brisk, wagging finger of the approaching new century. Nevertheless he made the decision, devoted himself to it, and within a few short years had earned enough money to never have to work again.

How did he do it? How does anyone amass a sudden fortune: luck, a bit of chicanery, the strength to risk everything on an idea that glows in the moment, and, in Jean Pierre Michel's case, the efficacy of trout acacia resin for making spearmint chewing gum. But what mattered more than any of these factors—including luck, which figures in everything—was will. Once Jean Pierre Michel determined himself to become a millionaire, there was little left to do but count the money as it leapt into his pockets and the objects as they accumulated, from the Lacroix boxes to the Limoges porcelain to the beads to the birds to the bells to the pumice moon.

Jean Pierre Michel raised his bony knees, and the pumice moon bobbed gently on the surface of the water. When he looked at his new toy a thrill coursed through his body, but also a trace of irritation. Why hadn't he thought of it before? To possess the moon. What was the use of all his money if there were things still beyond his reach?

Jean Pierre Michel clasped the floating ball in his hand and lowered his legs. "Cassandra!" he cried. "The water's getting cold!"

For a moment there was silence. Then, somewhere in the mansion, a door slammed. Then silence again. Then the door to the bathroom swung open and a large, coffee-colored woman (a finger of cream, four teaspoons of sugar) wearing an elegant set of gold lamé lounging pajamas entered the room. She was carrying a stack of folded garments, and she looked at Jean Pierre Michel as if he were a highly impressionable, if somewhat demanding, child.

"I told you not to stay in there so long," she said. "If that body o' yours gets any more wrinkled, I'll have to take you to the cleaners and get you pressed out."

Cassandra Nutt was Jean Pierre Michel's companion. She'd been in his service for twenty-five years, having come to him, in 1904, as a girl of sixteen and having worn, in the interim, every possible title from scullery maid to personal assistant. The only role she had consistently managed to avoid was that of mistress, although Jean Pierre Michel had tried everything he could think of to make her yield. When he'd come to her the first time, in the second-floor pantry, wearing nothing but a vast, salacious grin, the young girl had simply stared; she had seen a man's penis before, even an erect one, but she had never seen one so pale and so pink. It seemed comical to her, and strangely innocent, like the flexed, flailing arm of a petulant child. And though she'd gone on to have her share of white lovers, she could never quite take Jean Pierre Michel's penis seriously, no matter how many times, or in how many settings, he had presented it to her over the years.

In spite of her refusal to sleep with him, however—or perhaps because of it—Jean Pierre Michel lavished Cassandra Nutt with gifts. Jade-and-ivory brooches, pheasant feather hats, evening dresses trimmed with Spanish goat. Cassandra Nutt was fitted out in greater style than many of the women on the New York Social Register. More significant, she wore her finery both day and night, sporting chiffon tea dresses to do the morning shopping and hand-stitched furs to post Jean Pierre Michel's correspondence in the afternoon. She was so refined, so always elegant, that it was assumed by virtually everyone she encountered that she *was* Jean Pierre Michel's mistress. Cassandra Nutt, however, cared nothing for what people thought. She liked her clothes and she liked her work, despite her employer's frequently proffered penis. If she wished to wear a Paris gown to take out the trash, whose business was it but her own?

Jean Pierre Michel placed his hands on the ledge that surrounded the tub and raised himself to a standing position. "You can press me out now, Cassandra," he said. "If you like."

Cassandra Nutt placed the clothes she was carrying on the crystal stand that stood beside the sink and reached for one of the large salmon-colored towels that hung behind it. "That thing o' yours don't need pressin', Monsieur C. It needs cold storage."

Jean Pierre Michel took the towel and began to dry himself, beginning with his head and then working his way down his thin, loose-skinned body. When he was done he handed the towel back to Cassandra Nutt, who placed it in a wide-mouthed basket that sat in the corner.

"Is the Hispano-Suiza ready?" he said.

"Yes," said Cassandra Nutt.

"Then help me dress."

Cassandra Nutt reached for the garments she'd lain on the crystal stand and began to layer them over Jean Pierre Michel's naked body; they were the crisp robes of an Arabian sheikh, complete with turban and veil.

"Seems mighty early in the day to be goin' to a dress-up party," she said.

"We're not going to a party," said Jean Pierre Michel. "No one can afford to give a party besides me. And if I gave one, no one could afford to come." He raised his arms as Cassandra Nutt placed the paneled sash about his waist. "We're going to have our own party," he said. "Just the two of us." He lowered his arms. "One does the best one can, Cassandra. No matter the circumstance."

There were several interesting things about October 31, 1929. The first was that it was Halloween, a day that had special significance for Jean Pierre Michel. For though he relished beautiful things, and reveled in the splendid clothing with which he graced Cassandra Nutt, he himself always wore a black waistcoat, a pair of gray trousers, a white, wing-collared shirt, and a black-and-silver cravat. He had dozens of each, never wearing one out, never tiring of what, to someone else, might seem a prison of sartorial monotony. Only once a year, on Halloween, did he allow himself to deviate, to indulge in fancy dress, to become himself one of the elegant objects that he preferred only to look at the rest of the year. This year, however, Halloween fell precisely one week after the collapse of the New York Stock Exchange—the second interesting thing about October 31, 1929. As most of Jean Pierre Michel's friends either had leapt from one of the city's recently constructed skyscrapers or remained frozen, over their week-old coffee, in various positions of shock, a party seemed improbable, if not totally lacking in taste. So Jean Pierre Michel decided to dress for himself and to drive, like a visiting potentate, through the ruined city.

Jean Pierre Michel had not lost a penny in the stock market crash, partly because he did not believe in the stock market and partly because he did not believe in pennies. He kept his money in the country where he made it, convinced that billions of *ducatos* were even nicer than millions of dollars. He had what he needed wired to him regularly, and if things continued in the direction they were going, with prices plummeting and the bulk of the nation's fortunes disappearing overnight, the stock market crash would most likely end up tripling or even quadrupling his worth.

He would have to stop at Cartier and buy Cassandra Nutt a new pair of earrings.

There was one thing Jean Pierre Michel desired that could not be purchased in a shop—the third interesting thing about October 31, 1929. It was not entirely triggered by the pumice moon, yet the pumice moon had helped him to articulate it: yes, Jean Pierre Michel wanted the moon, but, more than the moon, he wanted a son. The thought had not occurred to him before, nor, more surprisingly, had it been thought of by any of the countless women he had been with. Now, however, at the age of seventy-one, that old, inevitable instinct had kicked in—and the rest was simply a matter of *ducatos*.

Cassandra Nutt adjusted the two veils that floated out from either side of the white turban. "Valentino lives."

Jean Pierre Michel looked into the mirror. The outfit was arresting, but even the flowing veils could not camouflage the thick folds above the eyes, the deep creases about the mouth, the tough, lived-in quality of the skin.

"Go start the motor," he said. "Before I expose myself again."

Cassandra Nutt adjusted the pearls about her neck and moved toward the bathroom door. "Nothing like an incentive," she said—and like a great, gold lamé gust of wind, she was gone.

the hard wood chair

BENJAMIN KNEW THAT HE WAS expected to remain in the hard wood chair until Mr. Petersen returned for him, regardless of the fact that the bumps in the seat cushion pressed into his bottom and his feet could not touch the ground. He'd wanted to sit on the ledge that footed the window and look down at the street; he'd never been up so high in a building before, and when he'd passed by the window and had looked down, the people had looked like the tiny figures from his train set and the cars had looked like the ones that he kept in the shoebox under his bed. Mr. Petersen, however, had told him to sit in the chair, and as he did not know Mr. Petersen very well and as he was wearing his very best trousers (the gray ones, with the flaps on the pockets), he did as he was told—even if the bumps in the seat cushion pressed into his bottom and his feet could not touch the ground.

It was an awful room. The walls were covered with dark printed wallpaper, and the furniture was heavy and ominous looking. And even though it was only ten o'clock in the morning, it was mostly dark: the sunlight that came through the one lonely window seemed to stop a few inches after entering. The only thing that alleviated the gloom—the only thing that kept Benjamin from minding how uncomfortable the chair was and how long Mr. Petersen was taking in the other room—was the large oil painting on the wall across from him. It was a picture of a storm at sea, with a large boat crashing on the waves and a smaller boat carrying a group of survivors to safety. Benjamin had seen the ocean only once, on an ill-fated outing to the Jersey shore that had included a flat tire, a very bad chicken sandwich, and about forty-five minutes to actually look at the water. But he knew from that brief visit how wonderful it was, so the painting helped him take his mind off the interminable wait.

Benjamin was an astonishingly beautiful child. His body was strong and lithe, his face the product of a sculptor's chisel, perfect and radiating light. His only flaw—although a wise eye would not have seen it as such—was a large strawberry birthmark that spread, like the Russian steppes, across his right cheek and throat. When his parents first saw him, the contradiction of it stunned them into silence: the startling beauty, even as a newborn, and this strange, sprawling mark across its surface. Whatever they called it—spot, stain, blotch, smear—it stole away their joy at the birth of a wonderful child.

As Benjamin grew, his beauty grew, too, so that the strawberry birthmark eventually began to seem like a natural balancing mechanism: a silk scarf thrown up against the light of God. The more beautiful he became, however, the more his parents hated the birthmark. His mother, Lavinia, interpreted it as a punishment. It reminded her of the stain on the bedsheet in the morning after she'd made love with Benjamin's father, the dried insignia of her husband's seed that spilled out of her as she slept. At least one of those seeds had managed to find its way up into her womb, and Lavinia was convinced that the mark on the body of the child that it had grown into was intended to chastise her for the pleasure she'd taken in the embarrassing act that had produced him. Benjamin's father, Edward, had a different interpretation. To him the birthmark was a sign not of what had been, but of what was yet to come: Benjamin was the future, and there was a stain upon it.

Had Benjamin looked into the mirror for the first time in a world in which neither his parents nor anyone like them had ever lived, he would have liked what he saw tremendously. The cerulean blue eyes were strong and clear. The nose was straight and the mouth delicately curved. The dark blond hair feathered softly into neat, attractive waves. And the strawberry birthmark was really quite fascinating—a splash of color on a pale canvas, a burst of good cheer like the wine that spilled from the goblet turned over at a wedding. Edward and Lavinia, however, were most decidedly in Benjamin's world. So when he looked into the mirror and saw the strawberry birthmark, the only thing he could feel was his parents' shame.

At first he tried rubbing it off, using terry-cloth toweling, soap detergent, cotton batting, rubbing alcohol, and half a jar of what his mother referred to as, but was obviously mistaken in calling, vanishing cream. When this didn't work he tried covering it over with a paste he concocted of bourbon and baking soda, using the bottle of bootleg his father kept in the broom closet, being careful to top it up with water. When this didn't work he tried spreading strawberry jam across the rest of his face, though by the time he'd emptied the jar he realized that the strawberry birthmark was not really strawberry, but more like stewed cherries or twisted candy whips or the small glass relish dish that his mother brought out whenever company came to dinner.

It was when all these methods failed that Benjamin, tired of being sticky and seedy, stumbled upon his fate. He was sitting on the large, flowered sofa in the sitting room of the small Brooklyn brownstone where he and his parents lived. His mother had told him to wait there while she answered the doorbell, and from the emphasis in her voice he understood that she wished him to remain hidden rather than to accompany her and produce that look of amazement that always appeared on the face of whoever was at the door. As he tucked his legs up under him and listened to the conversation through the wall, he wished that he could curl up tight enough to disappear. And for a moment he did. He closed his eyes and entered a half-world—a blue zone—a limbo. And when he opened them again he found himself on the kitchen floor between the icebox and the stove. He was quite confused and had to concentrate feverishly to return himself to the sitting room before his mother came back. But the next morning, after he had transported himself from his bedroom to the bathroom, and the bathroom to the back garden, he knew that, whatever was happening, it was more than just chance.

For the next few weeks Benjamin refrained from wishing himself to be anywhere other than where he was. It was strange enough to have a strawberry birthmark; what could be the meaning of the ability to transport oneself through space? He tried to convince himself that it had not really happened. As his father always liked to say, people constantly imagined the most ridiculous things. But the vast possibilities that it held finally tempted him to test it again. So he transferred himself from the basement to the attic—from the front porch swing to the second-floor landing—and he saw that, bizarre and vaguely dangerous as it seemed, these powers were actually his.

The one thing Benjamin felt certain about, however, was that he dared not reveal his discovery to his parents;

Edward and Lavinia were beleaguered enough without having to process their son's new abilities. Their problems were mostly a product of their insecurities: they had money, but they were convinced that it wasn't enough; they had a satisfying sex life, but they felt horribly guilty about it; they had a beautiful son, but he had a strawberry birthmark on his face. They were therefore poised, like a pair of overripe apples, to fall to the ground with a resounding splat should the appropriate wind blow in. And though Benjamin did his best to see that his new gift did not provide the shock, on the morning of October 24, 1929, something else did: the New York Stock Exchange collapsed into panic, and their entire life's savings were lost. Compared with the losses of others, Edward and Lavinia's losses were meager. And perhaps if they had felt good about how good they felt when they made love, or their son's skin had not looked like the backdrop to one of Macy's Christmas windows, they would have been able to sustain the shock. But they didn't, and it did, so on October 25, while Benjamin was at school, they sealed the windows, turned on the gas, and promptly asphyxiated themselves.

"Benjamin!"

Benjamin looked up to find Mr. Petersen, a few strands of hair bravely combed up over his balding head, standing grim-faced in the doorway.

"Feet off the upholstery and look sharp!" he said. "Mr. Feinstein will see you in five minutes."

Mr. Petersen turned and reentered the office, and Benjamin lowered his feet so that they dangled, once more, above the ground.

Benjamin had no parents now. He also had no brothers,

15

no sisters, no aunts, no uncles, no grandparents, and no cousins. Mr. Petersen was a social worker, the office he sat in belonged to the law firm of Wittman, Waxman, and Feinstein, and Benjamin, although he did not know what it meant, was about to be made a ward of the state.

Benjamin closed his eyes and tried to block out the dank, musty smell that filled the room. He wondered what it would smell like in the place they were going to take him, the place they had told him he was going to have to live in now that his mother and father were dead. When he opened his eyes, he looked at the painting across from him. There were twelve men in the small boat being led away from the wreckage; there were people on the boat that was sinking beneath the waves; there was a faint rainbow arcing between the two crafts. Benjamin did not know if it was possible, but he decided that he would try to enter the painting, to disappear from the darkness of the law office waiting room and enter an alternate world. He realized that he might miss his mark, that he might will himself onto the wrong ship, that he might get trapped on the sinking vessel and be pulled beneath the waves. But even that seemed better than the dull, gray fate into which Mr. Petersen was about to usher him.

He closed his eyes. He breathed in deeply. He concentrated.

Then Benjamin disappeared.

the Hispano-Suiza

WHAT IS THE SHAPE OF A MIRACLE? Is it slender, compact, able to fit, like a silver bead, within the palm of your hand?

So dense, so deeply concentrated, that it carries an entire universe inside its smooth, brittle shell? Or is it fluid, ephemeral, an invisible substance that pours out over the moment, releasing upon its subjects a whiff of the sublime, transforming them, man and child and thing, forever?

Jean Pierre Michel sat in the back of his Hispano-Suiza V8 convertible with his veils carefully arranged about him and his fingertips poised, on either side of his body, upon the taut red leather interior. The top was down, and Cassandra Nutt was at the wheel: massage therapist, tax accountant, pastry chef, chauffeur, it was but another of her roles in Jean Pierre Michel's service, though one she enjoyed a good bit more than the rest. The Hispano-Suiza was superb to handle. On weekends, when Jean Pierre Michel decided to drive out to Connecticut or Long Island, Cassandra Nutt imagined herself to be a bold aviatrix, piloting the red-and-white vehicle on a sleek course through the sky. She felt the heft and grace of the automobile as she felt them in herself: powerful when necessary, fleet and subtle when she desired. It was never a chore to be asked to go driving. All she needed was the road, the car, and a destination.

Now she was purring down Fifth Avenue on a late-October morning with a pseudo-Arabian sheikh in the backseat. The traffic was light; with the industrial average still plummeting like a suicidal finch, the streets of Manhattan were open wide to the solitary Halloween parade of Jean Pierre Michel Chernovsky. They continued down Fifth Avenue until they came to Fourteenth Street, where they turned and headed west. When they reached the corner of Fourteenth and Seventh, they stopped to allow a woman pushing a dark blue baby carriage to cross over to the south side of the intersection. And that was when the miracle—solid or fluid—occurred. For when the Hispano-Suiza stopped to allow the pram to pass, it held a stunning black woman in her early forties wearing a sleek beaver coat and an aviator's cap and an elderly white man dressed in a set of flowing robes. But when it started again, turning left on Seventh Avenue into the heart of Greenwich Village, it suddenly held, in addition to these two, an exquisite young boy with a strawberry birthmark on his face.

When Benjamin saw the red leather interior of the car and the crisp white veils of the man beside him, he knew that he had not entered the painting. Yet he felt that his efforts had not entirely failed: he had definitely willed himself into something more interesting than what Mr. Petersen had had in mind. When Jean Pierre Michel became aware of the young boy beside him, he did not question where he had come from or how or when or why he had entered his car. He only knew that he had found his son—or, rather, that his son had found him. And when Cassandra Nutt glanced into the rearview mirror and saw the ravishing child with the extraordinary light in his eyes, she could only think that veils or no veils, Halloween parade or not, Jean Pierre Michel Chernovsky had finally met his match.

2/(How He Did It)

HIS IS HOW HE DID IT:

Closing his eyes, he imagined himself to be free of his body, to be an impulse inside of Benjamin rather than the perfectly proportioned nose or the soft down at the back of the neck or the ecstatic strawberry birthmark. To be free of the cellular world and part of the molecular, like the scent of a rose or a ripe melon, which can pass through a crack in the window of a room though the rose or the melon itself remains trapped inside. First he would concentrate until the impulse became entirely free of the shell; then he would picture a destination; then he would slip through the crack. When the transfer was complete, he would think again of Benjamin: nose, down, birthmark. And when he opened his eyes, he would find himself transferred to wherever it was that he'd imagined.

This is the way that he defied the laws of nature. That he out-Houdinied Houdini. That he confounded space and time.

This—though he could not yet fathom the reason why—is how he did it.

3/A New Home

three days

ROM THE TWENTY-EIGHTH-FLOOR offices of Wittman, Waxman, and Feinstein to the backseat of the Hispano-Suiza was in some ways easier passage than from recently orphaned about-to-be-made-ward-of-the-state to adopted millionaire's son. There were endless telephone calls to be made, affidavits to be filed, hearings to attend, judges to be persuaded, and, with everyone well aware of Jean Pierre Michel's financial status, a considerable number of *ducatos* to be paid. No effort was too great, however, when Jean Pierre Michel set his mind on something, and by mid-February of the new year—bald, empty-pocketed 1930—Benjamin was officially his.

At first he did not know what to do with him. When he brought him home from the boarding facility where they'd kept Benjamin after his parents had died, he installed him in the large suite of rooms on the second floor beside the

even larger suite that belonged to Cassandra Nutt. (As
Cassandra Nutt had risen from role to role over the course
of her service to Jean Pierre Michel, she had also risen
from bedroom to bedroom, until finally she took posses-
sion of the vast cluster of rooms on the second floor that,
in size and elegance, were second only to Jean Pierre
Michel's own living quarters.) He sat him down on the
large bed that centered the main room, told him to wait
there, and then promptly left the house. It was customary
for Jean Pierre Michel to do this when he acquired something new; it gave him the opportunity to shake it from his
mind and then return to it with a fresh perspective. And
though Benjamin was neither a Persian rug nor a pair of
silver candlesticks, he stayed just as Jean Pierre Michel
had left him: perched on the edge of the enormous bed,
waiting, as he had waited for Mr. Petersen.

Fortunately for Benjamin, Cassandra Nutt came to
check on him not long after Jean Pierre Michel had gone
out.

"How long you figure you can sit there?" she said as she
stood in the doorway, a casual hand on her hip.

"He told me to wait," said Benjamin.

"You don't know him. He could be gone for days."

Benjamin rubbed his forehead and shrugged. "He told
me to wait," he said again.

Cassandra Nutt folded her arms across her bosom and
stared at this strange child who seemed to have been delivered, like a wayward Christmas present, to the wrong
house. Benjamin sat on the bed and stared back. Neither
of them could think of a thing to say, yet neither could
break away—for though Cassandra Nutt had never seen a
face so beautiful and Benjamin had never felt a warmth so

radiant, each felt the sense that they already knew one another. It was as if two separate lines were moving through time to meet in that same moment: a line moving forward that led to astonishment, a line moving backward that triggered a strange recognition.

"Belgian waffles," said Cassandra Nutt, finally breaking the silence. "What you need is some Belgian waffles."

Benjamin, not knowing precisely what Belgian waffles were, said nothing as Cassandra Nutt raised her cream-and-burgundy silk shawl about her shoulders, left the series of elaborate, interconnecting rooms, and went down to the kitchen to prepare the most delightful version of the unheard-of food that any man, woman, or child had ever tasted. (Years later, when Benjamin visited Bruges for the first time, he was instantly transported back to that cold winter morning when he'd arrived at Jean Pierre Michel's mansion and had first sampled Cassandra Nutt's cooking. Even from a distance of thirty-seven years he had to confess that her waffles—poured, beaten, and crisped with her particular brand of joy—were better.) For the next three days this was the pattern: Benjamin sitting on the bed while Cassandra Nutt brought him food—barbecued spareribs, cheese ravioli, pecan-walnut-cinnamon rolls, spaghetti bolognese—and he tried to figure out what Jean Pierre Michel meant to do with him. Perhaps the old man intended to tag him and put him on display beside the bronze busts and the carved elk heads and the enormous marble statues. Perhaps Cassandra Nutt had been instructed to fatten him up so that he might fetch a good price on the black market.

Eventually, in an effort to quiet these thoughts, Benjamin decided to memorize the room, thinking that perhaps, when Jean Pierre Michel returned, he was going to be tested on it. One by one he studied the cluster of fat angels that crowned the center of the ceiling, the silhouetted deer that stamped the border of the carpet, the geometric knobs that graced the drawers of the small writing desk, the slender panes in the large French windows that fronted the park across the way. He would focus upon each item until it began to shimmer and blur. Then he would close his eyes and try to re-create it in his mind. By the end of the third day there was not an object in the room that he could not describe at length, from its color to its dimensions to the way it changed character in varying lights of the day.

On the morning of the fourth day, just as he was sitting up (Benjamin allowed himself to lay back upon the bed to sleep at night, although he was careful not to wrinkle his clothes or drool upon the satin bedding), Jean Pierre Michel returned.

"Good morning," he said.

"Good morning," said Benjamin.

"How have you been getting along?"

"Fine, sir," said Benjamin.

Jean Pierre Michel moved closer to the bed, and Benjamin noted that he was wearing precisely the same clothes he had worn each time that he had seen him, except for that first day, when he'd been dressed as an Arabian sheikh.

"Cassandra Nutt has been taking good care of you?"

"Yes, sir."

"And you've had enough to eat?"

"Yes, sir."

Jean Pierre Michel pressed his lips together tightly. "Don't call me 'sir,'" he said. "What about your rooms?"

"What about them, sir?"

"Are they spacious enough? Is your bed large enough?"

"Large enough, sir?"

"Don't call me 'sir,'" said Jean Pierre Michel.

"What should I call you?" said Benjamin.

"What would you like to call me?"

Benjamin thought about this for a moment. "Cassandra calls you Monsieur C."

Jean Pierre Michel narrowed his eyes a fraction of an inch. "That will not be acceptable."

Benjamin remained silent, so Jean Pierre Michel crouched down before him. As his face came level with his own, Benjamin considered that it was the face of an eagle: the watery eyes, the large, swooping nose, the narrow, firmly fixed mouth.

"What about 'Father'?" said Jean Pierre Michel.

Benjamin looked at the eagle face and thought of his real father; in his memory he seemed more like a bear or a large, tired dog. He knew that this man was not his father—and there was something faintly disturbing about the tightness of his lips—but he figured that he could learn as much from an eagle as he could from a bear, and even more than from a tired dog, and that perhaps love would come.

"All right," he said.

Jean Pierre Michel rose and walked to the door. When he reached it he turned back to Benjamin. "Perhaps you'd prefer a smaller bed," he said.

Benjamin nodded.

"Or a smaller set of rooms?"

"Just one would be fine," said Benjamin.

Jean Pierre Michel stared at him. "You can have the study down the hall," he said. "And you can wait until"— he removed a small leather notebook from the pocket of his waistcoat, opened it, closed it again, and then returned it to the pocket—"next Thursday to call me 'Father.' We needn't rush things."

Benjamin nodded again. Then Jean Pierre Michel exited the room and disappeared into some other corner of the mansion.

When he'd gone, Benjamin looked about the room again: the lamp, the chair, the desk, the windows. He saw, for the first time, that there was a stain upon the carpet near the corner of the bed, a faint discoloration approximately the size of a fig. He did not know if it had been there all along, but he did his best now to memorize it. For though he hadn't been tested yet, he knew that the game, whatever it might be, was just beginning.

ghost dance

THE NEXT FEW WEEKS were like a strange, hybrid fairy tale, as if pages from *The Arabian Nights* had been torn from their binding and interspersed with some chronicle of the Jazz Age. Although the financial panic of the preceding fall had been devastating, there was still no awareness of the Depression that loomed on the horizon. It was therefore quite easy—particularly when fueled by a limitless supply of *ducatos*—to continue the extravagant lifestyle that had been enjoyed before the crash. If the atmosphere had something of a ghost dance to it, Benjamin didn't notice; he was too busy trying to adjust to the hectic pace his new father seemed to live by. For despite the wrinkled body and the un-pry-openable lips, Jean Pierre Michel was showing him a wonderful time.

He took him to see his first talking movie, *Say It with Songs*. (The talking was more like barking or shouting, and the songs were so loud that Benjamin had to put his fingers in his ears.) He took him up to the construction landing of the enormous new skyscraper, the Empire State Building, that was being erected on Thirty-fourth Street. He took him for egg rolls in Chinatown and hot dogs on Coney Island, and in the evenings he introduced him to the assortment of people who came to the mansion to eat and drink and argue. Jean Pierre Michel loathed arguing himself, but he loved to listen to others argue. He therefore selected his dinner guests from all walks of life, and whether the sparks that eventually flew were between the bank president and the Baptist minister or the opera singer and the liquor-racket moll, Jean Pierre Michel savored the conflict. It was like a tart sauce for the Cornish hen or a dark espresso to follow the crème brûlée. Benjamin quickly discovered that the arguments were not serious and that listening to them quietly was a useful way to learn how people think.

While Jean Pierre Michel and Benjamin held down the dinner table—sometimes quite literally—Cassandra Nutt was in full swing. For after having invited the guests, devised the seating, arranged the flowers, and prepared the food, she spent the evening itself at the piano, serenading the guests. Jean Pierre Michel preferred Strauss before dinner and Brahms or Tchaikovsky to accompany the main course, but by the time dessert arrived Cassandra

Nutt was generally wheeling into ragtime or Tin Pan Alley. Some evenings, when an argument threatened to become especially vehement, she would skip the classics
entirely and head straight for Irving Berlin.

Benjamin was aware at these dinners, as he was wherever he went, that the people he encountered were aware
of his remarkable looks. The guests at Jean Pierre
Michel's dinner parties, however, were not like the people
who rang the doorbell at his parents' house in Brooklyn.
They never gawked, and they never looked stunned; they
seemed to accept Benjamin for what he was—a beautiful
child with a spectacular birthmark—and in those very first
weeks a fraction of his shame washed away. Only once did
someone actually make mention of his strange beauty.

"Thank God you've got that mark, honey," exclaimed
Edna Van Tillsdale, the voluptuous young wife of a Texas
oil magnate. "Otherwise I'd have to ditch ol' Albert an'
keep my legs crossed till you grow up!"

Benjamin blushed so deeply, his strawberry birthmark
almost disappeared.

On weekends Cassandra Nutt took Jean Pierre Michel
and Benjamin out in the Hispano-Suiza or the Packard
640 or the Bugatti Type 45. Benjamin loved these excur-
sions, but even more he loved the times, during the week,
when Cassandra Nutt took him with her to Lazy Joe's, her
favorite Harlem speakeasy, and ordered him lemon-lime
sodas while she sipped her sloe gin fizz.

"No matter what life do to you," said Cassandra Nutt, "a
sloe gin fizz can always help undo it."

Where Jean Pierre Michel, despite his officially docu-
mented status as Benjamin's father, remained a stranger
to Benjamin, Cassandra Nutt, from the very first waffle,

was like blood. Benjamin especially liked her smell: it reminded him of one of those oranges stuck with cloves that his mother used to place on the mantel in the sitting room at Christmas. He liked to lean in close to her when they played backgammon at midnight (Cassandra Nutt was a backgammon whiz, and when Benjamin couldn't sleep he'd creep into her room and they would play for hours). When she left her scarf in the conservatory one afternoon, Benjamin took it upstairs and slipped it beneath his pillow so that he could smell her when she wasn't there.

As the months slipped by, Benjamin began to explore the mansion, uncovering an infinite number of nooks and crannies that were excellent places to hide. For the most part, however, he felt happiest when he was alone in his room. Jean Pierre Michel, as he had promised, had converted the small study on the second floor into a perfect boy's bedroom with a sleigh bed, a set of electric trains, and an enormous radio with two sets of speakers and a polished mahogany cabinet. Benjamin loved his radio; he would listen for hours to *The Shadow* and *Amos 'n' Andy* and *Whiteman's Old Gold Orchestra*. Benjamin felt the safest when he was alone, because that was when he felt most like Benjamin—not Edward and Lavinia's orphan, not Jean Pierre Michel's adopted son. He could not quite forget the Brooklyn brownstone, but neither could he quite believe in the Fifth Avenue mansion. When he was alone in his room, listening to the radio, it was almost as if nothing had changed.

At the same time that Benjamin was investigating the mansion, he also began to explore his gift. When he had tried to transfer himself into the painting at the law office, he had not really failed: his body had impelled itself forward toward the seascape but, unable to recompose itself into a two-dimensional form, had rematerialized inside Jean Pierre Michel's Hispano-Suiza as, at precisely that instant, it had passed beneath the window. Now, in an effort to discover the parameters of his powers, he transferred himself farther afield: to the toy department at Macy's, to the observation deck of the Statue of Liberty, to the dinosaur section of the Museum of Natural History. What he soon found, however, was that he was not always able to control his new skills. When he tried to transfer himself to the lake in Central Park, for example, he wound up at the tea shop near the boathouse. When he tried to transfer himself to Grand Central Station, he wound up on a train for New Rochelle. He realized that such imprecision could end up being quite dangerous. What if he wound up in an intersection instead of in an automobile? An elevator shaft instead of an elevator? A fireplace instead of the couch or the bear rug before it?

Still, he experimented. His gift was too rich with possibilities to ignore, too full of excitement, too laced with a sense of autonomy. And though he always made certain to return to wherever he started, both Jean Pierre Michel and Cassandra Nutt began to gather that something was going on. Why were Benjamin's cheeks flushed with cold when he returned from the bathroom? Why were his shoes covered with mud when he came down from the library?

They said nothing about it to one another and nothing about it to Benjamin. Yet the feeling kept growing, in each of their hearts, that Benjamin was no ordinary child.

in lieu of Cointreau and milk

IT WAS WELL INTO THE dark hours of the night, and Jean
Pierre Michel could not sleep. For the most part, throughout his seventy-two years, sleep had not been a problem;
he needed little of it, and when he beckoned it generally
came. On the rare occasions that it didn't—being unaware
of Cassandra Nutt's enthusiasm for midnight backgammon games—he would go down to the kitchen and fix
himself a small glass of Cointreau and milk, with a dash of
triple sec. He would sip this as he returned to his bed, and
by the time he'd placed the glass upon the nightstand and
had removed his robe and slippers and had lain his head
upon the pillow, he was halfway to slumber. (Even during
Prohibition Jean Pierre Michel kept every kind of liquor
in the house. The bootleggers he dealt with were especially
fond of Pablito's Spearmint Chewing Gum—which Jean
Pierre Michel had named for the young boy who had first
shown him the acacia tree and the marvels of its resin—
not to mention the neatly folded one-hundred-dollar bills
that Jean Pierre Michel slipped between the sticks.)

Tonight, however, even Cointreau and milk could not
ease Jean Pierre Michel to sleep. So he rose again, slipped
back into his robe and slippers, and went to the former
study on the second floor that was now his little boy's bedroom. The door gave a loud creak as he pushed it open,
but the sound did not wake Benjamin. As Jean Pierre
Michel crossed the floor he was careful not to trip over the
stuffed lion, the miniature milk truck, or the team of Spanish donkeys that littered his way. When he reached the
small bed beneath the window he stood there for a mo-

ment, looking down at the sleeping figure. He could not see him very well among the thick night shadows, but even the suggestion of the small fists curled up beneath the chin and the soft cheek pressed down against the pillow brought Benjamin's startling beauty back to him. From the moment he first saw him, he was perfect to Jean Pierre Michel, and the strawberry birthmark was the seal of that perfection. Like the stamp of a watermark on a sheet of linen stationery. Like the crest of a king upon his robes.

Benjamin shuffled beneath the covers and rolled over against the wall; Jean Pierre Michel remained standing in the darkness. He watched the rise and fall of the child's little body as his breath moved in and out. He smelled the sweet scent that rose from his bedclothes, like milk mixed with freshly cut grass. And though he wanted to reach out and pat his little head, or tuck the rumpled covers up under his chin, he could only stand there, frozen, like the cadaver that he imagined he soon would be, and wonder.

4 / School Days

the state flower of Texas

HE EXTRAVAGANT holiday that followed Benjamin's arrival in Jean Pierre Michel's life continued throughout the summer. Only when the temperature began to drop did Cassandra Nutt, busy with transferring the goldfish from the fountain in the garden to the reflecting pool in the atrium, suddenly realize that it was time to enroll the new member of the household in school. Benjamin had begun the first grade the year before, at P.S. 263 in Brooklyn. He had gotten only as far as "three plus one equals four," however, when his parents had self-destructed. Now, after an exhausting year of foster care, law courts, and the elaborate Fifth Avenue revels, Jean Pierre Michel set about to enter him in the illustrious Berbin Academy, the most prestigious day school in Manhattan. Founded in 1883 by John Wesley Berbin, the academy was noted for its *fin de siècle* architecture, its exclusive Park Avenue address, its progressive coeduca-

tional policies, and the well-known fact that the combined wealth of the parents of its students exceeded the national budget. Even with the previous year's stock market crash, places at the Berbin Academy were difficult to come by; Jean Pierre Michel had to pull a number of strings and in the end was able to secure Benjamin a place only by offering to build a brand-new gymnasium with a sixty-foot heated swimming pool.

Despite the splendor of this noble institution, despite its prestige, to Benjamin it was still just a school. So when he passed through its doors on that cool September morning (having been driven to the curb by Cassandra Nutt in the white Isotta Fraschini), he was neither joyful nor downcast, but merely a bit nervous. The first thing he did was to go to the admissions office, where an elderly gentleman snatched up his papers. Then he wound his way through the thick maze of hallways until he reached the room where he'd been told he would find his class. When he opened the door he discovered sixteen desks, each peopled with an attentive eight-year-old, and a tiny woman with aggressive hair standing menacingly beside a large blackboard. For a moment there was silence as Benjamin stared at them and they stared at Benjamin. Then the woman at the blackboard suddenly turned and shouted:

"The infirmary is on the second floor!"

Benjamin was as startled by the loudness of her cry as he was baffled by its meaning. Not wishing, however, to make trouble on his first day—and thinking that perhaps a health examination was a routine part of the admissions process—he left the room and made his way to the infirmary. Only when he entered and the attending nurse inquired if she could put some ointment on his rash did he

understand that his new teacher had mistaken his birthmark for some sort of affliction, and that the six months of
acceptance by Jean Pierre Michel's dinner guests was a
grace period that had come to an end.

Benjamin returned to his classroom with the hope of
making light of the matter. As the day progressed, however, it became clear that such thinking was in vain. When
it was time for the art lesson, eight of the children drew
faces with strawberry birthmarks on their cheeks. When it
was time for the geography lesson, a tall, gangly boy in the
back of the room announced that "Texas was like a giant
splotch across the face of the United States." When it was
time for recess, Benjamin was excluded from all forms of
play with the explanation that he might be contagious.

Benjamin realized, with a certain uncomfortable pride,
that had he been homely, or worn thick spectacles, or been
possessed of a massive limp, the children would have
pitied him or at least have been too ashamed to mock him
so openly. He knew that it was as much for his alarming
beauty as for his birthmark that he was shunned; the intensity of the extremes was too much for the other children and could be soothed only by the exercise of a
tremendous cruelty. Being Jewish didn't help. On the
third day of school a girl named Sally Crenshaw asked him
if he had developed his condition from eating too much
matzo. Benjamin considered trying to explain that although Jean Pierre Michel was Jewish, he, technically,
was not. In the end, however, he decided not to bother. He
was used to being taunted—and he sensed that Sally
Crenshaw was serious.

By the end of the first week several things had emerged.
The chief offender in the onslaught against Benjamin was

the tall, gangly boy, whose name was Snyder Stevens and whose family was said to own half the real estate in lower Manhattan. The rest of the class was under his sway, from Elizabeth Bates Morgan, the large pigtailed girl whose entire wardrobe was patterned over with horses, to Alexander Fobbs, the pale, spectacled boy who always farted during roll call. They nicknamed Benjamin "Texas," and every day at recess Snyder Stevens would stand at the top of the jungle gym and guide the others through the new class litany:

"What's the state flower of Texas?"
"The spotted orchid!"
"What's the state tree of Texas?"
"The spreading oak!"
"What's the state fruit of Texas?"
"The strawberry!!"

Benjamin did his best to ignore the entire thing. He would sit on the bench near the water fountain and pretend that he was in the African hunting grounds or the heart of the Amazon or the snow-covered peaks of the Himalayas. He suspected that with a bit of experimentation he might actually have been able to transfer himself to these places, yet he somehow understood that he had not been given his gift in order to run from his adversaries. No one he had met at any of Jean Pierre Michel's dinner parties—not the championship skier or the French couturier or the assistant secretary of the defense—seemed likely to have run from anything in their entire lives. To remain in the playground amid the storm of slurs was to grow stronger by what was meant to diminish him.

When Benjamin had first discovered his unearthly powers, he'd had visions of becoming a superhero. Dressed in a bright cape and a form-fitting mask, he would roam the world, doing battle against the forces of evil. As time passed, however, he'd begun to understand that his dreams were too vast—that before he could solve the problems of the world, he had to meet the challenges of his eight-year-old life in New York. It wasn't until he met Petrie Woolrich, however, that he discovered a way to use his powers to confront his own situation.

Petrie Woolrich was the only member of Benjamin's class not to participate in his mockery, largely because, prior to Benjamin's arrival, it had been him the other children had delighted in tormenting. (Snyder Stevens called him "Pee-Tree," and the class joke was to run to the nearest oak when he passed by and pretend to urinate.) Small and somewhat rodentlike, Petrie was, besides being astonishingly intelligent, completely amoral. He was convinced that laws existed only to guide the dull and the foolish and that a wise man's pleasure consisted in carefully and creatively subverting them. Yet although he would have easily stolen Benjamin's pocket watch or pencil case had he taken a liking to either one, he refused to join in the malice of the other children now that their attention was turned from him toward someone else. For the first several weeks he merely stood on the sidelines, observing the scene. Only as he began to perceive Benjamin's implacability in the face of his persecution did he take an interest in him, and only on Thursday of the fourth week, a sultry day of Indian summer, did he cross to the bench by the fountain where he sat and address him.

"It all falls into place when you understand that Snyder Stevens has only one testicle," he said.

Benjamin, who at that moment was trying to resist the pull of Morocco, turned to look at him. "How do you know?"

"Filched the nurse's report," said Petrie, keeping his eyes on the schoolyard. "At the right moment the use of this fact will level poor Snyder so completely, it will take the rest of his days at Berbin to recover."

Benjamin invited Petrie to sit with him and by the end of the recess period had learned his entire history: that he was not eight but eleven and that for the past three years he had methodically flunked his exams in the hope that a growth spurt would occur and he would begin to look like the other children; that only recently had he given up all thoughts of greater size and revealed his vast intelligence, which only made everyone despise him more, as they felt that he had made complete and utter fools of them, which he had; that he was in love with mathematics and was convinced there was nothing that could not be translated into a set of precise algebraic equations; that, like Benjamin, he was an orphan, though in his case there had been no wealthy benefactor to swoop down and magically transform his life. He had instead been placed in the Baines' Home for Boys and sent, as a poverty case, to the Berbin Academy, where he'd proceeded to make everyone he encountered extremely uncomfortable.

Benjamin and Petrie soon became inseparable. The latter supplied the former with an insight into the world that was as thrilling as it was wicked, while the former restored a trace of innocence to the latter's jaded life. As both were equally on the outskirts of their classmates' affections, they had nothing to lose by their alliance. The only alteration was an addition to the class litany:

"What's the state animal of Texas?"
"The rat!"

To Benjamin it was victory enough to be able to withstand the gibes and jeers of the other children. The idea of taking revenge would never have occurred to him. For Petrie, however, revenge seemed perfectly natural, and the more he talked of it, the more he aroused a hunger for it in Benjamin.

"Imagine how it would feel," he said, "to see Snyder Stevens impaled on one of the spikes of the schoolyard fence. Or to inject strychnine into Elizabeth Bates Morgan's third or fourth helping at lunch."

It was a brisk October morning, and the bench, which was made of a heavy wrought iron, was uncharacteristically cold. Just opposite the bench, on the jungle gym, Snyder Stevens was doing his impression of the school's headmaster, Calvin Simon Fisk, which resembled an ailing chimpanzee.

"I don't know," said Benjamin. "It sounds a bit extreme to me."

Petrie pressed his hands down into the bench and began squishing the air in and out of his cheeks. "Then what," he said, "in the case of our primate friend here, would you suggest?"

Benjamin looked across at Snyder, who was now hanging upside-down and rolling his eyes while the other children doubled over in laughter.

"Complete and total humiliation," said Benjamin.

"An acceptable compromise," said Petrie. "The question is how to do it. What can we come up with to make his bullying body tremble? To strike a note of terror in his malicious little heart?" Petrie looked away for a moment, a shiver of excitement distorting his features. "What can we do," he said, "that will reduce him to Cream of Wheat?"

Benjamin kept his eyes on Snyder Stevens, who had jumped through the bars to the sandpit below and was now wriggling his bottom in the air like an amphetamine-addicted fan dancer. He knew that his gift was exactly the sort of thing Petrie was looking for, yet he had never told anyone about it and was not at all certain that he should do so now. He sensed, however, that if he could entrust his secret to anyone, he could entrust it to Petrie, so he decided to take the risk and tell him.

"I can disappear," he said as nonchalantly as it was possible to make such a statement. "It can be very effective."

Petrie neither turned to look at him nor registered the slightest surprise at what he had said. He merely continued squishing the air in and out of his cheeks: left and then right, left and then right. "Show me," he said.

Benjamin looked about the schoolyard in search of a place where no one would be able to observe them. There were children everywhere, from the mittened kindergartners to the laconic upper-level boys and girls whose awareness of one another was as complete as their disregard for everyone else. Eventually, however, his eyes fell upon the small alcove that lay between the boys' gymnasium and the east wall. Only a few feet wide and a few feet deep, with a section that jutted away behind the building, it seemed as good a place as any to demonstrate his powers to Petrie.

"Follow me," he said, and then he started across the schoolyard, and Petrie followed, until they reached the tiny alcove, where they ducked out of sight. "I don't know if I can do it with anyone watching."

Petrie slipped his hands into his pockets. "I suppose we'll find out."

Benjamin closed his eyes and stood very still. Then he opened them again and added, "Don't scream or anything."

Petrie nodded quickly and squished his cheeks in and out. Then right before his amazed eyes, Benjamin disappeared. It wasn't like the girl in the magic show: now you see her, now you don't. There was an intermediate phase when Benjamin was both there and not there, when Petrie could see the leaves and the fence through the lens of his dissolving body and when nothing, as he had ever conceived it until then, made sense. Then, in a flash, he was gone.

Petrie stood there, suddenly aware of the crisp October air and the scattered leaves, some yellow and red, some brown and starting to decompose. Then a chill ran through him—the two worlds collided—and the state flower of Texas reappeared where he had been standing before.

"I'm still working on the middle part," said Benjamin. "I'd like to be able to do it without going see-through."

Petrie let his arms drop to his sides and nodded again quite slowly. "It'll do, Benjamin," he said in a soft voice. "It most certainly, most definitely, will do."

breakfast in bed

THE LIGHT THAT POURED into the second-floor bedchamber did not know what to grace first: the nips and folds of the blue satin bedsheets; the sea of open newspapers; the cherrywood tray heaped with pork-and-apple sausages, cinnamon-buckwheat biscuits, and chèvre-scrambled eggs; or the large, hazelnut-butter-colored woman in the white linen caftan who was perched at the center of it all. Mornings were precious to Cassandra Nutt. There was nothing she liked more than to lie in bed, surrounded by food and information. She subscribed to fourteen daily newspapers—eight of them in languages that she did not even speak—and she was never content until she'd spent a little time with each of them. These mornings, with Benjamin to take to school and Jean Pierre Michel to escort to the Russian embassy, she was unable to return to the house until almost ten o'clock. (Jean Pierre Michel's latest love affair was with a defected Russian princess whose obsession with Fabergé eggs resulted in his spending his mornings either scouring the New York auction houses or pestering the foreign embassy to help her retrieve her private collection from Kursk.) By the time she had cooked her breakfast, and had slipped into her caftan, and had spread out her newspapers, it was almost time to begin preparing Jean Pierre Michel's lunch (borscht these days, or blini with black caviar) and to return for him and the princess wherever she had left them. She proceeded, nevertheless, as if the day were entirely hers and savored the ritual even if she had time only for a few bites of sausage and the opening section of *Le Monde*.

It was not only a thirst for information that made Cassandra Nutt drape her bed with foreign journals. With the amount of newsprint that came off the *Corriere della Sera* — not to mention the *New York Herald-Tribune* — she would never have bothered with the first rag had it not been for her dreams. Cassandra Nutt's dreams were like no one else's: rich webs of symbol and metaphor that left her breathless in her sleep. She was never the protagonist; indeed, she rarely made an appearance in them at all. She was simply the canvas upon which they were painted, the vessel into which their odd, fraught messages were so freely and generously poured. For Cassandra Nutt's dreams always contained a message — cancel the picnic, quarantine the cat, beware falling objects — though it had taken her much of her life to be able to decipher them. A scene in which Jean Pierre Michel was swimming in a hospital gown through a multicolored sea, for example, was a warning that he was about to eat a bad piece of rainbow trout. While the vision of him running down a dark alleyway as a fleet of heavy soup tureens rained down meant only that he should sell his shares of Anaconda Copper. (After the Wall Street crash, Jean Pierre Michel had gamely decided to gamble some of his precious *ducatos* on the still declining market — and had managed, of course, to pick the one or two stocks that continued to make a gain.) Whether or not Cassandra Nutt could interpret what her dreams were telling her, however, did not really matter, for no one ever believed her when she tried to warn them. Jean Pierre Michel could be rushed to the hospital to have his stomach pumped or watch his *ducatos* drain away like a molten river, and he would still scoff the next time she approached him with one of her prophecies.

So she read newspapers. The *Miami Herald*. The *Denver Post. Der Süddeutsche Zeitung*. They helped take her mind off the terrorizing images that flooded her brain while she slept. For there was another aspect to Cassandra Nutt's dreams: they intensified, rather than faded away, upon awakening. Like a network of veins gradually filling up with blood, like a text slowly bleeding black from a surfeit of printer's ink, the images that visited her in the depths of the night grew stronger as the day continued on. The only thing she had found that could block them out was a stream of information from around the world. Dry facts or lurid sensation, English or Swedish or Danish or Dutch, a fresh stack of papers was her best shot at acquiring peace of mind.

On this particular morning she was immersing herself in a lengthy article from the London *Guardian* about the decline of agriculture in the eastern sectors of Brazil and how it would affect the world economy. Cassandra Nutt had little interest in either agriculture, the economy, or the affairs of Brazil. She was unusually eager, however, to press her latest dream from her mind. It took place in a large garden with fruit trees and banks of flowers and a curving stone wall. Benjamin was running through the grass, holding the string of a kite, and his joyfulness seeped from the edges of the dream like syrup upon Cassandra Nutt's pillow. Only when he reached a large fountain by the far wall, and began to circle it, did that joy turn to horror—for just as he was about to complete his first revolution, he began to disappear. Like an ice cube in warm water, he slowly dissolved, until nothing was left of him at all. The balloon floated off into the perfect blue sky, and on the grass, beside the fountain, lay a small piece of metal that glowed like a radioactive mah-jongg tile.

Most of Cassandra Nutt's dream was lovely, a Wonderland-like vision of a golden afternoon. The disappearance of Benjamin, however, made her heart race with fear. Her only recourse was to bury herself more deeply in the agricultural conditions of Brazil—and the political uprisings in Spain—and the latest beauty tips from France—until the picture of Benjamin fading away finally faded away itself.

the waters of the Black Sea

ON THE MORNINGS when Jean Pierre Michel was not off hunting eggs, he was in bed with Princess Larissa, savoring the joys of Russian womanhood. It was more than likely that Princess Larissa was not really a princess; anyone who left Russia before the revolution could claim to be royalty as long as they had the bravado—and the jewelry—to back it up. Princess Larissa had both, plus a thick mane of hair that she wore in a huge mountain on the top of her head and let down when she made love with Jean Pierre Michel. Princess Larissa always insisted on taking the top position when she made love; she would lower her hair as her passion rose and cry out the names of tiny villages in the Caucasus when it exploded. With the sound of these place names ricocheting across the room, and the rich hair pouring over him like the waters of the Black Sea, Jean Pierre Michel felt a strange nostalgia that he could attribute only to genetic memory.

At the age of forty-seven, Princess Larissa could easily have been the mother of Jean Pierre Michel's previous lover, Maria Constanza Garcia, the granddaughter of Juan Garcia, his twice weekly gardener. The princess's age, however, gave her scant distinction among the litany of Jean Pierre Michel's lovers. Over the course of his seventy-two years, Jean Pierre Michel had slept with women of every age, size, shape, religion, and color. Without statistics, figuring that he had made love an average of two times a night on an average of four nights a week over a period of fifty-eight years (beginning with his first experience with Dara Sue Pritchard, in a grain elevator when he was fifteen, and excluding the six months following his double hernia operation when he was fifty-three), he had probably achieved orgasm in the vicinity of twenty-four thousand times. And although the duration of his affairs ranged from a single encounter to, in one or two cases, six or seven years, he always found each individual act of lovemaking to be a revelation. Each woman's body was different, but even the same woman's body was different each time that she made love. It was in finding that subtle alteration—the slight tension in the small of the back, the sudden responsiveness in the buttocks—that Jean Pierre Michel took his greatest pride as a lover. Each encounter required a careful attentiveness, a listening, a presence. Indeed, by the time he was in his mid-forties his own orgasms began to seem superfluous. It was only in recent years, when he realized that his life was drawing to a close, that he took to appreciating them again, aware that in their pitch and fury they were a sort of dress rehearsal for that final, departing spasm.

Today, however, it was neither Princess Larissa's shouts nor her hair that caused Jean Pierre Michel to tumble over the edge of his passion. It was a sudden rapping on the bedroom door, followed by the unexpected sound of Cassandra Nutt's voice.

"Telephone call from Benjamin's headmaster, Monsieur C.! There seems to be a problem with Benjamin!"

Jean Pierre Michel lay still for a moment, the waters of the Black Sea subsiding all around him. "Thank you, Cassandra," he called back. "I'll be right there."

The princess shifted her body, and for a fraction of an instant Jean Pierre Michel considered setting back out to sea. In the name of duty, however, and his newfound fatherhood, he rose, threw on his robe, and went to find out just what was the problem with Benjamin.

up a tree

THE PROBLEM WITH BENJAMIN was in its own way the climax to a situation that had been escalating for weeks. For just as Benjamin had expected, his ability to disappear had provided Petrie Woolrich with the perfect means to humiliate Snyder Stevens. Petrie's plan developed in three stages, the first of which involved finding moments in which Benjamin could be alone with Snyder and use his powers to confuse him. If Snyder volunteered to go to the arts supply room, for example, Benjamin would volunteer to go with him and then vanish along the way. If Benjamin and Snyder were alone in the boys' bathroom, Benjamin would fade out while he and Snyder were standing at the urinal. If Snyder was chosen to do the head count when they went in the bus on a field trip, Benjamin would sit alone at the back, disappear just a moment before Snyder began counting, and then reappear just before he had finished. Snyder, who was not that bright to begin with, assumed that Benjamin was playing tricks on him and simply increased his attacks. "Stand too close to the heat register?" he'd whisper while they were standing in the lunch line. "Jam jar explode?" he'd mutter as they lined up for gym. Benjamin did his best to act as if everything were normal, but over the course of the fall term Snyder began to suspect that something odd was occurring in the state of Texas.

The second phase of the plan—to actually reveal his gift—was initiated during the Berbin Academy Annual Christmas Pageant. The entire school was involved in the pageant, which was composed of a series of carols, a reading from the Bible, and a full-scale depiction of the Nativity. While it would seem that the point of any such affair would be to celebrate the singularity of the Holy Family, Headmaster Fisk, in order not to lose any of the parents' substantial Christmas donations, allowed for five Marys, four Josephs, and fourteen Baby Jesuses. The rest of the children (with the exception of Foster Hewitt and Elizabeth Bates Morgan, who, along with Headmaster Fisk, portrayed the Three Wise Men) were relegated to being livestock, and it was while impersonating a sheep on a simulated midnight clear that Benjamin revealed his powers to Snyder.

It was very crowded on the Berbin Academy auditorium stage; with so many Marys, Josephs, and Jesuses hugging center, there was little room for all the pigs, cows, horses, geese, and sheep. Benjamin and Snyder were therefore stranded on the upper left-hand corner of the set, between a huge mountain of straw and a six-foot cardboard olive tree. At first, with so much activity going on—

with the lights beaming down and the school choir singing—Benjamin could only stand there in his little lamb outfit and absorb the spectacle like others. About half an hour into the proceedings, however, as the Wise Men began to bow before the cluster of Holy Children, he turned to Snyder and spoke.

"There's something I ought to explain to you," he whispered. "It might clear things up."

"The only thing that needs clearing up," said Snyder Stevens, "is your face."

Benjamin, who by now was used to such comments, continued on calmly. "I can disappear," he said.

Snyder turned, the sweat dripping down beneath his fuzzy-wool hood over his forehead. "You're weirder than I thought."

"Watch closely," said Benjamin, and with several hundred eyes upon him, but none really looking, he slowly began to fade away.

It was only later that Benjamin appreciated what a stroke of Petrie's genius it was to have him demonstrate his gift in the middle of the Christmas pageant. With so much else going on, no one noticed the lone wavering sheep in the upper left-hand corner of the stage. The effect on Snyder Stevens, however, was undeniable. As Benjamin dissolved, so did control of Snyder's bladder—making him the first yellow lamb to be present at the birth of Christ.

Once Benjamin revealed his gift to Snyder, he did not let up. In the cloak room, on the stairwell, he always managed to do it in such a way that he was the only one who could see what was happening. The tricks themselves were fairly innocuous, yet it was in the execution of them that

Benjamin began to gain a real confidence in his powers; despite the occasional blunder (like when he aimed for the janitor's office and arrived in the girls' lavatory), he began to experience a consistency to his efforts that only made him wish to do more. And though Snyder grew angrier and more frustrated with each demonstration, what could he do? Tell people that Benjamin Chernovsky could disappear? That he was not really an eight-year-old child, but a warlock? A druid? A creature from another planet?

The situation came to a head in late February, when Snyder, Jack Sanders, and Billy MacDonald decided to climb a trio of great oaks in the schoolyard in an attempt to beat the record of the current national fad known as tree sitting. The teachers who discovered them tried to threaten them with expulsion if they did not come down. When Headmaster Fisk found out about it, however, he set up a team to watch them, sent them food at mealtimes and blankets during the night, and adjusted all activities around the hope that a record-breaking stay might bring national headlines.

Benjamin, under Petrie's guidance, waited until the excitement had died down before taking advantage of the situation. It was only on the third day, after Jack Sanders had grown bored and weary and had descended from his perch, that he initiated the final phase of the plan: to demonstrate to Snyder that, as well as disappear, he could transfer himself to any place he liked. While the rest of the students were eating lunch, Benjamin wandered off to an empty corridor and transferred himself to a branch of the oak tree in which Snyder was sitting. By this time Snyder was tired of the whole thing; he'd had no idea, when he'd first climbed the tree, that winning national fame could be so boring. When he heard a voice say, "Hello, Snyder," however, and turned to see Benjamin materializing beside him, he screamed so loudly that people thought he'd been bitten by a snake. (The oak trees in the Berbin Academy schoolyard were not known for being inhabited by snakes, but even snakes were more likely than disappearing-reappearing eight-year-olds.) Benjamin vanished again before anyone else could see him, and when Snyder clambered down from the tree, babbling insanely that Benjamin was the Cheshire Cat, they called Snyder's parents and Jean Pierre Michel down to Headmaster Fisk's office to analyze the problem.

There wasn't much to analyze. Even Snyder seemed stunned at the rabidness of his accusations, and the docile manner in which Benjamin bore them only made them seem more absurd. By the time Snyder had finished explaining how Benjamin had "turned shadowy and then see-through and then goddamn disappeared," the case was closed. They carted him off, never to be heard of again.

As they followed him away, Snyder's parents looked relieved. But Jean Pierre Michel and Cassandra Nutt (who, though not technically a parent to Benjamin, had insisted on joining Jean Pierre Michel in his defense) were not. For although Snyder Stevens's accusations were clearly the product of a deluded mind, both Jean Pierre Michel and Cassandra Nutt knew that somewhere within them was an undeniable, if not yet comprehensible, grain of truth.

5/A Grand Tour

little suitcases

ITH SNYDER STEVENS removed from his life, Benjamin found his days at the Berbin Academy far less oppressive. He discovered that he liked reading, hated math, was good at geography, was not so good at drawing, and when given the space to do so could hang from the monkey bars with every bit the ease of his arrogant former antagonist. By the time spring arrived, the other children had adjusted to his arresting looks. By the time summer did, he'd expanded his circle beyond Petrie to include Ralph Westingholme, a large, egg-faced boy whose only interest was bugs, and Betsy Cherney, who, as she was destined to be seated beside him for the remainder of their school days, had decided that she and Benjamin might as well be friends. Betsy's mother, Teresa May Cherney, was a former Louisiana homecoming queen whose bouncing good spirits augmented Benjamin's and Betsy's playtime with bird-watching, treasure

hunts, and lessons in how to make the perfect blueberry cobbler. ("The secret," she confided, "is to soak the little devils for three days before baking in a quart of Jack Daniel's.") Benjamin would invariably return from a day at the Cherneys' with a slight southern drawl and a desire to lounge upon the sofa. A day with Ralph, on the other hand, launched Benjamin into a world of microscopic detail, where the measurement of the wingspan of a South African tsetse fly could absorb an entire morning. That summer Ralph was particularly interested in hard-plated beetles, of which he kept a variety in his room in a series of glass jars and which he proceeded to illuminate for Benjamin as if they were a minor order of angels. ("Look how the shell of the musk beetle glitters. Even the pronotum of the click beetle can't match such iridescence.")

It was only after a day with Petrie, however, that Benjamin felt truly content. It wasn't Petrie's interests that nourished him (his current preoccupation being the laws of positive integral exponents and the simplification of radicals), and it certainly wasn't his surroundings (although the room Petrie shared was one of the least oppressive in the orphanage, it felt like a prison and smelled like a hospital to Benjamin). It was Petrie himself: toxic and cynical and, to Benjamin, utterly fascinating. Together with Cassandra Nutt—who chauffeured them about town in a variety of outfits that were often more exciting than the places they went—they managed to keep boredom at bay.

If anything seemed missing from Benjamin's summer, it was Jean Pierre Michel, for as time went by, and the novelty of having a son began to fade, he lost track of the impulse that had made him wish for him in the first place.

Princess Larissa didn't help matters. Having grown tired of the superficiality of American culture, the princess was in a funk. The waters of the Black Sea were therefore stilled, and Jean Pierre Michel was left to spend the better part of his time trying to stir them up again. He engaged a world-renowned violinist to play Rimsky-Korsakov while they dined. He kept buckets of herring, flown in from Finland, on ice in his customized bathtub. He hired a horse-drawn carriage to drive them through Central Park while a small boy, crouched upon the roof, tossed artificial snow in their path. Princess Larissa simply sighed and declared that it must be a punishment for her great beauty that she be forced to live in a country whose president had the same name as a vacuum cleaner.

It was not until Benjamin had begun his second year at the Berbin Academy that Jean Pierre Michel stumbled upon a solution to his problem. It was a quiet evening in late October; the violinist was ill, and everyone was relishing the uncustomary silence as they dined on a hearty beef Stroganoff. Eventually, however, Jean Pierre Michel spoke.

"How are things at school, Benjamin?"

"Fine," said Benjamin.

"What are they teaching you this term?"

Benjamin paused for a moment. "Fractions," he said. "And the planets of the solar system." He scooped up a forkful of noodles. "And war."

"War?" said Cassandra Nutt.

"Miss Daniels says that we must understand the events that have shaped our destinies."

The princess lowered her wineglass to the table. "Is true," she said. "You not know meaning of life until you look bastards in face who steal your land and butcher your brothers like dogs."

Benjamin stopped chewing for a moment.

"War is a fact," said Jean Pierre Michel. "There's no point in pretending it doesn't exist."

"War," said Cassandra Nutt, stabbing a large chunk of beef, "is a load o' hogwash. Don't let nobody get you goosed up for war, Benjamin."

"What else are you learning?" said Jean Pierre Michel.

"We learned about Governor Roosevelt," said Benjamin. "How he has polio and is in a wheelchair. And how he married his cousin."

"Is terrible," said Princess Larissa. "Whole Crimea is ruin because of people marry cousins. One village is complete idiots because of people marry cousins."

"And we've gone on a lot of field trips," said Benjamin.

"Field trips?" said Cassandra Nutt.

"Last week we went to New Jersey."

"New Jersey?"

"To visit some cows."

Jean Pierre Michel looked up. "You went to New Jersey," he said. "To visit some cows."

"We took them medicine," said Benjamin. "We always take someone medicine when we go on a field trip."

Jean Pierre Michel placed his fork beside his plate. "Medicine," he said.

"In little suitcases," said Benjamin. "They're always lighter on the way back."

No more was said about either cows or New Jersey, but the next day Jean Pierre Michel set off to discover what was in the little suitcases; and on the following Thursday—after a field trip to Connecticut to look at some horses—and a field trip to Delaware to look at some pigs—he revealed to the superintendent of education (with the aid of the school bus driver, who was able, with the amount of *ducatos* Jean Pierre Michel paid him, to retire to a small home in Fort Lauderdale) that Headmaster Fisk was using the first- and second-grade children to transport bootleg liquor across state lines. When the story broke, the school was dubbed "the Bourbon Academy," and its doors were promptly closed.

As a result of this incident, on the following evening, as Jean Pierre Michel, Cassandra Nutt, the princess, and Benjamin were dining upon a turkey tetrazzini, Jean Pierre Michel announced that he was taking them all to Europe.

"Europe!" cried the princess. "Is blessing! Is miracle!"

"It's time Benjamin sees the world," said Jean Pierre Michel.

"What about his education?" said Cassandra Nutt. "You can't just whisk a nine-year-old child off to Europe."

"What better education could he have than the National Gallery—the Vatican—the Louvre?" said Jean Pierre Michel. "Shy, of course, of smuggling bootleg liquor to a band of chickens in Rhode Island."

"Well, you better hire him a tutor," said Cassandra Nutt. "They got laws about these things."

Jean Pierre Michel took a sip of his wine. "You've never failed me in any of your other capacities, Cassandra. I'm certain you'll do just fine."

Jean Pierre Michel returned to his dinner, delighted that he had at last found a way to reinvigorate the princess. Before either she or Cassandra Nutt could sink into contemplation of the trip, however, Benjamin posed a new question.

"Can Petrie come?" he said.

"Who?" said Jean Pierre Michel.

"Petrie Woolrich," said Benjamin. "He's my best friend. I think he'd like Europe a lot."

Jean Pierre Michel wiped his mouth with his napkin. "I suppose that we can speak to his parents about it."

"Petrie Woolrich doesn't have any parents," said Benjamin.

"I see," said Jean Pierre Michel. He turned to Cassandra Nutt, who was in the process of serving herself another portion of turkey tetrazzini. "Do you think you can handle another pupil, Cassandra?"

Cassandra Nutt shrugged. "Why stop at two?" she said. "Might as well take ten. Might as well take the whole damn school."

Jean Pierre Michel turned back to Benjamin. "Petrie can come."

The dinner continued on in silence, each of the diners immersed in his or her vision of the adventure to come. That evening, however, Cassandra Nutt had another dream. It began with Benjamin, now grown to adulthood, running through a field. Just as in the first dream, he began to fade away, only this time he reappeared, running through the streets of a dark city. Again he faded, this time to resurface running down an illuminated corridor, his feet, as they beat upon the bright white floor, leaving behind them a rich trail of words. Cassandra Nutt could not read what the words said, but as Benjamin ran faster she felt a kind of panic build inside her, until suddenly—like a pot pie in a too hot oven—he exploded.

Cassandra Nutt had had many troubling dreams in her life, but nothing had ever thrust her into such sweat-drenched wakefulness as the dream of Benjamin exploding. So even though she knew that he was only a child, she decided, the following morning, to tell him about it.

"Maybe it's just a warning that you should keep off the track team. But I thought I ought to tell you. Just in case."

Benjamin listened carefully to what Cassandra Nutt described and promised that he would try to remember it. As soon as she was gone, however, he searched out Petrie Woolrich in the hope that he might help him to interpret what it meant.

"I agree with Cassandra Nutt," said Petrie. "It seems more of a warning than a prediction. And the fact is, it doesn't come as much of a surprise."

"What do you mean?" said Benjamin.

"Every gift has its price," said Petrie. "It seems to me you're being warned about the potential danger of these powers you've got. Warned that if you don't manage them properly, something awful might happen."

"What should I do?"

"Go slowly. Try to learn what you can and can't do. Maybe if you figure out the rules of your gift, and the reasons you were given it, it won't explode."

"You mean I won't explode," said Benjamin.

Petrie slipped his hands into his pockets. "Let's hope it's a metaphor, Benjamin."

Benjamin tried to think about what Petrie was saying. He had never considered that his gift might be dangerous or gotten too far in trying to determine what its purpose might be. As he packed his bags, however, and made ready for the departure, he suspected that the trip to Europe would provide him with at least a few clues.

big suitcases

BY THE FOLLOWING MONDAY Jean Pierre Michel had booked three large staterooms on the *Queen Isadora,* secured permission to take Petrie on leave from his orphanage (the board of trustees having tried to coerce him into signing a document promising never to return him), and carefully instructed the little band of travelers on how to prepare for the trip. The greatest challenge seemed to be the coordination and transportation of Cassandra Nutt's and Princess Larissa's suitcases; they had a combined total of twenty-three pieces, not to mention a pair of large, empty trunks to hold what they planned to buy when they got there. When they gathered at the mansion on the morning of their departure and Princess Larissa got a look at Petrie Woolrich, she pointed out that, with the addition of a small cap, he would make an excellent porter. Petrie responded by announcing that the only baggage he would consider transporting was the princess herself and only then if she promised to travel in one of the trunks. This interchange established a line of demarcation between the two that was not to be crossed for the remainder of the trip.

The passage to England was, for the most part, quite easy. Jean Pierre Michel managed to secure the captain's quarters for himself and Princess Larissa, and they spent most of their time there with the doors locked, making love. With the Atlantic surging beneath him and the Black

Sea churning above, Jean Pierre Michel felt blissfully wa-
terlogged; when he left the cabin at all it was to give his
old, splintery bones a chance to dry out. Cassandra Nutt
befriended the displaced captain, who taught her cross-
coordinate navigation by day and who sat, astonished, at
the poker table by night as she demonstrated her wizardry
with a deck of cards. Benjamin and Petrie were therefore
left to their own devices, and by the end of the crossing at
least two-thirds of the passengers were ready to jump
overboard when they saw either of the two boys coming
toward them.

When they arrived in London, Jean Pierre Michel installed them in a trio of connecting suites on the top floor
of Claridge's, and then, one by one, they set out to conquer
the town. Cassandra Nutt turned her attention to politics
and in a matter of days knew more about the Laws of Succession than most of the members of Parliament. Benjamin
and Petrie headed directly to Baker Street, as Petrie suggested that Benjamin's powers might be a form of higher
mathematics and that by studying the methods of Sherlock
Holmes they might discover some of the secrets of its
workings. Jean Pierre Michel made his way to the shops
in Mayfair and the galleries along Piccadilly. And Princess
Larissa discovered the British Museum, where she insisted, at all times, God was present.

"We must all go to British Museum," she announced
one morning at breakfast. "Is holy experience."

The others were unmoved by the princess's exhortation,
but Jean Pierre Michel knew better than to tempt the
fates—so the following morning he hired a limousine to
take the entire group to Great Russell Street, where the
curator of the museum was waiting to take Benjamin,

Petrie, the princess, and Cassandra Nutt on a personally guided tour. (Jean Pierre Michel himself abstained, having discovered many years earlier that museums were places of conflict—the ecstatic, almost erotic ecstasy he felt in the presence of great art made bitter by the fact that he was unable to take any of it home with him. He spent the hours, instead, in the Bloomsbury antique shops, acquiring a cherrywood gramophone cabinet inlaid with Japanese panels and a seventeenth-century Bavarian horn cup with twisted pewter mounts.) Benjamin, Petrie, and Cassandra Nutt had to admit that the museum was wonderful. They had difficulty, however, comprehending the effect that it had on Princess Larissa. As she walked from room to room she became light-headed and woozy, and when she reached the Elgin Marbles she fainted dead away. Benjamin, knowing Jean Pierre Michel's sensitivity to art, suggested that this was evidence that she was indeed his father's match. Petrie, however, offered a distinctly different theory.

"Too much makeup," he said. "When that stuff gets into your bloodstream, it knocks you out cold."

They remained in London for several weeks, allowing enough time for Cassandra Nutt to familiarize herself with the Royal Courts of Justice, for Jean Pierre Michel to begin a collection of Dunhill lighters, and for Benjamin and Petrie to terrorize the London Zoo. As November rolled into December, however, the princess began to exhibit signs of depression again, the rain making her dwell on the death of Pushkin and the food making her yearn for another helping of Cassandra Nutt's beef Stroganoff.

"In Kursk we eat better even during famine," she said.

Jean Pierre Michel agreed that it was time to move on, so they packed their bags and made their way to Paris, where the princess nearly died of joy. Not only were there the Louvre and Versailles and Notre Dame and Saint Chapelle, there were *blanquette de veau, lapin à la moutarde, confit de canard,* and a dazzling array of desserts that ranged from *tarte tatin* to *marquise au chocolat à la pistache.* Jean Pierre Michel even discovered a pastry called *la princesse,* a frothy meringue concoction laced with almonds, vanilla cream, and grains of nougatine, which the princess, once having tasted it, insisted on being served each morning in bed with a large bowl of café au lait.

Like the princess, Cassandra Nutt was impressed with France's gastronomic offerings. Her chief obsession, however, from the moment she arrived, was fashion. With Jean Pierre Michel busy pampering the princess, Cassandra Nutt had to do all her shopping herself. She found, however, that her employer's *ducatos* changed as nicely into francs as they did into dollars and that there was no limit to the possibilities that Mademoiselles Chanel, Lanvin, and Lemonnier offered her to spend them. By the end of the first week she had purchased a midnight-blue-and-silver silk opera cape, a handbag made of brushed kangaroo leather, and an emerald-and-amber velvet-and-pheasant-feather hat.

"Miss Josephine Baker," Cassandra Nutt remarked to Benjamin, "better stay on her toes!"

It was in Paris, while Jean Pierre Michel and the princess were eating *soufflés de grenouille* and Cassandra Nutt was playing dress-up, that Benjamin and Petrie set out to explore Benjamin's powers. At Petrie's suggestion they headed up to Montmartre, where an underworld of artists and dwarfs and amputees roamed the narrow streets that wound through the heights of the city.

"Life's strange, Benjamin," said Petrie. "And the fact is, so are you and I."

Petrie's idea was to test Benjamin's powers under a variety of different circumstances—by day and by night, in fair weather and foul, when he was hungry, when he was sleepy, when he was in a crowd, when he was alone—in order to find out if they harbored any limitations. Over the following days Benjamin therefore transferred himself into hidden courtyards and smoke-filled cafés and misty street corners in the process of being hazily painted. It wasn't until they had almost given up, however, that a significant finding emerged. Benjamin had transferred himself from the steps of the Sacré Coeur to a bench in the *Place des Abbesses*. He'd promised Petrie that he would return in fifteen minutes, but shortly after arriving, he was joined on the bench by a slender gentleman who announced that his name was Gustave and then proceeded, in broken English, to expound his philosophy of the art of piano tuning. Benjamin listened politely, but when it came time to leave, Gustave would not allow it; he insisted that he had not reached the heart of his discourse and, grasping Benjamin's sleeve, proceeded to go on. Twenty minutes passed. Then thirty. Then forty. And then Benjamin began to experience a pounding in his head and the vague smell of something burning. When he realized that the odor was coming from him, he decided that whether or not it would create permanent psychological damage for Gustave, he had no choice but to return to Petrie.

It was in this manner that Benjamin first came to consider what Petrie soon christened "the Cinderella factor."

"Can't we call it something else?" said Benjamin.

Petrie shook his head. "It's the classic example of the limited-time constraint," he said. "In her case, failure to leave by the appointed hour meant rags and a pumpkin. In your case . . ." He paused. "Well, I don't think we want to find out."

"Boom," Benjamin said glumly.

"The burning smell is not a good sign, Benjamin."

In order to be certain of his thesis, Petrie sent Benjamin on several more trips with time as the operative factor. And in the end, the evidence was fairly conclusive.

"I'd say fifty minutes is your outer range," said Petrie. "If you return to where you started from within forty-five, you shouldn't have any problems."

Benjamin tried to grasp the idea that he was like a sleeping hand grenade. "Why didn't I explode," he said, "when I transferred myself into the Hispano-Suiza?"

"I don't know," said Petrie. "Maybe if the need to escape is strong enough, a one-way transfer is possible. Maybe if you have no intention of ever returning to the place you started, you cancel out the time factor. I'd be careful about testing it out, though."

Benjamin agreed. In fact, having isolated "the Cinderella factor," he decided to put his gift on ice for a while. He and Petrie therefore spent the remainder of their time in Paris making ordinary mischief: running through the Tuilleries, stealing ashtrays from the cafés along the Place de l'Opéra, dropping eggs off the Pont des Arts upon the passing *bateaux*.

As the journey continued, the sights began to blur. They took a train to Marseilles, where they left the better part of their luggage, then a boat to the Genovese coast. Then they hired a car, and Cassandra Nutt whipped them through the back roads of Liguria and the bright Tuscan hills until they reached the sprawling madness of Rome. By now, having been abroad for several months, their senses were beginning to dull. This time it was the princess who went shopping and Cassandra Nutt who ate. This time it was Jean Pierre Michel who dragged them to the museum, having decided that as it would be impossible to transport it even if he could purchase it, it was safe to view the ceiling of the Sistine Chapel. When they reached the vast room where it was painted, Benjamin felt a storm that he had been unaware of grow quiet inside him, and for the first time he felt that he understood Jean Pierre Michel's relationship to beauty. The princess became delirious, and even Petrie was awed. When Benjamin pointed out the scene of God creating man, he could only nod, very slowly, as if some complex logarithm had just been solved.

It was in Rome, during a snowstorm, that Benjamin stumbled upon one of the keys to his future. It was late one evening, and the princess couldn't sleep; after a grueling day of shopping, her system was imbalanced and she insisted that she needed some liver salts. Under normal conditions Cassandra Nutt would have been sent to find them. Cassandra Nutt, however, was in her own bed, recovering from a venomous portion of *spaghetti putanesca*, so Benjamin was dispatched instead.

He was quite sleepy as he entered the tiny elevator, his clothes on over his pajamas, a paper that read *"bicarbonato di sodio"* clutched in his left hand. When the cage reached the lobby, however, he was lured from his sleep by two strange impressions: the sight, through the window, of snow falling up and the sound, from a doorway across the

65

lobby, of a soft, insinuating music. When he crossed to that
doorway he found a trio of musicians on a plush little
stage, a handful of patrons at a scattering of tables, a cluster of lights casting beams through a filter of smoke. But
though he registered the piano and the large set of drums,
the sound that drew him in was the rumble—the swoon—
the sweetness—of the tenor saxophone.

Benjamin stood in that doorway for close to an hour.
Only when one of the waiters brushed by him and the paper slipped from his hand did he remember the liver salts
and scurry back to the lobby, where he was shaken from
his stupor by the sight of Petrie, wearing a black fedora
and conversing with a heavyset man. They exchanged a
few words; then the heavyset man nodded; then they
moved to the door and sauntered off into the night.

Benjamin could not fathom where his friend could be
heading after midnight like some miniature mafioso. He
went to the concierge, however, to get the liver salts for the
princess, delivered them to her room, and then returned to
his own room and tried his best to get some sleep.

The following morning, when Benjamin awoke, he
found Petrie sleeping snug in the bed beside him. When he
asked him where he had gone, however, Petrie was reluctant to explain himself.

"It's a big city," he said. "It's hard to keep track."

When Benjamin pressed him further, Petrie finally said
that he would rather show him than tell him, so the following afternoon—while Jean Pierre Michel roamed the
Forum and the princess visited the Vatican and Cassandra
Nutt continued her relentless search for the perfect osso
buco—Petrie led Benjamin down a series of winding side
streets to a small, enclosed courtyard, strewn with broken

glass, where a group of teenage boys stood waiting. There were nine of them all together, each tiny and wiry like Petrie himself, and they glared at Benjamin suspiciously.

Petrie stepped forward. *"Mi amico,"* he said in a thick, heavy voice.

The boys exchanged looks. One of them mumbled something. Then they moved toward Benjamin and began to encircle him, studying him as if he were a figure made of wax. One of them pulled a hair from his head and ran it across his tongue. One of them rubbed his thumb across his cheek to see if his birthmark would wipe away. When they were finished looking him over, they conferred for a few moments; then the leader of the group muttered something; then Petrie announced to Benjamin that he could go with them.

The adventure turned out to be an afternoon of petty thievery. Benjamin followed along as they made their way through the city and into the bags and pockets of the unsuspecting. Their methods were crude but effective: they split up into pairs, one person acting as a distraction, the other as a concentrated wad of grease that slithered the possessions away. They had speed on their side, plus a certain unsavoriness that made their victims eager to hurry off once the unknown deed was done. It did not take long, however, to discover that Benjamin was not cut out for this sort of work. His looks made it difficult for him to get lost in the crowd, let alone casually slip his hand into a stranger's pocket. Petrie, on the other hand, was a natural. His tiny body could slip into the small space between the arm as it reached for the handle of the door and the pocket that housed the plump billfold, while his swift intelligence could always discern who had had too much wine with his lunch. By the end of the afternoon he had demonstrated to Benjamin that he was a bona fide pickpocket prodigy.

Later that evening Benjamin took Petrie to the lobby to share his discovery of the saxophone. Petrie agreed that it was an excellent sound and encouraged him to learn how to play. For the next few days things went on in this fashion: Petrie sneaking off in the afternoon to do a bit of thieving, Benjamin sneaking off at night to listen to the sinuous music. The following Wednesday, however, Petrie began to behave rather oddly. At breakfast he embarked upon a lengthy conversation with Jean Pierre Michel regarding the Pakistani funeral steles in the Pontifical Missionary and Ethnological Museum. At lunch he presented Cassandra Nutt with a Boucheron brooch, which he claimed to have found in the gutter of the Piazza del Popolo. He even managed to give a little smile to Princess Larissa—although the princess, accustomed to his bile, interpreted it as indigestion. Toward the end of the meal Petrie whispered to Benjamin that he needed to speak with him and asked if they might slip away again late that afternoon.

It was almost dusk as they crept from the hotel, made their way along the Tiber, and headed out toward the seedy quarter where the teenage pickpockets gathered. It was a cold, misty day, and as they walked along the river Petrie was as strangely silent as he'd been chattery and animated earlier. Only when they reached the outskirts of the quarter, where the buildings closed in tightly upon each other, did he stop, turn to Benjamin, and speak.

"You're the best friend I've ever had, Benjamin," he said. "The fact is, you're the only friend I've ever had. But this is the first time in my life I feel like my life makes sense. Like I belong somewhere. If I don't do this, I'm just going to wind up back at that stinking orphanage."

Benjamin felt the damp fog burn against his cheeks. "What about my powers?" he said.

"What about them?" said Petrie.

"How am I supposed to figure out how to use them without you?"

Petrie shook his head. "You don't need me to help you, Benjamin. Just keep experimenting. Just keep watching. You'll figure it out yourself."

Benjamin kept his eyes on Petrie, hoping that if he did not break the contact, his friend would not go. After a moment, however, Petrie thrust out his hand, which Benjamin took, and then he strode off into the gray afternoon, his compact body already possessing the quiet confidence of a hoodlum. And though it was Benjamin who yearned not to be there, and Benjamin who possessed the gift, it was Petrie—like a puff of smoke into the damp winter air—who disappeared.

And unlike Benjamin, he did not return.

the dance of the bleu cheese

DESPITE BENJAMIN'S insistence that Petrie had vanished on his own, Jean Pierre Michel initiated an extensive search for him the moment he learned of his disappearance. Only after spending several suitcases full of lire (not to mention exhausting the entire carabinieri) did he accept the fact that the odd little fellow was gone. Benjamin, Cassandra Nutt, and even Princess Larissa subsequently descended into a deep melancholy (once Petrie disappeared he became the princess's dearest object, like the purse or the fan one suddenly finds one's left behind at the opera), which Jean Pierre Michel could think to assuage only by repairing to the small villa on the Côte d'Azur where his mother, Alma Esther Rosenberg Chernovsky Chevalier, now lived. Jean Pierre Michel's father, Isaac Aaron, had died in 1905 in a skiing accident in Chamonix; he was crossing the slopes to the sauna when a pair of Swiss slalom champions came swooping around a corner and leveled him in his tracks. Alma Esther immediately relocated to Nice, where she met and married the French industrialist Gilbert Chevalier. When he too died the following autumn, she purchased a villa in Cap d'Antibes and, having at last acquired a French surname, settled in for the duration. As the years went by she grew thinner and thinner and more and more translucent, so that by the time Jean Pierre Michel and the others came to visit, she was like an exceptional piece of Roquefort: ninety-eight years old and generously veined with a deep filigree of blue.

Jean Pierre Michel, who was visiting for the first time, was delighted with his mother's surroundings. The villa was spacious but intimate, offering spectacular views from almost every window and a path that led down the face of a cliff to the sea. Alma Esther said nothing about the fact that it had taken her son over a quarter of a century to visit; she seemed to accept this as unquestioningly as she accepted the fact that when he finally arrived he brought with him a Russian princess, a magnificently dressed colored woman, and a beautiful, birthmarked child. They were all welcome at the Villa Chernovsky-Chevalier, and, heavy with the loss of Petrie (not to mention the steak-

and-kidney pie and the *confit de canard* and the *tortellini in brodo*), they were all deeply grateful for the quiet and the chance to rest.

Over the next few days each of the weary travelers followed his own path toward restoration. Jean Pierre Michel spent his time at a local café, where the proprietor engaged him in a series of discussions concerning the relative merits of the interior designs of Georges Champion and Robert Mallet-Stevens. Cassandra Nutt challenged Alma Esther's chauffeur, Henri, to car races along the coast: she took the Pic-Pic, he the Peugeot, the winner of each day's contest treating the loser to champagne and truffles. And Benjamin, who had convinced Jean Pierre Michel to buy him a 1924 Selmer tenor sax, wandered down the narrow path to the sea, where he sat upon a rock and discovered just how hard it was to play it. The sounds that issued from Benjamin's horn were nothing like the graceful music he'd heard in the lobby of the hotel in Rome. Each squawk, however, each blast, each bleat, expressed another bead of his anguish at losing Petrie. The rocks may have crumbled—the birds relocated to another stretch of the coast—but the dissonant music kept Benjamin from being swallowed by his pain.

Benjamin discovered something else as he sat by the sea and wailed at the horizon. Although the shoreline was mostly rock face jutting out into the water, there were a few grains of sand within the crevices that were formed where those jagged rocks met, and every so often Benjamin would lay down his saxophone, lick the tip of his forefinger, press that finger against the sand, and place the sand upon the surface of his tongue. To feel the sharpness of the grit—to taste the faint saltiness—to feel the rush of saliva rise up inside his mouth—soothed him as much as his terrible wailing on the horn.

Princess Larissa was another story entirely. For while Benjamin and the others were off in their separate sanctums, the princess was being swept into the mad, exotic world of Alma Esther. With both of her husbands' fortunes at her disposal, Alma Esther had devoted the latter portion of her life to becoming a patroness of the arts, turning the Villa Chernovsky-Chevalier into one of the favorite watering holes of the flock of creative geniuses who passed through France in the first quarter of the century. Everyone who was anyone had paid her a visit—from Isadora Duncan to Igor Stravinsky, from F. Scott Fitzgerald to Picasso to Freud—and Alma Esther had grappled with each theory that they had espoused between bites of brioche in her salon. Her most recent guests had been the young choreographer Martha Graham and the German Expressionist stage director Gustav Meyerhold, and although their visits had occurred several weeks apart, their philosophies had overlapped in Alma Esther's mind so that she felt compelled to somehow forge them together. Draping herself with transparent veils of yellow and green chiffon (which transformed her from a sliver of Roquefort into a wedge of Gorgonzola), she would float, in a near trance, from one room to the next, stopping every so often to freeze in a position that suggested the inner workings of a machine. Cassandra Nutt was convinced that Alma Esther had lost her mind; the old woman's bizarre tableaux opened an entirely new window into the eccentricities of Jean Pierre Michel. Princess Larissa, however, was captivated. In short time she was donning veils of her own and following Alma Esther about the villa.

"Is so liberating!" cried the princess. "Is so wonderful avant-garde!"

This period of recovery lasted twenty-six days, at which point Jean Pierre Michel announced that it was time to return to New York. When he informed the others of this decision, however, he learned, to his sorrow, that the waters of the Black Sea would be remaining, like a small eddy, along the glittering shores of the Mediterranean. The princess made no bones about it: dancing with Jean Pierre Michel's ninety-eight-year-old mother gave her even greater pleasure than making love with Jean Pierre Michel. And nothing that either Jean Pierre Michel, Cassandra Nutt, or Benjamin could think to say to her could convince her to leave her side. (Alma Esther said nothing, having learned many years earlier not to try to control other people's behavior, which was one of the main reasons that she was still alive at the age of ninety-eight.)

It took several days to sort out the luggage, which Henri and Cassandra Nutt retrieved from Marseilles and delivered, two or three pieces at a time, to the villa. The princess insisted that all of her suitcases be opened so that she could make unwanted presents of the various articles she had acquired to Benjamin and Jean Pierre Michel and Cassandra Nutt. When this ritual had been completed, the rest of her things were taken to her room, while the others' things were carefully labeled for shipment back to New York. Then the departing trio said a series of swift goodbyes—which were met, on the part of Alma Esther and Princess Larissa, by a brief pas de deux in the foyer—and set out for their voyage home.

There was little said on the return passage. So much had been eaten, so much had been seen, it would be months before they would be able to digest it all properly. They had new clothes and new books and new ways of thinking. They had plaster casts of important monuments and reproductions of their favorite works of art. As they sat on their deck chairs, however, and stared out at the water, they could not help but think that, whatever they had gained on their trip to Europe — including, for Benjamin, his new insight into his gift — it was nothing compared with what they had left behind.

6/The Ghost of Hamlet's Dad

the scent of cherry tea

HEN JEAN PIERRE MICHEL, Cassandra Nutt, and Benjamin returned to New York, they were startled to discover how the city had deteriorated in their absence. The streets were lined with beggars and panhandlers, shops and restaurants had boarded up their windows, and an eerie silence pervaded the air as construction was halted and the roar of the riveters ceased. Worst of all were the dull expressions on everyone's faces, the series of glazed looks that said they all knew, no matter what anyone told them, that things were only going to get worse.

"Things got to be awful," said Cassandra Nutt, "if everybody be wearin' them Eugenie hats."

To Jean Pierre Michel, however, the atmosphere of poverty was more an annoyance than an inconvenience, for by the fall of 1932 the value of his *ducatos* was greater than ever before. There was little fun in entertaining, however, when your guests either burst into tears over the vichyssoise or pocketed the silver, so Jean Pierre Michel did away with his dinner parties and threw himself, unstintingly, into collecting. This time the focus of his attention was antique weaponry. While having lunch one day with the ambassador to Germany in his small brownstone on West Sixty-third Street, he admired a beautiful eighteenth-century hunting rifle inlaid with tiny scallops of mother-of-pearl. When the ambassador took it down from its cabinet and placed it in his hands, Jean Pierre Michel experienced a sexual thrill that surpassed anything he had known since Lillian Oppenheimer in 1926. He immediately returned to the mansion, transformed the billiards room into a weapons gallery, and set about to fill it with exotic arms.

Cassandra Nutt was horrified. Besides the fact that she loved playing billiards (she and Juan Garcia, Jean Pierre Michel's gardener, had had a standing game each alternating Thursday that dated back to the spring when he'd put down the hydrangea bushes just after the war), she could not bear the thought of living in a house that contained so many instruments of death. Benjamin, however, was just plain scared. It was difficult enough to have a father as old as Methuselah; a father who could purchase anything he wanted; a father with an endless stream of lovers. To have a father who was obsessed with guns and knives made life a somewhat tentative experience. How could he be certain that in a moment of pique he might not use one of the weapons on him?

It was in this atmosphere of yearning and apprehension that something occurred that completely changed the dynamic of life in the Chernovsky household. It was a Saturday morning in early January, and though the holiday decorations had already been taken down and the enormous Christmas tree had been removed from the foyer, there was still a trace of pressure in the air and the lingering scent of pine. Jean Pierre Michel was in the weapons gallery, inspecting a recently acquired Turkish saber with a black-and-magenta velvet-covered scabbard and a handle encrusted with pearls. Cassandra Nutt was in her bedroom, eating chiles rellenos and leafing through the pages of *La Vanguardia*. And Benjamin, feeling bored with his new school (a venerable institution called the Breckinridge School, which, after his adventures in Europe, seemed impossibly dull), was in Ceylon. Upon returning from Europe, Benjamin had sunk into a depression even deeper than the one that had hit New York. He missed Petrie terribly, and though he tried to do what he'd told him—to experiment with his powers and see what he could find—the only thing he came up with was the fact that wherever he went he wished that he were somewhere else. He finally decided that the only thing to do was use his gift to search for Petrie.

He wasn't, of course, certain that he could travel that far. So he began to devote himself to building up his stamina, trying trips to Massachusetts—and Miami—and Madrid—until he was finally able to transfer himself to that courtyard in Rome where Petrie had introduced him to the pickpockets. By the time he got there, the pickpockets were gone. Over the following months, however, he transferred himself in and out of each corner of the Eternal City in the hope of finding his friend.

By the end of September Benjamin had made eighty-three trips to Rome—each one lasting no more than forty-five minutes—and had decided that if Petrie was still there, he was not going to find him. It suddenly occurred to him, however, that he might have gone somewhere else. So he borrowed an atlas from Jean Pierre Michel's library and set out on a global mission. It was a bit like looking for a needle in a haystack, yet Benjamin was convinced that if he concentrated hard enough, the answer to Petrie's whereabouts would come to him. For hours and hours he sat with the large volume propped open upon his lap—tracing his fingers along the rivers and the mountain ranges—scanning the borders of the countries and the continents—in the hope of receiving some sign of where Petrie might be. He usually settled upon places with odd-sounding names, like Kolhumadulu or Qeqertarsuatsiaat or Llanfairpwllgwyngyll. But none of his efforts seemed to lead him to his elusive friend.

Despite Benjamin's failure to locate Petrie Woolrich, his tireless search for him ultimately led him to a different discovery. For as he began to use his gift on a regular basis, he became more and more fascinated by the etheric space of that moment before he disappeared. In that place of dissolving—that space of nonbeing between here and there—he felt a lightness, an emptiness, that was a welcome relief from the chaos of his usual existence.

Benjamin might have gone on searching forever—enjoying his brief moments of incorporeity—had it not been for the cherry tea. It was not the only thing to scent the air on his visit to Ceylon; indeed, there seemed to be a sweetness everywhere, a rich perfume of figs and fennel, a fragrance of candied limes. He'd transferred himself to the moonlit garden of a glittering palace, where an elaborate meal was being served. There was soft, reedy music playing in the distance, there were men with shining skin carrying large trays of food, there was a warm, coaxing breeze floating by. Yet it was not so much what Benjamin experienced while he was there that was significant as what happened when he tried to come back. Benjamin always knew when it was time to return. A few minutes before the burning smell there came a shimmering sensation, like a field of butterflies rising across the surface of his skin. When this occurred he would close his eyes and in a matter of seconds he would be back wherever he had begun. This time, however, just as he was about to go, he caught a strong whiff of cherry tea. And he hesitated. And just like the day that he appeared in the car instead of the painting, he rematerialized at the center of the foyer instead of in the privacy of his own room.

Had Jean Pierre Michel exited the weapons gallery or Cassandra Nutt stepped out onto the second-floor landing one moment later, they would have thought little of finding Benjamin beside the railing where the Christmas tree had recently stood. At precisely the moment they did, however—as their eyes interlocked across the entrance to the mansion—Benjamin rematerialized before them.

And they thought of Snyder Stevens.

And they thought of the Hispano-Suiza.

And they thought of the dozens and dozens of other times they'd suspected that something was going on.

Had they not had each other's stunned faces to look into, however, they would never, ever have believed what they'd both just seen.

Timbuktu to Taiwan

BENJAMIN SAT ON THE COUCH in the east sitting room, the blue winter light filtering in through the door to the garden.

"Say it again," said Jean Pierre Michel.

"I can disappear," said Benjamin.

"You can disappear," said Cassandra Nutt.

"I can disappear," said Benjamin.

The sitting room was divided into two separate areas: a place for conversation that looked out onto the garden and a place for sitting alone by the fire. At the moment, Benjamin's eyes were focused upon the large rug that divided the two spaces, a geometric confusion of black and white intermingled with splashes of gray.

"Just like that?" said Jean Pierre Michel.

"Just like that," said Benjamin.

"You close your eyes," said Cassandra Nutt.

"You think about a place," said Jean Pierre Michel.

Benjamin nodded. "Just like that."

Benjamin knew that he was in trouble when Jean Pierre Michel ushered him into the east sitting room. The majority of Jean Pierre Michel's recently acquired collection of modern furniture had been installed there—from the polished zinc coffee table to the red lacquer bar to the frosted-glass-and-chromium piano—and under normal circumstances it was strictly off-limits to Benjamin.

"And you've been doing this since you first came to us?" said Jean Pierre Michel.

"It's how I first came to you."

"In the car?" said Cassandra Nutt.

"In the car," said Benjamin.

Jean Pierre Michel pursed his lips together. "In the car," he muttered to himself.

Benjamin focused his attention upon the steady ticking of the ivory-and-amber clock upon the wall. He was willing to answer all of their questions, but what was there to say?

How?
By becoming a thought wave.

Where?
Timbuktu to Taiwan.

Why?
I've been asking myself that since it first began.

"How?" said Cassandra Nutt.

"Where?" said Jean Pierre Michel. "Why?"

Benjamin just sat there, his eyes moving evenly from the polished steel lamp that stood in the corner to the cork cigarette box on the mantelpiece. Knowing that it was neither Jean Pierre Michel's nor Cassandra Nutt's fault that they were asking so many questions. Understanding that when you had a gift like his you had to be kind, and clear, and very, very patient.

a glass garden

IT TOOK SEVERAL WEEKS for Jean Pierre Michel and Cassandra Nutt to fully accept the idea of Benjamin's gift. It was too bizarre, too incomprehensible; they were afraid that it marked him as the instrument of some dark, demonic power. In time, however, their curiosity outweighed their fears and they began to ask for small demonstrations. Go to the pantry. Go to Penn Station. Go to the south of Peru. The more they explored it, the more fascinating it became, and if Cassandra Nutt was mostly interested in the moments of coming and going ("Do it again," she'd say when Benjamin returned; "I got to see that part where you go all soft an' see-through, like the ghost of Hamlet's dad"), Jean Pierre Michel was mostly eager to discover whether Benjamin could bring things back from the places he visited. Benjamin himself had never thought of this possibility, and when Jean Pierre Michel suggested it he felt a wave of nausea pass through him. Jean Pierre Michel, however, insisted that he try it, so while the old man waited in the second-floor library, Benjamin transferred himself to the toolshed in the garden, pocketed a pair of pruning shears, and willed himself back to the mansion. With the success of this mission, Jean Pierre Michel sent him off on a series of expeditions: Go to Havana and bring back some cigars. Go to Vladivostock and bring back some vodka. He suddenly saw Benjamin as a device that could help him obtain virtually anything he wished for. And what Jean Pierre Michel wished for, at that particular moment, was weapons.

Lances from Spain.

Muskets from Denmark.

Sabers from Czechoslovakia.

He wanted the best and the most beautiful weapons in the world, and he wanted Benjamin to use his powers to get them.

This time it was Benjamin who was horrified and Cassandra Nutt who was frightened. Bringing guns and knives into the house was awful enough; the thought of using Benjamin to gather them made her bones shiver. She had another dream: On a cold winter's day, a golden snake was writhing through a field of fresh snow. Slowly and methodically it made its way forward, until it reached the center of the field and rose to strike, and out of its mouth sprang a slender, double-edged blade. As the blade sliced the air, the field filled with blood, and Cassandra Nutt knew that she could not remain in a house filled with weapons.

She also knew, however, that she could not abandon Benjamin. And the answer came to her—the way to both leave and stay—one morning while she was preparing Jean Pierre Michel's toast and coffee. Like so many other details in Jean Pierre Michel's life, his toast and coffee had to be made in a fanatically precise manner. The bread had to be a particular shade of brown, with just the right degree of "scrape" should one test it with a knife; the butter had to be applied between fifteen to thirty seconds after toasting, as too soon created sogginess and too late caused clumps to form that were flecked with tiny crumbs; the angle of the cut had to follow from the upper left-hand corner to the lower right and be performed in a single sweep. The coffee had to be freshly ground from beans that had been roasted within the previous seventy-two hours; the water had to be filtered through a charcoal-based purification system; and the temperature of the coffee and milk, respectively, had to be exactly one hundred sixty-five and one hundred forty-eight degrees.

Cassandra Nutt knew this procedure as thoroughly as she knew the way to fold Jean Pierre Michel's socks or remove the footprints from Jean Pierre Michel's carpet or circulate the air, according to season, through Jean Pierre Michel's bedroom suite. On this particular morning, however, as she brought the knife toward the toast to make the perfect cut, she suddenly thought of the other knives that were gathering in the mansion, and she found herself hurling it clear across the kitchen to stick in the wall above the waffle iron. She realized then that as long as there were knives in the house and walls to stick them in, she was going to be in trouble. And then it came to her. She would build a glass garden on the roof of the mansion and live there until Jean Pierre Michel's obsession had passed. She knew that it would pass—like his obsession with Aztec jewelry or his obsession with twelfth-century maps—but until it did, a rooftop garden would allow her to remain safe from the burgeoning war museum and yet still keep an eye on Benjamin.

Once the idea came to her, she had a wonderful time bringing it into being. She hired a prominent New York architect to design the structure, which consisted of six glass walls and a hexagonal glass ceiling piece whose panes folded down to allow fresh air and sunlight to enter. She had Juan Garcia put in soil for a bulb garden (her father, Erasmus Chester Nutt, had always been fond of saying, "Get some dirt on your hands, Cassandra," and though Cassandra Nutt knew that he had been speaking metaphorically, she felt that she was pleasing him whenever she did a little gardening), and she installed a large Victorian divan, where she proceeded to take a succession of lovers. Cassandra Nutt had had many lovers over the years, from the various denizens of Jean Pierre Michel's dinner parties to an assortment she'd discovered on her own. And though her list was not as long as her employer's, it was every bit as exotic: over the course of her forty-five years she had slept with oil barons, taxi drivers, presidents of textile companies, grocery clerks, slide trombonists, and an entire Australian crew team.

"A woman may not be as loose-hipped as a man," said Cassandra Nutt, "but even Heinz got fifty-seven varieties."

Because of the vast parade that had passed through Jean Pierre Michel's bedroom, Cassandra Nutt had never brought any of her own lovers to the mansion. Now, however, with Jean Pierre Michel more infatuated with knives than with women, she finally broke custom: Max, the postal worker, who licked the stamps for her while she waited at window number seven; Billy, the chimney sweep, whose smile was like a fistful of coins; James, the bank financier, whose fine silk undergarments were even fancier than her own.

They came to the glass garden to lie naked beneath the sun. To taste Cassandra Nutt's cinnamon skin. To sprinkle joy upon the rooftop of a lavish mansion that was slowly filling up with rage.

7 / An Affair to Remember

the Velvet Phantom

ENJAMIN STOOD in the doorway of the bedroom and gazed at the great scimitar that hung upon the wall over the bed. The bed belonged to Dr. Seymour Kleinberg, the most prominent obstetrician in Boston, who was currently in the adjoining bathroom, brushing his teeth. Benjamin had approximately two and a half minutes to tiptoe across the room, climb upon Dr. Kleinberg's pillow, retrieve the weapon, and transport himself back to the mansion. The scimitar was encased within a polished nephrite sheath, yet Benjamin found it difficult to believe that Dr. Kleinberg could sleep a wink beneath the dangling blade. One startled cry from a dream too dark, one jostling of the bed from a moment of too great passion, and the chain might break, the blade become unsheathed, and the scimitar fall with a deadly slice into the bed. Benjamin wondered, in fact, if that was what had happened to the obstetrician's wife: only the

sound of a single toothbrush emanated from the bathroom, yet the room seemed to echo with the memory of Mrs. Kleinberg.

Benjamin's efforts to retrieve the scimitar were but the latest in a series of such endeavors. For while Cassandra Nutt had been taking lovers on the roof, Jean Pierre Michel had been busily putting his plan into action. With the aid of a history professor at Columbia University who had a fondness for whips and flintlocks, plus access to a cache of reference materials from the New York Public Library, he was able to discover in which museums, royal armories, and private collections the world's finest weapons were housed. Benjamin would go to a given destination (the private study, say, of a magistrate in York), retrieve a given object (a Persian hunting knife, for example, with open goldwork on the hilt), and return with it to the mansion without anyone noticing that he had been there. In place of each object he would leave a velvet sack containing three times its value, in disposable currency, which generally served to temper the owner's outrage at its disappearance.

Unfortunately things did not go quite as smoothly as planned. When Benjamin tried to transfer himself to Bucharest to steal a hand-hammered slaughtering knife, he wound up in a thermal bath in Razgrad. When he tried to transfer himself to West Virginia to steal a Revolutionary War musket, he wound up in a stable in Kentucky. At first he thought that he was losing his powers, but then he realized that another quality of his gift was that it could not actually take him to where he did not wish to go. So in order to continue doing Jean Pierre Michel's bidding, he had to find ways to inspire himself to visit the places where the weapons were kept. The thought of seeing a real Scottish castle, for example, allowed him to retrieve a Mongolian hatchet, pavé-set with precious stones, that was on display in a small museum in Edinburgh. The thought of visiting the whaling museum helped him to fetch a pair of Russian pistols from the mantelpiece of a manor house in Nova Scotia. His efforts eventually settled into a pattern: he came, he saw, he took a silver *golek* with a horn-and-ivory handle. And though there were moments when these objects stirred in him a trace of the excitement that Jean Pierre Michel felt, his chief consolation was the thought that his thieving somehow connected him with Petrie Woolrich.

Benjamin did not mention "the Cinderella factor" to Jean Pierre Michel, and except for a close call in Cairo, when the removal of a scarab-studded ceremonial knife brought him dangerously down to the wire, he always managed to pull off his heists in less than half an hour. After several months word of his exploits began to spread; the newspapers dubbed him "the Velvet Phantom," and he began to hope that with the attendant notoriety, he might be released from his labors. All that occurred, however, was that a few choice pieces were placed under greater surveillance. As Jean Pierre Michel had no interest in letting anyone else see his collection, there was no danger of his being connected with the thefts. And with the amount of money that he left in their place, he preferred to think of them as purchases anyway.

As time passed, Benjamin became quieter and more intense. The house seemed lifeless without Jean Pierre Michel's dinner parties, and he put little energy into making friends at school, having decided, after Petrie, that it was pointless to make them if you were just going to lose them in the end. The only thing that managed to cushion his loneliness was his passion for the saxophone. Cassandra Nutt bought him a portable Victrola, and Benjamin spent hours listening to Tex Beneke and Elmer Williams and his favorite of all, Coleman Hawkins. No one could make a saxophone soar like Hawk; his luminous tone and hot-buttered phrasing sent Benjamin to the moon. When it came to his own playing, however, it was another thing entirely: no matter how he tried, what came out of his instrument was an awkward, erratic mess. It wasn't a question of learning technique, for he convinced Jean Pierre Michel to hire him a first-rate instructor who worked with him three times a week. It was that the music that Benjamin heard inside his head was not like any other, and no amount of practice seemed to bring him any closer to playing it.

As if these things weren't confusing enough, Benjamin also began changing chemically: he grew several inches taller, his voice began to swoop like a vertiginous bird, and his face became visited by violent eruptions of scarlet and mauve and maroon. For the first time in his life, Benjamin's birthmark drew no attention; beneath the battlefield of his acne, it was hardly noticeable at all. Most significant, however, was Benjamin's sudden awareness of the opposite sex. He seemed to be in a constant state of arousal that was fueled by nearly every female that he encountered: Susie Figgis, the curvaceous blonde who sat beside him in history class; Mrs. Daltry, the diminutive girls' gym instructor; Anabel Wren, the alternate lunchtime monitor. Everything about them was perplexing and divine—the way they walked, the clothes they wore, their smiles as they passed him in the hallway. What troubled him, however, was a more immediate attraction, for with the fragrance of all those love affairs wafting down from the roof, Benjamin discovered that he could not take his mind off Cassandra Nutt. Her voluptuous brown body burrowed its way into his fantasies, and there was nothing he could do to make it vanish.

So he went to Nepal to get a marcasite dagger. He went to Madagascar to get a wood-and-nickel spear. He went to west Java to get a forged iron kris from the era of Sultan Agung. And he went to the Boston bedroom of Dr. Seymour Kleinberg to get an emerald-encrusted, Middle Kingdom, twelfth-dynasty Egyptian scimitar. Dr. Kleinberg's bedroom was filled with glittering objects, yet Benjamin understood that to contemplate even the least of them might delay him fatefully. So as the sound of brushing gave way to the sound of rinsing and spitting, he made his way across the Persian-carpeted floor, climbed upon the pillows of the canopied bed, and lifted the weapon from where it was carefully mounted on the wall.

It was extremely heavy. Yet before he could transfer himself back with it to the mansion, the door to the bathroom opened and in walked Dr. Kleinberg. He was a small, balding fellow, wearing burgundy slippers and tan-and-black-striped pajamas, and though Benjamin was planted firmly upon his pillow he walked right past him, went to the bureau on the opposite side of the room, removed a teak hairbrush from the upper left-hand drawer, and carried it back to the bathroom without even noticing him.

Benjamin considered that perhaps Mrs. Kleinberg's recent death had thrust the doctor into so deep a despair, he was unable to register a thief upon his bed pillow. He nevertheless decided to remove both himself and the scimitar as swiftly as he could and to leave Dr. Kleinberg to process his grief on his own.

the Saint of Hooverville

HAD CASSANDRA NUTT had the slightest idea how her rooftop exploits were affecting Benjamin, she would have boarded up her glass garden and checked into the Plaza Hotel. What she eventually discovered without any prompting was that even perpetual lovemaking was not enough to counter the evil that was gradually infiltrating the mansion. It was more than just the violence that the weapons evoked; it was the sudden awareness, after all these years, of the pervasiveness of Jean Pierre Michel's greed. When times had been high, her employer's avidity had seemed nothing more than a slight exaggeration of the national character. Now his acquisitiveness seemed positively obscene—and Cassandra Nutt was determined to make up for it.

Cassandra Nutt, like the rest of the country, had seen a lot in the last year. The Twenty-first Amendment had brought an end to Prohibition. Fred Astaire and Ginger Rogers had given grace to the movies. Governor Roosevelt had swept into the White House on the breathless strategies of the New Deal. But just as quickly as hope came in, it went swiftly rushing out—and by the winter of 1934 it was clear that the breezy, jazzy good times were not coming back. Cassandra Nutt therefore decided that the time had finally come for her to offer her services to her country. She began with an extensive letter-writing campaign to the new president, in which she pledged her support and offered him a few tips on policy management.

"The man can't even walk," she said, "and already they be tryin' to make him trip."

By the end of the summer she was communicating regularly with the assistant secretary of state and considered herself to be a fundamental agent of the ultimate resurrection of the country.

Despite such efforts, Cassandra Nutt craved a more immediate way of helping the down-and-out. And the answer came to her one November afternoon while she was making love with Ernie Johnson, the handsome hansom cab driver who liked to give her passage across the park. They were lying together on the antique divan—Cassandra Nutt savoring Ernie's lime-scented body, Ernie lazily tracing circles around the areola of Cassandra Nutt's right breast—when Ernie suddenly lifted his head and said, "Cassandra Nutt, if you could give some of your honey to every hungry man in this city, you could wipe out the whole damn Depression." Cassandra Nutt, of course, had no intention of making love to the entire city, but Ernie Johnson's words struck a chord in her. By the time he'd slipped on his clothes and sauntered blissfully out of the mansion, she'd decided to make it her mission to feed New York.

She began with the breadlines. Each morning she would rise at four and bake six or seven honey-wheat loaves, which she would pile into sacks and take to the various churches where food was distributed to the poor. She started in Harlem but soon discovered that Father Di-

vine's Peace Mission had that territory covered and that
Father Divine was not interested in competition. So she
wandered instead through the streets of lower Manhattan,
handing sustenance to whoever seemed to need it. For the
first few months this seemed to be enough; she always returned to the mansion by ten, and she always left a few
loaves on the counter to explain the extraordinary aroma.
As time went by, however, she began increasing her efforts—starting earlier and earlier—installing extra
ovens—until the hours of the night became an endless
frenzy of mixing, pouring, kneading, and baking and her
deliveries lasted until two.

"She must be a social worker," said Arlene La Foy, who
waited for her on West Twenty-third Street.

"She must be a politician," said Wilbur MacLaine, who
waited at Thirteenth and Third.

"She must be an angel," said Charlotte Ann Dodd, who
stood on the corner of Hudson and Bleecker like a child
waiting patiently to see Santa.

The only thing that everyone could agree upon was that
she was stunningly, fabulously dressed. For if the end of
prosperity had had any real advantage, it was in how it
had changed women's fashions. Gone were the boyish
haircuts and the sexless, waistless dresses; curves were
back, and Cassandra Nutt was in heaven. She wore moun-
tains of chiffon and hats piled with fruit. She wore enormous clip earrings and open-toed, sequined high heels.
The newspapers called her "the Saint of Hooverville," and
photographers followed her everywhere. But Cassandra
Nutt always managed to stay a few steps ahead of them
and, with the addition of a dark veil, was able to preserve
her anonymity.

Although it was not her intention, Cassandra Nutt's self-lessness brought with it a reward. For by the third or fourth month she realized that if she was up all night baking, out all morning distributing bread, and busy tending to Jean Pierre Michel, Benjamin, and her lovers the rest of the afternoon and evening, there was very little time left to sleep. With no time to sleep, there was no time to dream—and with no time to dream, there was a feeling of lightness that almost made up for the gathering of sharp objects that had started the entire process in the first place.

what Jean Pierre Michel saw

WHAT JEAN PIERRE MICHEL saw in the swords and daggers—in the maces and muskets—in the rifles and lances and hatchets and pistols and sabers and stilettos and spears—was neither death nor danger, neither power nor cunning, but, as with everything else he collected, beauty. The way the light glinted off a silver blade. The way a jeweled hilt offered itself to the hollow of an open hand. The conflict implicit in the dressing of tools of bloodshed in the articles of a woman's boudoir.

He found them erotic. And mesmerizing. And devastatingly beautiful.

So he did not concern himself with what they were doing to his household, with how each gun placed a bullet in Benjamin's well-being, each knife another gash in Cassandra Nutt's peace of mind. He knew that it was happening; he could feel the air growing thinner and the life slowly draining from the mansion. But all he could think of was the smoothness of satin, the richness of carved ivory, the coolness of sharpened steel. The elegant surfaces of a lavish collection—and none of the destruction they held.

machine guns and matzo ball soup

AS THE MONTHS SLIPPED BY, and the weapons accumulated, Benjamin began to find himself, more and more, craving sand. If his travels happened to take him to where there was a nearby beach, he would escape for a few moments to rake his fingers through the grains. If he passed through the park on his way back to the mansion, he would slip off to the playground and plunge his feet into the children's sandbox. He tried to resist actually swallowing the stuff; the most he allowed himself was to place a small pinch upon his tongue. With the knives at his heels, however, and the world closing in, it brought some measure of relief.

By the time Benjamin's thirteenth birthday arrived, the members of the Chernovsky household were leading three delicately overlapping yet ultimately separate lives. It therefore came as a complete surprise when Jean Pierre Michel announced that he was making arrangements for Benjamin to be Bar Mitzvahed. The first thing he had to do was to explain to Benjamin what this meant, to which Benjamin responded by pointing out that, first, he was not really Jewish, and second, despite a variety of new feelings that he would prefer not to go into, he did not really feel that he was on the threshold of manhood. There was no changing Jean Pierre Michel's mind, however; a Chernovsky was a Chernovsky, whether by blood or by legal document, and a Chernovsky had to be Bar Mitzvahed.

Cassandra Nutt suggested that Benjamin view it as an introduction into the world of high finance, for with the guest list that Jean Pierre Michel was assembling he was guaranteed to garner a tidy sum. All that mattered to Benjamin, however, was that it brought his fractured family back together, as the guns and the baking soda made way for the coming of the Torah.

Neither Benjamin nor Cassandra Nutt could figure out why Jean Pierre Michel had waited until only three weeks before the event was to occur to begin making preparations. Jean Pierre Michel's only answer was that "the nature of the Covenant is not governed by time"—which, as far as Cassandra Nutt was concerned, explained absolutely nothing. What was clear was that there was a tremendous amount of work to be done and not a single moment to lose. A team of rabbis was hired to work day and night to cram an entire year of talmudic training into the space of twenty-one days. In addition to teaching him what was required for the ceremony, they gave Benjamin a comprehensive overview of Judaism itself—for though he was familiar with the holidays, and a few of the precepts, being Jewish had always seemed to him to be more about food than about faith. When Benjamin learned about the other rites of passage in a Jewish boy's life, he was grateful it was only a Bar Mitzvah he was being prepared for and not a *bris*.

If Jean Pierre Michel was responsible for organizing the religious side of things, Cassandra Nutt was in charge of the festivities. The first thing she did was to secure the grand ballroom of the Waldorf Hotel, which took every bit of her talent (and no small number of Jean Pierre Michel's *ducatos*) to accomplish with only three weeks' notice. Once this had been done she sent out the invitations, hired the caterers, helped plan the menu, hired the musicians, shopped for Benjamin's clothing, wrote out the place cards, and personally decorated the cake.

"It ain't every day a boy becomes a man," she said to Benjamin as she pinned up the trousers on his new serge suit. "I been with fellas three times your age it ain't happened to yet."

Despite the meticulousness of the preparations, however, on the morning of the event there was absolute panic in the mansion. Benjamin woke at dawn and began wandering through the hallways, trying to remember his haftarah speech. Jean Pierre Michel closed himself up in the conservatory to make final changes in the seating arrangement. And Cassandra Nutt, who had a thousand last minute tasks to oversee, stood before her mirror, tucking her hair beneath a platinum blond wig. Like everyone else in the country, Cassandra Nutt had become mesmerized, over the previous year, by the dazzling adventures of the G-men and the Mob. She therefore decided to scrawl, at the bottom of each invitation:

Come as your favorite Public Enemy!

Benjamin's induction into manhood, she reasoned, would come only once. Why not make it as memorable as possible?

Jean Pierre Michel did not see Cassandra Nutt as she slithered down the staircase in her blue satin gown and slipped out the front door; he and Benjamin were to leave an hour later with Rabbis Horowitz, Hertzberg, and Korn. When they arrived at Temple Emanu-El, however, he was stunned to see what looked like half the New York underworld streaming into the synagogue. Only as he began to recognize some of the faces—the governor of Kentucky—the chairman of U.S. Steel—did he begin to guess what was going on, though by the time he found Cassandra Nutt and confirmed his suspicions, it was too late to do anything about it. When Benjamin finally took his place before the ark, the consortium of rabbis took cover; they feared that if his voice should crack, the temple would be sprayed with bullets.

Benjamin was too busy trembling to worry about how the guests were dressed. As he stood at the front of the synagogue, he felt as if various pairs of hands were gripping his arms and throat and ankles. When the service began, a great quiet came over the room; then Benjamin stepped forward to the open Torah and that silence became a sea of listening. As he began to speak, he felt a buzzing above his head—he heard the words come from his mouth, but they were someone else's words—it was someone else's mouth.

Somehow he made it through to the end. Then everyone hurried off to the Waldorf and the feasting and celebrating began.

It was an affair to remember. Benjamin was seated at the head table with Jean Pierre Michel, Cassandra Nutt, a fake Bonnie Parker, a bogus Baby Face Nelson, and a not-so-pretty Pretty Boy Floyd. (Had the press known that "the Velvet Phantom" and "the Saint of Hooverville" were seated together at a Bar Mitzvah at the Waldorf, they would have slapped the event on the front page of every newspaper in town.) But though the music was swinging and the food superb, Benjamin remained numb throughout the entire thing. The majority of the guests were total strangers, and he could not help thinking that they had dressed like criminals because he had lately become a criminal himself. His only real pleasure came from watching Jean Pierre Michel; he had not seen him so happy since the days when he'd first arrived at the mansion. It was not until the event was nearly over, however, as the coffee was being served and the band was launching into its fourth rendition of "Stardust," that Benjamin discovered the reason for the old man's joy.

"My congratulations, Mr. Chernovsky," said Rabbi Horowitz as he approached the table with Rabbis Hertzberg and Korn.

"It's been a most unusual Bar Mitzvah," said Rabbi Hertzberg.

"*Most* unusual," said Rabbi Korn.

"Machine guns in the temple?" said Rabbi Hertzberg. "This I never heard of."

"But if we've learned anything by now," said Rabbi Horowitz, "it's that we should never question the ways of the Lord."

"And besides," said Rabbi Hertzberg, "we can build an entire new rabbinical school on what you paid us to teach Benjamin."

"So who's complaining?" said Rabbi Korn.

"You understand, Benjamin," said Rabbi Horowitz, "that even with all this gangster *mishegas,* a Bar Mitzvah is a serious thing. You're responsible now for what you do."

"On Yom Kippur," said Rabbi Hertzberg, wagging a long, arthritic finger, "God takes notice."

"But because we know you're a good boy," said Rabbi Horowitz, drawing a package from his robe, "we have a little present for you."

Michael Golding

Rabbi Horowitz handed the package to Rabbi Hertzberg, who handed it to Rabbi Korn, who handed it to Benjamin. It was a small box wrapped in bright blue paper with a white-and-silver bow on top.

Benjamin looked to Jean Pierre Michel to see if he might open it. Jean Pierre Michel nodded.

"Might as well start inspecting the spoils," said Cassandra Nutt.

Benjamin weighed the box in his hands; it seemed extraordinarily heavy for its size. Then he pulled aside the ribbon, tore off the paper, and eagerly opened the lid.

"According to Rabbi Hertzberg, it's for cutting the meat at seder," said Rabbi Horowitz.

"But I personally think it's a *yad* for the Torah," said Rabbi Korn.

"Either way," said Rabbi Hertzberg, "you don't want to know how valuable it is."

Benjamin looked down, and on a small velvet cushion sat a slim golden dagger with an asp coiled around its handle.

"They say it belonged to Rabbi Eliezer Ashkenazy ben Elie Rofe," said Rabbi Hertzberg.

"Who carried it from Egypt to Prague," said Rabbi Korn.

"So when your father told us you collected knives," said Rabbi Horowitz, "we knew this was the one for you."

Benjamin stared at the object in the box. It was really quite beautiful—the gold glimmered with a soft, pinkish cast and the eyes of the asp were studded with tiny rubies. When he looked at it, however, he suddenly understood what was in all the other boxes on the table by the en-

100

trance and why Jean Pierre Michel had been so eager to have this Bar Mitzvah.

"Thank you," he said softly as he placed the box on the table beside the wrapping.

The three rabbis shook Jean Pierre Michel's hand, patted Benjamin's head, nodded to Cassandra Nutt, and then wandered off in search of their coats. When they'd gone, Benjamin turned to look at Jean Pierre Michel: his lips were fixed more tightly than he had ever seen them before, and though his eyes were focused firmly upon the weapon, they betrayed no shame at the discovery of what he had done. He turned to look at Cassandra Nutt: her mouth was slack, and her skin had gone ashen at the sight of the dagger from her dream. But it was only when he turned to look at his Bar Mitzvah present, that sensuous snake glittering venomously in its box, that he understood that if he was now responsible for his actions—if he was now, officially, a man—he could not allow himself to steal weapons, or anything else, ever again.

8/Chernovsky's Total History of the World

HEN BENJAMIN announced to Jean Pierre Michel that he would no longer serve as an intercontinental pirate—that he was hanging up the velvet sacks and turning off his gift—Jean Pierre Michel could only stare at him for a few moments and then retreat to another part of the mansion. He knew that he could not force Benjamin to continue; the entire operation had been founded on the pretense that the young boy had enjoyed the adventure of it. Once Benjamin established that he detested the whole thing, Jean Pierre Michel could only lock up his cabinets and consider his collection complete. A chill, however, soon descended over the household. The lines were drawn. Father and son were at war.

For Jean Pierre Michel it was a quiet offensive. Questions were responded to in as few syllables as possible, and attempts at conversation were immediately cowed down with an icy, impenetrable stare. Dinners thus became a series of non-sequitous monologues by Cassandra Nutt, with topics ranging from "The Long-Term Implications of the Farm Mortgage Moratorium Act" to "The Pros and Cons of Mae West's Salary." Neither the silence nor the speeches, however, had the least effect on Benjamin, for Benjamin had finally decided to devote himself to discovering the purpose of his gift. Each day after school he would go to the library, where he would study the lives of the greatest men and women who had ever lived. From ancient Greece to Italy during the Renaissance, from the Age of Reason to the Age of Political Revolution, he searched for those people who, through their insights or their actions—their understandings—their gifts—had somehow altered the course of human history. He was convinced that by examining the threads of their lives, he would figure out what to do with his own.

It took him six weeks to winnow down the field to a list of worthwhile subjects, which he ultimately divided into five separate categories: Statesmen and Leaders, Artists and Poets, Philosophers, Scientists, and Inventors. Beginning with the Statesmen and Leaders, he found that most of the great conquerors were convinced that they were bringing order to a chaotic world; the amount of blood they shed had therefore to be balanced against the beauty and fruitfulness of the societies that grew up out of the destruction. Alexander the Great, for example, was as interested in art and architecture as in the devising of battle maneuvers. Charlemagne was cruder, and perhaps even bloodier, yet when Benjamin considered what must have been required to bring an entire civilization lurching out of the Dark Ages, he could not help but admire his tenacity. Only the great Napoleon refused to inspire, perhaps because all of his endless looting reminded Benjamin of Jean Pierre Michel.

The lawgivers were no less impressive than the conquerors—yet what could a thirteen-year-old boy really implement from the fiery God-colloquys of Moses? Solon seemed more practical, stressing the harmony of the state, while Elizabeth I taught that niceness was subordinate to decisiveness in accomplishing an aim. From Jefferson he learned equanimity and from Lincoln humility, but of all his country's statesmen it was Franklin who delighted him the most. He felt certain that if he could demonstrate his gift to the man who had devised both the flexible catheter and the glass hemisphere harmonica, he would have had a wealth of ideas about what to do with it.

If the Statesmen and Leaders increased Benjamin's sense of scale, the Artists and Poets set him spinning. From Rembrandt he learned the difference between looking and seeing, from Leonardo the sanctity of the human face. There were figures in these painters' works that linked Benjamin with the divine: only angels and saints seemed to materialize more suddenly than he did. There were equally kindred spirits in the plays of Shakespeare, witches and fairies who vanished on whim and then swiftly reappeared to wreak mischief. From Mozart he learned the virtues of virtuosity, from Bach the significance of balance and form. Bach's mathematical perfection made Benjamin think of Petrie Woolrich; he imagined his lost friend in a garret somewhere, composing toccatas and fugues for the underworld.

No one suggested to Benjamin that he was too young to be reading Dante. That he should be out playing stickball, or dropping sacks filled with water off the post office roof, instead of studying the perspectives of Vermeer. He seemed as natural behind his stack of books as a sixty-year-old professor. Day after day, month after month, he sat quietly constructing Chernovsky's Total History of the World.

As his fourteenth birthday passed, Benjamin entered the world of the Philosophers: Confucius, Socrates, Aristotle, Lao-tzu. He studied Cause and Effect, the True and the False, Faith versus Reason, the Real versus the Fantastical, the Concept of Identity, the Properties of Solidity, and the Illusory Nature of Forms. The more he studied, however, the more confused he became. There seemed to be as many explanations to the meaning of life as there were seeds in a pomegranate, and if he was unable to narrow the field to just one, he at least devised a motto: "I disappear, therefore I am."

On the heels of the great philosophers came the great religious leaders, and though Benjamin found himself more attracted to the nonattachment of Buddha than the submission of Muhammad, it was Jesus who fascinated the most. He was surprised to discover how little he actually knew about him; as far as he could tell, the Jews did not so much reject Jesus as simply behave as if he had never existed. He recollected a few Christmas stories that his parents had told him, and there was that memorable Nativity scene in the Berbin Academy auditorium, but it was only now that Benjamin actually studied Jesus' words. He ultimately decided that, whether or not he was the son of God, he was a brilliant and invigorating teacher.

After the world of religion came the world of science, and here Benjamin's heart quickened: in the ice-cold realm of formulas and proofs he glimpsed the sweet possibility of a rational explanation for his powers. Marie Curie's discovery of radium, for example, made Benjamin wonder whether his ability to disappear might be the result of some strange new element. Louis Pasteur's use of paratartaric acid crystals to deviate polarized light provided a framework by which he might study his own fluctuations. From Galileo he learned that the accepted order of things could be reversed: perhaps everyone possessed the power to disappear and Benjamin was merely the first to actualize it. From Einstein he took reassurance that space and time were not what they seemed. And from Freud he took to wondering whether some subconscious force could have propelled him to transcend the laws of nature.

On the eve of his fifteenth birthday, Benjamin turned to the great Inventors. As he studied their achievements, however — Gutenberg and his printing press, Whitney and his cotton gin — he began to wonder about the people who had invented the things that the world took for granted. Who had invented the alphabet, for example? Or the toothbrush? Or the shoe? Who — naive, unknowing — had invented the wheel? He realized that he could spend the rest of his life mulling over such things without reaching recorded history. So he decided to devote himself to more recent discoveries: the cinema, the telephone, the light bulb. There was some secret in these things that held a key to Benjamin's gift — the ability to transcend time and space, an awareness of the nature of the electronic world — some principle of the twentieth century. Was it possible that Benjamin's gift was the seed of some new invention? Or had all his endless studying begun to warp his brain?

The more Benjamin tried to penetrate the mystery of his

gift, the more he began to glimpse the mystery behind all things. As he made his way from subject to subject, however, skipping across the continents and traveling among centuries, he began to see that his categories were artificial. Was Marcus Aurelius a statesman or a philosopher? Leonardo an artist, a scientist, or an inventor? Benjamin Franklin a philosopher, an inventor, a statesman, or a poet? He saw that the greatest men and women transcended categorization, that what bound them together was a common conviction that their lives were about something greater than themselves.

Perhaps it was all just an elaborate way of avoiding the dinner table—or the terrible music that rose from his sax—or the constant, insistent, unflagging erection in his pants. For when all was said and done there was still no explanation as to why an unsuspecting child had been given such extravagant capabilities. The only thing Benjamin felt sure of was that his destiny awaited him—and that sooner or later its brash, birthmarked face would appear.

9/The Tenor's Daughter

Cupid's prize

HROUGHOUT THE LONG HOURS that Benjamin spent in the library, he never lost sight of Cassandra Nutt's dream of him exploding. At times he was afraid that it would happen at any moment, whether or not he used his powers. When explosions actually occurred, he felt oddly responsible; in the spring of 1937, for example, when the passenger dirigible *Hindenburg* collided with its mooring and burst into flames, Benjamin didn't sleep for a fortnight. It wasn't until the following spring, however, a few weeks after his sixteenth birthday, that an explosion occurred that significantly altered his life.

Benjamin had accompanied Jean Pierre Michel and Cassandra Nutt that evening to a performance at Carnegie Hall of the famed Irish tenor Conal O'Shaughnassy. None of the three was much interested in opera, but Jean Pierre Michel liked to attend opening nights, and he liked Ben-

jamin and Cassandra Nutt to go with him. This time it
proved to be a very long evening; O'Shaughnassy, a tiny
fellow with a tender, limpid voice, offered not only the
great arias of Verdi and Puccini, but an extensive selection
of Irish lullabies, including three full encores of "Danny
Boy." It was after the performance, however, when they
went backstage, that Benjamin's eyes fell upon the tenor's
daughter and he instantly exploded into a violent parox-
ysm of love.

She was like nothing he had ever seen before: pale skin,
emerald eyes, flaming hair, and a body like a fountain
flowing. He'd read about this feeling in Dante, and Shakespeare, yet he had never expected it to be so absurdly bio-
chemical. He felt a host of sensations that even poetry
could not describe, and what startled him most was that,
from the way she looked at him from across the room, she
seemed to be feeling them, too.

While Benjamin had been in the library studying the
lives of the great, significant changes had been occurring
in him: his shoulders had broadened, he'd grown strong
and tall, his voice had lowered into a rich, clear baritone.
His face had changed as well—the bones were more
prominent, the beard growth more dense—and when the
adolescent acne finally faded away, his birthmark had
grown several shades lighter. The most significant
change, however, was the way in which Benjamin wore
that birthmark. When he had not been in the library
studying Erasmus and Euclid, Benjamin had been in the
street, studying faces. And though some were quite obviously more pleasing than others, the ones that intrigued
him the most were the ones with the imperfections. The
woman with the gigantic wart upon her chin; the man

with the furry patch upon his cheek; and those, like him, with some congenital discoloration: dark stains upon the forehead, bright splotches across the throat, or a mottled quality to the entire surface of the skin. He eventually concluded that it was the shame these people felt about their imperfections that made them unattractive and not the imperfections themselves. So he decided that he would never again apologize for his birthmark—and it was this absence of self-consciousness, as much as his startling looks, that made Lorna O'Shaughnassy stare at him from across the room.

Benjamin thought that he would go up in flames. But instead he merely stood there as Cassandra Nutt praised Conal O'Shaughnassy's singing and Conal O'Shaughnassy praised the audience and the accompanist and the acoustics of the hall. Then they filed out of the dressing room to allow the next group of acolytes to enter.

Benjamin did not sleep that night; instead he lay in the dark, picturing troops of soldiers marching endlessly across the desert toward the ever-vanishing figure of Lorna O'Shaughnassy. By the end of the week he was convinced that he would die if he did not see her again, but before he could actually make arrangements for the funeral, Jean Pierre Michel announced that they'd been invited to a party the following evening at Conal O'Shaughnassy's apartment at the Sherry-Netherland.

Benjamin was overjoyed—so much so, in fact, that he could not remember a single thing that happened from the moment of Jean Pierre Michel's announcement to the moment he found himself standing beside the hors d'oeuvres table in Conal O'Shaughnassy's penthouse. It was an

enormous apartment, extravagantly decorated, yet everything in it, from the calfskin furniture to the parchment-
covered walls, seemed to Benjamin but a backdrop for
Lorna. It was her entrance into the room that reignited his
awareness: as she appeared from around a corner he was
shaken from his stupor into a sudden realization of where
he was. He was content just to look at her as she made her
way through the crowd: her hair pinned up into a scattering of curls, her lips and cheeks gleaming with a faint
touch of rouge, her throat and shoulders exposed above
her strapless gown. When their eyes met again he felt the
flush come over him—which increased to a fever when he
saw that she was moving toward him.

"I hate these parties," she said as she approached.
"There are too many people. And they always serve the
stupidest food."

Benjamin was holding a cheese puff in his hand and
could not figure out whether to put it in his mouth or place
it back on the table. "Then why do you come?"

"My father," said Lorna. "He'd be crushed if I didn't. So
I figure what's a few more Swedish meatballs?"

She turned as she said this, and as she did, Benjamin
stole a look at her breasts, which peeked from the bosom
of her dress like a pair of schoolboys.

"I'm Lorna," she said, turning back.

"Benjamin," said Benjamin.

"Chernovsky," said Lorna. "Jean Pierre Michel Chernovsky's son. I asked my father all about you after you left
his dressing room."

There was an awkward silence, so Benjamin popped
the cheese puff in his mouth and reached for a pig-in-a-
blanket.

"God, I hate this music," said Lorna, referring to the treacly sounds coming from the nearby piano.

"It's pretty awful," said Benjamin.

"I wish they'd play swing," said Lorna. "That's all I listen to. My father thinks I've gone off the deep end."

Benjamin felt his heart quicken. "Who do you like?"

"Hal Kemp . . . Artie Shaw . . . Benny Goodman . . ."

"What about Coleman Hawkins?"

"Of course. But I like Lester Young better."

"*Nobody's* better than Hawk!"

"Have you *listened* to Lester Young? You couldn't say that if you'd really *listened* to Lester Young."

They paused for a moment and then began to laugh.

"Why don't we get out of here?" said Lorna. "Ben Webster's playing the midnight set at the Vanguard. We could be there in twenty minutes."

Benjamin hesitated. "I'm not supposed to stay out past eleven."

"I'm not supposed to stay out past ten-thirty," said Lorna. "But I don't think they'll notice tonight."

Benjamin looked across the room to find Conal O'Shaughnassy fielding compliments on the terrace, Cassandra Nutt telling stories on the couch, and his father drinking whiskey with a leggy brunette at the bar.

"I think you're right," he said.

"Then we're off," said Lorna.

She turned and began to weave her way through the thick crush of bodies. Benjamin followed—perfectly content to be Cupid's prize—and then they made their way out of the overcrowded apartment, down the elevator, and off into the velvet night.

Burnt Roses

LORNA O'SHAUGHNASSY had spatulate thumbs. Stubby
and wide, they were the one thing about her that she
truly detested. Penelope Jenkins had said that they were
criminals' thumbs, that the very same gene that was responsible for their blunt ugliness was also known to appear in most ax murderers. Lorna had as yet shown no
criminal tendencies, but she always feared that they were
but an arm's length away, dangling at her sides like the
squashed, swollen digits that protruded from either
hand.

Perhaps it was her thumbs that gave Lorna O'Shaughnassy such a feeling of kinship with the birthmarked Benjamin. That, and their mutual passion for swing. Lorna
insisted that swing was revolutionary, that it "expressed
the proletariat longing to make contact with life's primitive
urges." Over the following months she and Benjamin went
not only to the Vanguard, but to the Savoy and the Cotton
Club and the Apollo and the Regency. They heard Art
Tatum and Roy Eldridge and Dizzy Gillespie and Kenny
Clarke, but most of all they heard the big men on sax:
Benny Carter and Johnny Hodges and especially Lester
Young. Lorna felt that Lester Young's innovations pointed
the way to something new, and the more Benjamin listened
to him, the more he began to agree. When Benjamin
played for Lorna himself, however, it still had the quality
of a mud slide, a train wreck, a fourteen-car pileup. Lorna
was convinced, nevertheless, that there was talent beneath
the chaos and that one day Benjamin would break
through.

"You never know when inspiration will find itself in form," she said. "The best you can do is to just keep trying."

Lorna O'Shaughnassy was not your average sixteen-year-old. Having lost her mother to diphtheria at the age of five, she'd spent her childhood with her father in the operatic circles of New York, London, Paris, and Milan, acquiring opinions on everything from Russian constructionism to the Japanese cinema, plus a perspective on the times that kept Benjamin as captivated as the swell of her breasts beneath her sweater. She took him to see *Tobacco Road* and *You Can't Take It with You*. She discussed the merits of "Fallingwater" and the meaning of *Guernica*. She argued the role of women in literature and the significance of Marxism and, unlike anyone else Benjamin had met, she talked about war in Europe.

"Only a fool can keep his eyes closed to what's happening," she said. "Even if you don't take Hitler seriously, there's Mussolini, there's Franco. It's not going to just go away."

"We'll never get involved in another big conflict," said Benjamin. "That's why we signed the Neutrality Act."

"We'll never be neutral," said Lorna. "We can't help ourselves. And if somebody doesn't step in soon, there'll be no end to the slaughter."

Benjamin thought about Petrie and the princess and Alma Esther. "Do you really think there's going to be a war?"

"There already is a war, Benjamin. They just haven't come up with a name for it yet."

The sophistication of Lorna's thinking made Benjamin wonder if he'd been merely gathering cobwebs while he was cooped up in the library. Yet the up-to-date sociopolitical theories were but a part of the education that Lorna offered, the other part being lessons on the nature of the female form. Lorna was well aware of the effect that her body had on Benjamin; he studied it as carefully and diligently as he had studied Plato's *Republic* or the evolution of the steam engine: the sloping shoulders, the curving belly, and those breasts, those breasts, those breasts. At all times—whether they were walking down Broadway or sitting in a soda shop, strolling through Central Park or swimming at Coney Island—she could feel his eyes roaming over her. And though Benjamin tried his best to hide his staring, Lorna was secretly delighted. For she had sworn to herself, on her sixteenth birthday, that she was going to become a woman before her seventeenth arrived—and Benjamin Chernovsky had been elected to do the job.

Benjamin, however, knowing nothing of this decision, could only keep telling himself that he must be patient, that she was only sixteen, that he mustn't allow himself to take advantage of her innocence. One evening, however, at the beginning of August, he found that he could no longer control himself. They were lying on the floor of Lorna's father's penthouse, smoking cigarettes and listening to *The Camel Caravan*. Lorna had taught Benjamin to smoke a few weeks after they'd met, explaining that in Paris people began smoking at the age of seven and that one could not begin to appreciate things like Hemingway or Matisse if one could not appreciate the subtleties of a decent cigarette. In the absence of Gitanes or Gauloises, she settled upon Camels—mainly because they sponsored her favorite radio show, *The Camel Caravan*, which she insisted on listening to while lying on the floor, surrounded by a sea of candles.

It was a warm, sultry evening, and with the terrace doors open the noise of the Fifty-ninth Street traffic filtered in beneath the sound of the Big Band beat. Lorna was lying on her back with her shoes off and her feet upon the sofa, so that her skirt fell back to reveal her right thigh, which Benjamin, who was lying on his stomach, could not take his eyes off. The room reeked of cigarette smoke, but beneath the fumes lurked the sweetness of Lorna's toilet water, and together the two odors were like some strange new perfume that Benjamin half expected to hear advertised on the radio. ("Looking for something special on those hot summer nights? Try 'Burnt Roses.' Now available in the new atomizer bottle. . . .") Benjamin lay on his stomach to camouflage his erection, which was as much a part of these candlelit evenings as the music of Count Basie and his Orchestra. He only worried that if the room grew any hotter, or the music any louder, he would begin making love to the carpet.

Lorna, on the other hand, was lost in contemplation about the former King Edward and Mrs. Wallis Warfield Simpson, who were still in the headlines more than a year after their monarchy-shattering marriage. "It can't possibly last," she said to the strains of Benny Goodman. "There's too much pressure on them to prove an ideal. I admire their courage, though, and their ability to seize love while it's right there in front of them."

Benjamin needed no further encouragement. As the music grew louder, he began to inch himself toward her, and as the sound of a tender ballad gave way to a hot boogie-woogie, he raised himself over her and kissed her. Lorna was so startled that she bolted forward, which sent the ashtray that had been perched upon her stomach flying clear across the room. Before Benjamin could pull away, however, Lorna returned the kiss, and this time it was Benjamin who went flying. His entire body rocketed away beneath him, and for a moment he thought he was going to disappear. When they separated, however, he was still in the penthouse, whirling in circles, adrift in a sea of crushed Camel butts.

The kiss became a regular feature of their evenings together. Benjamin would wait through the concert or the movie or the long walk home for that moment when their lips made contact. What he never realized, however, was that beneath the demureness, and the show of restraint, Lorna was waiting for him to pounce.

Blue Mama's Suicide Wail

WHEN JEAN PIERRE MICHEL had adopted Benjamin nearly a decade earlier, he'd been certain that he'd had but a few scant years left to live. As time went by, however, the old man seemed no closer to dying than he had been on the day he'd signed the adoption papers. His skin became more spotted—his hands a bit bonier—but his spirit remained as stubborn and vigorous as ever. And so, to his own astonishment, did his sexual drive. During the period when he had become inflamed with weapons collecting, Jean Pierre Michel's sexual activity had waned. When that period ended, however, and the women returned, he found himself possessed of a greater stamina than at any previous time in his life. Sex seemed to rejuvenate him. He passed his eightieth birthday like a racehorse at the steeplechase.

Like her employer, Cassandra Nutt found that the passing years did little to decrease her interest in sex. It was the men themselves who began to bore her. She grew tired of their stories, and their liquor, and their lies. She grew tired of them falling asleep on her divan and, too often, on top of her. So while Jean Pierre Michel was taking on more and more lovers, Cassandra Nutt gradually diminished her ranks and turned her attention to the blues. She'd resisted this music for years and years—resenting the idea that she was supposed to like it because she was colored, resenting that it said things like "Gwine lay my head on de railroad tracks," not only because the sentiment was so hopeless, but because it suggested that colored folk actually said things like "gwine." Cassandra Nutt had never experienced anything to make her feel as low-down awful as the words to those songs, and she was convinced that if she ever did, she would not go around wailing about it in some twelve-bar bobtailed refrain.

One evening, however, after an unusually difficult day, something happened that changed her mind. Jean Pierre Michel's current lover, a svelte dolphin trainer named Adelouise Foster-Fontaine, had insisted that he install a large aquarium at the foot of his bed, as she liked to pretend, while she was making love, that she was submerged beneath the sea. Cassandra Nutt had thus spent the entire day hooking up intricate pumps and filter systems, arranging synthetic sea vegetation along the floor of the tank, and carrying bags of tropical fish from the pet shop, on Madison Avenue, home to the mansion. At about six o'clock, as she was returning with the last pair of paradise gouramis, she happened to pass by the door of a record shop when she heard a deep, gravelly voice cry out —

> *Gonna set a hex — on his baldin' head —*
> *Gonna lay a curse — in his lumpy bed —*
> *Gonna tip some lye — in his evenin' stew —*
> *Gonna fill his boots — with some old dog doo —*
> *Gonna 'rouse dat man — with some tellin' news —*
> *Oh he's fixin' to have*
> *A serious case*
> *O'dem Shouldn't-Have-Been-*
>   *Such-a-Mean-Rotten-Dirty-*
>   *Skunk Blu-u-es!*

—and she fell into a fit of laughter so satisfying, it completely removed the tensions of her day. Rather than put dog doo into Jean Pierre Michel's boots, she took the record home and listened to it until three o'clock in the morning. The next day she returned to the store and bought half a dozen more, and from then on she was hooked. She listened to the blue-gummed blues, the pool-house blues, the schoolyard blues, and the blind man blues. She discovered W. C. Handy and the various Smiths: Clara, Trixie, Laura, Mamie, and empress of them all, Miss Bessie. She learned that the blues were a way to turn your sorrows into joy, that to sing about your troubles was to kick them. And though she found out from Benjamin that she was behind the times — that jazz was "hot" — that swing was "happening" — Cassandra Nutt didn't care. When the weather grew cold she wrapped herself in ermine and listened to "Aunt Hagar's Children." When it got warm again she lay naked in the sun and played "Got

No Mo' Home Dan a Dog." Cassandra Nutt loved to sun-bathe nude. Her body, at the half-century mark, was still a thing to behold, and the warm sun lent it a dusky, ashen quality that brought out the high notes in the shades of her summer wardrobe.

It was a lively house. For while Jean Pierre Michel was in his bed setting records, and Cassandra Nutt was on her rooftop playing them, Benjamin was in his room trying to transcend his limitations with the saxophone. Lorna had convinced him that if he just kept at it, he was certain to break through. The more he tried, however, the worse he became, until finally Jean Pierre Michel hired a contrac-tor to soundproof his bedroom.

The only thing that managed to distract Benjamin's at-tention from the frustration of his soul was the pent-up en-ergy in his pants. For a while now he'd accepted the fact that he always had a hard-on and trusted that, sooner or later, it was bound to go away. When Lorna entered his life, however, the situation only intensified, and if he was able to resist laying a hand on her, he finally discovered the sweetness of laying one on himself.

Benjamin's studies had not ended when he stopped go-ing to the library; he continued them instead, before bed, after his evenings with Lorna. Lit up with the energy that he could not expend with her, he drank in Didymus and Cicero, Frederick II and Adrian VI, Milton and Goethe and Wordsworth and Shelley and Keats. He found, how-ever, that the more he studied, the more aroused he be-came — until one night, while reading about the adventures of Genghis Khan, he threw the book across the room, tore open his pajamas, and confronted the situation directly. A few strokes revealed the pleasures of his own touch, and from then on there was no turning back. He whacked off over everything from *The Canterbury Tales* to *The Mayor of Casterbridge*, from the French Revolution to the Spanish Civil War. And whenever he became frustrated in his efforts to play the saxophone, he turned to himself to release the tension.

It went on like this throughout autumn, throughout winter, and there were times when Benjamin feared that it would go on like this forever. One day, however, toward the beginning of spring, something happened that changed everything. Benjamin had been in his room all morning, struggling with his saxophone and trying to keep his mind off the heat of the previous evening. He'd taken Lorna to see *Gone With the Wind*, and when they'd returned to her apartment and he'd leaned in to kiss her, she'd suddenly pressed herself tightly against him—her incredible softness against his ever-present hardness—and Benjamin had nearly exploded in his pants. Now, the following morning, he was so lit up with desire that even the saxophone was unable to quench his passion, and he began to consider the thought of reactivating his gift. The more he thought about it, the more he longed to once more experience that rush of adrenaline—that gentle dissolving—that glorious feeling of freedom. So without even stopping to interrupt his playing, he decided to take a quick trip to Spain.

He closed his eyes. He breathed in deeply. He concentrated. But as the energy began to gather inside him, something quite unexpected happened. As his body started to vibrate, something opened in his chest—and released in his throat—and pulsed through his fingers—and just before he vanished, the most extraordinary music began to pour from the mouth of his saxophone. Urgent and raw, it was precisely the sound that Benjamin had been after for years. A moment later he was swept off to Seville, but when he transferred himself back and began to experiment, he found that if he concentrated, he could channel his powers into his music instead of into disappearing.

It was a heady discovery. And the first person he wanted to share its implications with was Lorna. When he thought of her, however—charged as he was with both the excitement of his discovery and the heat of the previous evening—he became so aroused that he almost blacked out. He decided that a quick session with himself would release some of the tension, but as he took himself in hand something even more unexpected occurred. His eyes closed as always, his ankles flexed, his body slid down so that his head touched the bottom of the headboard. As his ecstasy grew, however, he began to disappear—and when he rematerialized he found himself standing in the garden, on the rooftop, before a naked Cassandra Nutt.

Benjamin felt the warm sun stream in. He heard the sound of the mournful-joyful music. But all he could do was stare. Cassandra Nutt's body was so luxurious: the breasts so pendulous, the belly so inviting. He wondered if her name were somehow linked with her nipples, which rose into the air like a pair of giant toasted acorns.

As for Cassandra Nutt, she was no less astounded. To have Benjamin suddenly materialize in her garden was peculiar enough. But to do so as he did now—his pants around his ankles—his thing exposed like a catfish out of the creek—was more than she could process. All she could think of, as she looked at him standing there, was that her little Benjamin was certainly not little anymore.

From the wobbly Victrola came the sound of the woeful music: Clara Smith singing "Blue Mama's Suicide Wail." And though the irony of the title was not lost on Cassandra Nutt, she could not seem to make herself reach for the needle to remove it. Benjamin was not familiar with the song, but he could hear the words—

Goin' up to the mountain top
Throw myself down in the sea
Goin' up to the mountain top
Throw myself down in the sea

—and as he looked at Cassandra Nutt she seemed like nothing so much as a great chocolate sea in which he was destined to drown.

Neither of them could stop it. The sun was too hot, the music too insistent. Only as their bodies made contact, and Benjamin smelled that old clove-orange fragrance, did a tremor of hesitation pass through him. By then, however, he was cast upon the waters—and it was much, much, much too late.

10/Repercussions

going

HE FOLLOWING MORNING Cassandra Nutt packed her satin blouses, her open-toed pumps, and her complete collection of Paramount, Emerson, and Pathé records and headed back to Rock Hill, South Carolina. She told Jean Pierre Michel that it was just for a visit, that she was long overdue to see her relations, but Jean Pierre Michel knew that if she was taking her records, it was more than just a visit and that after thirty-five years it was highly unlikely that any of her relations would still remember her. There had to be some other reason for such a hasty departure, and one look in her eyes told Jean Pierre Michel what it was.

Jean Pierre Michel knew. From the overbuttered quality of his morning toast to the way she lined up her suitcases in the foyer. From the dampness on her forehead as she stepped into the taxi to Benjamin's failure to come from his room to say good-bye. But most of all he knew from the strange vibration in his body—a strong admixture of alarm, arousal, and fury. To lose Cassandra Nutt was an unthinkable circumstance: how would he bathe, how would he eat, how would he move through the day? To lose her, however, because she had slept with his son— after having yearned for her himself for over thirty-five years—was more than he could bear. It made his bones tighten. It made his ears sweat. It made the blood in his eighty-year-old arteries churn like borscht on a turned-up flame.

He watched as the driver piled the suitcases in the trunk of the cab. He watched as Cassandra Nutt raised a white-gloved hand to the window and the taxi pulled away. But all he could think of was the clutching in his stomach— and the burning in his throat—and how grateful he was that the room where he kept the weapons was firmly bolted shut.

going

IF CASSANDRA NUTT raised her hand to the window like a departing monarch, inside she felt like a criminal creeping off from the crime. What had happened the previous afternoon had been as unfathomable as a dream; the only thing Cassandra Nutt could not understand was why she hadn't had a dream to warn her of it. The horror had set in almost as soon as the pleasure: this was Benjamin that she was lying with, the same Benjamin she had taken to the seashore and tucked into bed and helped do his long division. The fact that he was now a man did not obliterate those memories. The fact that he was not her son did not alter the fact that for almost ten years now he had felt like one.

When the lovemaking ended, there was a moment of emptiness—a pure, abstracted state in which there was no awareness of either what was coming or what had been. Then Benjamin raised himself up from her breast—their eyes connected—and it hit them. Benjamin quickly bolted from the garden, but Cassandra Nutt just lay there: the feel of the sweat dripping down from her belly, the sight of the needle grazing the label of the spinning record, the sound of the pigeon gently mocking her with its cooing from the edge of the open glass roof.

So she packed her things. And she bought a ticket to Rock Hill. And she tried not to think about what she was going to do once she got there. Or what Jean Pierre Michel was going to do without her. Or what Benjamin was going to do once the reality of what had happened sank in.

gone

BENJAMIN SAT in his bedroom, feeling lousy and wonderful. Wretched and glorious. Rank, foul, rotten, and horrid; flushed, elated, enchanted, and blessed.

In other words, Benjamin was confused. What he'd experienced with Cassandra Nutt was as blissful and satisfying as anything that he had ever known. The only problem was that it was Cassandra Nutt with whom he had experienced it. When she packed her bags the following morning, he was not the least bit surprised; the moment he'd raised himself up from her breast he'd known that they could not go on living beneath the very same roof. Yet Benjamin could not regret what had happened. It was too spine tingling, too soul quenching, too utterly, utterly delicious. His only concern was that Jean Pierre Michel would find out.

Benjamin was not very good at lying. Even the slightest concealment deepened his birthmark several shades, and he knew that the more he tried to camouflage the incident, the more suspicious Jean Pierre Michel would become. But that was only part of the problem—for how, after having tasted the pleasures of Cassandra Nutt, could he possibly hold himself back when it came to Lorna? The only solution was to avoid them both and to hope that, after a sufficient period to cool himself down, he might retrieve his former safe and uneroticized self.

He returned to the library and read D. H. Lawrence; he studied the Kama Sutra and the marquis de Sade; he found Chinese texts that preached the virtues of celibacy and Tibetan manuscripts that clearly differentiated between six different levels of love. Yet nothing that he found could align the vast contradictions that battled away inside him. A rapacious hunger. A yearning to be chaste. And the alternating images of Cassandra Nutt and Lorna O'Shaughnassy, over and over and over.

After three weeks of study, he felt the heat suddenly cool and the feeling of panic begin to filter away. And it was then that he realized he had hardly given a thought to how Jean Pierre Michel was surviving the sudden absence of Cassandra Nutt. He hurried back to the mansion, where he was greeted by Juanita Perez, the myopic Spanish woman Jean Pierre Michel had hired after Cassandra Nutt had gone. Juanita Perez was eager to please, but after thirty-five years of being taken care of by Cassandra Nutt, Jean Pierre Michel had been unable to explain to her what her duties were. She therefore spent her days making beef empanadas and wandering about the mansion in a daze—so that now, as Benjamin entered and asked where his father was, she could only shrug and mutter something about *cebollas*. When Benjamin realized that she was not going to help, he raced up the stairs and into his father's bedroom in the hope of finding him there.

At first he could feel only an incredible embarrassment, for there, in his bed, Jean Pierre Michel was making love with the latest of his conquests. With the sunlight streaming in through the open window, the scene was set into relief: Benjamin froze in fascination at the sight of the aged body coiled above the youthful one, the dry, voracious fingers clutching the bedsheets, the pale, wrinkled buttocks rising up and thrusting down. Only when the old man's body suddenly arched, and he threw back his head, and Benjamin was able to see the young girl's face, did his embarrassment turn to horror and then to rage.

It was Lorna O'Shaughnassy. Making love with Jean Pierre Michel. In a bed perched midway between the room where he'd had so many fantasies about her and the roof where he'd had Cassandra Nutt.

Benjamin stood there for exactly fifty-three seconds. Then he ran to his own room, gathered up his things, and headed off for somewhere—anywhere—that Jean Pierre Michel was not.

11/The Family Guildenstern

advice of a young hog

ENJAMIN STOOD along the curve of the Singel, just off the Konigslein, and drank in the sights and the sounds and the smells that rose from the banks of the canal. He'd been traveling for six days now, and the flood of impressions—the cobbled streets, the gabled rooftops, the ice-lined barrels of herring and lobsters and eels—was almost too much for him. He had to place his suitcase and his saxophone down and lean upon the iron rail that ran along the water. He had to close his eyes, and breathe in deeply, and try to find something to take his mind off his craving for sand.

The summer of 1939, from almost any perspective, was a strange time to go to Europe. Hitler's armies were storming the continent, and war was close at hand. To Benjamin, however, even the shadow of war was not as threatening as the shadow of Jean Pierre Michel: only by putting an ocean between them could he live with the horror of what he'd witnessed in the old man's bedroom.

The first thing he'd had to do was figure out how to get there, for after his deviation to the roof he felt he could not trust his powers, and when he fled from the mansion he had exactly seventy-three dollars and fifty-six cents to his name. (As Benjamin was still a minor, his considerable Bar Mitzvah funds were still in Jean Pierre Michel's name; all that he had was the assorted change that he'd managed to secret away inside the heat register behind the headboard of his bed.) Checking himself into a small hotel on the West Side, he proceeded to investigate his possibilities, the chiefest of which seemed to be flying. He'd never been on an airplane before, but he'd read in the newspapers about the new "Clipper" flights that could supposedly take one from New York to Lisbon in less than twenty-four hours. So he contacted one of Cassandra Nutt's former lovers—a gray-haired gentleman who happened to be the vice president of one of the world's major airlines—to arrange a particular deal. For more than six months after Cassandra Nutt had ended their affair, this fellow had tried to tempt Benjamin, with a variety of hand-crafted model fighter planes, into swaying the magnificent woman back to him. Benjamin had never succumbed to these lures, but now, inspired by his tactics, he snuck back into the mansion, filled a small suitcase with an assortment of Cassandra Nutt's undergarments, and offered it to the gentleman in exchange for a one-way ticket to Lisbon. (Although Benjamin had sworn after the weapons collecting that he would never again steal anything, he considered the undergarments to be an exception; he was certain that if Cassandra Nutt knew what Jean Pierre Michel had done, she would have gladly loaned him her panties to help him escape.) The airline vice president considered the deal a bargain, and Benjamin was on his way.

Lisbon was not Benjamin's actual destination, as was neither Paris, Rome, nor any of the other places he had visited with Jean Pierre Michel. He decided, instead, that he would go to Amsterdam, a city that seemed safely situated outside the Nazis' reign of terror, as well as the sort of place where he might be able to explore how his gift might be used for his music. It took him five days to get there—slow trains, rocky seas, and a particularly garrulous ticketing officer all conspiring to delay him—but finally, on the twenty-first of June, the longest day of the year and, for Benjamin, the most exhausting, he arrived at his new, watery home.

A small, stocky man rushed by carrying a basket of steaming rolls, and Benjamin suddenly realized how hungry he was. So he picked up his suitcase and his saxophone, found a nearby bank to change his dollars into guilders, and headed off in search of a place to eat. Within a few blocks he came to a large sign that showed a bright red gryphon holding a frothy mug of beer; entering the door beneath it, he found himself inside a small *bierencafé* with rose-colored walls, half a dozen tables, and a mahogany bar that was centered with a large bowl of oranges. Seating himself at the bar, he scanned the large chalkboard that served as a menu. Then, realizing that everything was written in Dutch, he waved over the bartender, held out his money, and pointed to the plate of herring and the tall, pale beer that sat before the fellow beside him.

"The same," he said.

The bartender nodded and fetched him the food and drink. Benjamin ate quickly and guzzled down his beer, which made him feel light-headed and giddy. Then he turned to the man beside him, a gaunt-faced fellow with a head of yellow hair, and asked if he spoke any English.

The man stared at Benjamin, chewing on a toothpick that protruded from his mouth. "Young Hog!" he grunted.

Benjamin felt that this was a rather rude thing to call someone whom you had only just met, so he turned to the bartender and asked him the same question. He, too, however, hurled the strange epithet at him. "Young Hog!" he shouted. "Young Hog!"

Eventually a fellow in the corner rose from his table, indicated to Benjamin that he should remain where he was, shuffled out the door, and then returned a moment later with a bearded, bulbous-nosed creature who cleared up the confusion.

"Jan Hoag," said the man as he approached Benjamin with a slight bow. "What can I do fer you?"

"I'm looking for a place to stay," said Benjamin. "And a way to earn some money."

Jan Hoag seated himself at the stool beside Benjamin and leaned in closely. "Are you sure?"

Benjamin drew back involuntarily at the warm, sour smell of the old man's breath. "I'm sure."

Jan Hoag stroked his beard quite slowly, and Benjamin saw that he was studying his birthmark, pondering it as if it were a pattern of tea leaves or a figure of the I Ching, some symbol that might explain who he was. "De question is," he said, screwing up the left side of his face, "do you got any problem wit Jews?"

Benjamin was somewhat surprised by the question, but he shook his head.

Jan Hoag paused for a moment. "De question is," he said again, "do you got any problem wit clowns?"

"Clowns?" said Benjamin.

"To be specific," said Jan Hoag, clearing his throat, "do you got any problem wit Jewish clowns?"

Benjamin assured Jan Hoag that he had no problem with either Jews, clowns, or, to be specific, Jewish clowns, so Jan Hoag explained that there was a family on the Groenburgwal, in the Oude Zijde, that was offering a room with meals in exchange for help mending the costumes that they used in their street circus act. "Dey're good people," he said. "And de mudder is an excellent cook." He leaned in again. "And you can have de address for only fourteen guilders."

"But I don't know anything about mending costumes," said Benjamin.

Jan Hoag shrugged. "You push de needle in, you pull de needle out. What can be so difficult?"

Benjamin suspected that he was getting himself into something that he might regret, but as he had no other options, he paid Jan Hoag the money for the address—plus two guilders more for directions on how to find it—and headed off to see what would come of it.

As he wandered along the banks of the Amstel and out through the Waterlooplein, Benjamin could feel a quiet come over him that he could attribute only to the prospect of a warm, clean bed. When he reached the address that Jan Hoag had given him, however—a narrow structure on the edge of a canal—and he rang the bell, there came no answer, and it was only then that it occurred to him that

Jan Hoag had taken him for a fool. Jewish clowns? He chided himself for being so gullible. Just as he was about to leave, however, the door swung open to reveal a slender girl of about fourteen years of age with a mass of black hair, a freckle-splattered nose, and a pair of painted figures on her cheeks: a crisp blue diamond on the left, a neat green triangle on the right.

"Excuse me," said Benjamin. "But I came about the room."

The girl stared at Benjamin with a look of pure astonishment, so he handed her the note that Jan Hoag had written him (for another two guilders), and she motioned him in, led him up a steep stairway to a large sunlit room, and then hurried away, presumably to fetch someone who was less overwhelmed by his presence.

Benjamin put his belongings down and looked about the room. It was a large space with a hearth at one end and a great deal of furniture and hoops and balls and musical instruments and seven purple bicycles hanging upside-down from the ceiling. He had never heard of Jewish clowns before, and he wondered if it meant that they were clowns who were Jewish or if in some particular way they were *Jewish* clowns. He tried to picture them davening on the high wire or telling stories from the Bible as they juggled a series of brightly painted matzo balls. As he was imagining this, a stout woman entered the room, wearing a flowered dress, a flour-covered apron, and a pair of yellow wooden shoes. There were no geometric shapes upon her cheeks, yet there was indeed something clownish about her—a flushed quality to the skin, an overexuberance, a sense that at any moment she might suddenly trip and go flying across the room into one of the bicycles.

"I'm sorry to disturb you," said Benjamin. "But I came about the room."

The woman came closer to Benjamin and looked him up and down; she tilted her head to the left and to the right; then she clapped her hands together and let out a great, resounding laugh. Benjamin tried to respond, but before he could do so the woman took his hand and led him across the room, up another flight of stairs, and into a small attic with a bed, a lamp, a desk, a sink, and an old wooden clothes maker's dummy, upon which was draped a purple-and-green shirt with an enormous rip down one side. The woman patted the dummy. The woman pointed at Benjamin. Then she laughed again, shuffled out of the room, and clambered back down the stairs.

Benjamin looked at the costume dummy. He looked at the bed. And though a part of him was convinced that he should race down the stairs and hurry out of the house, the rest of him could think only about slipping off his shoes, and pulling back the covers, and burying his face into the pillow. So he placed his suitcase and his saxophone in the corner and, trusting that he would figure out how to sew in the morning, went to bed.

a new life

IN THE MORNING there was no time even to think about sewing. Benjamin was awakened by a series of loud blasts on what sounded like a tuba rising up through the floorboards of his room. After throwing on his clothes, he stumbled down the stairs to find a family of seven—one for each bicycle—boisterously preparing their breakfast.

"Hallo!" shouted a strapping youth from the center of the chaos. "We're just about to eat. Come, we've made you a place."

The youth, who introduced himself as Abel, showed Benjamin to his seat as the others began to lay down plates of smoked whitefish, boiled eggs, whole-grain bread, tomatoes, onions, Gouda with nettles, Gouda with dill, blackberry jam, and chocolate. Then they all took their places, and Abel, who spoke surprisingly good English, explained that they were "the Family Guildenstern": Abram, the father, a squat man with an impressive beard who could juggle up to seven items while singing the "Marseillaise"; Hannah, the mother, who despite her bulk was an expert on the unicycle; he and Herschel, the late-teenage sons, who could walk on their hands, stand on each other's shoulders, and do a variety of acrobatic leaps; Henni, the eldest daughter, who could dance on toe while conversing with a cockatoo, named Stella, that was perched on her left shoulder; Hilda, the middle daughter, who played not only the tuba but the clarinet, the oboe, the trumpet, and the French horn; and Sara-Hilda, the youngest, the one who had met him at the door, whose talent, beyond a gift for doing cartwheels, had as yet not been discovered.

"We perform in de Vondelpark," explained Abel, "by de lake. We carry a big soup tureen—people toss coins—"

"*Het ein goede lief,*" said Abram.

"It's a good life," translated Abel.

The breakfast continued on in a bright, easy manner with lots of Dutch chattering and a good deal of laughter. No one seemed uncomfortable with this guest at their table, and no one seemed even to notice his extraordinary birthmark. When the food was finished the dishes were cleared, and while the hoops and the rings and the balls were being gathered, Hannah asked Abel to ask Benjamin to play something on his saxophone. At first Benjamin hesitated, for if he did not use his powers, he would produce his usual racket, and if he did, he might transfer himself away. He remembered, however, that one of his reasons for coming to Amsterdam was to explore the use of his gift, so he went to the attic, retrieved his sax, and while the Family Guildenstern gathered around the hearth, he prepared himself to play. He had not done so since that unexpected morning when he'd wound up on the roof, but as he closed his eyes and concentrated on the music, he found that, once again, he was able to channel his powers through the saxophone. He played "Hello, Lola" and "The Jamaica Shout" and "I Only Have Eyes for You." And the sound was as rich and as strange and as free as the first time.

When he was finished playing, the family just sat there. Then Abram turned to Abel, spoke a few sentences, and asked him to translate them for Benjamin.

"He says he's not sure if it's music," said Abel, "but whatever it is, he likes it. So he wants to know if you'd be interested in joining our act."

Benjamin was delighted and immediately said yes. As he was still uncertain, however, that he could control his new talent, he asked if he could wait a few weeks to settle in and adjust to his new life before beginning. Abram agreed. Then they hoisted their things and took him to the Vondelpark, where they gave him his first taste of what they did.

It was a simple affair. A white pennant, with their name written on it in bright gold letters, was thrust into the ground on a large metal stake. A groundcloth with a dark blue star at its center was carefully laid down and spiked into the earth. An orange-and-green blanket was strung between two trees to form a makeshift changing room. Then one by one they performed their routines, beginning with Abel and Herschel and continuing on through Henni's final dance with Stella.

At first Benjamin could not decide if they were a wonderful clown act or a terrible one; moments of complete awkwardness were followed by sweet glimmers of grace. When Abram stepped forward, however, and began to juggle, Benjamin lost all doubts. There was a sense as the old man stood there — his feet planted firm, his strong arms tossing eggplants and alarm clocks into the air — that he was the perfectly balanced center of the earth.

Later, as they made their way back to the Groenburgwal, Benjamin told this to Abel, who told it to Abram, who nodded with an almost biblical gravity.

"Balance," he said, via Abel, "is the secret to everything."

Benjamin had never thought of this before, for from the dullness of the Brooklyn brownstone to the glamour of the Fifth Avenue mansion, his life had been a series of extremes. The idea of balance seemed wonderfully appealing. Yet he somehow suspected that life with the Family Guildenstern was not going to teach him its virtues.

a doppelgänger

AS TIME PASSED, Benjamin's life with Jean Pierre Michel receded further and further into the distance. It was almost as if it were someone else's life, from its rousing commencement in the back of the Hispano-Suiza to its painful conclusion in the pair of disturbing sexual escapades. It was finally clear to Benjamin that he hated Jean Pierre Michel — hated the coldness, and the control, and the ever-more-elongated, ever-more-pressed-together lips. As for Lorna, he could not bear to think of her at all. So he blocked them both out and threw himself fully into his life with the Family Guildenstern.

At first Benjamin found it difficult to believe that the Family Guildenstern was Jewish. They ate heartily enough — their meals generally consisted of enough food to feed twenty — yet they lacked the air of suffering that Benjamin associated with Jean Pierre Michel and the three rabbis. On top of that their house was messy, they painted their faces, they had no safeguards for the future. As the weeks went by, however, Benjamin began to see that they were more truly Jewish than anyone he had ever known. For one thing, Hannah kept a kosher kitchen. For another, they discussed the scriptures as other people talked about the weather. More than anything, however, their Jewishness expressed itself in the warmth and immediacy with which they accepted Benjamin into the family. Abram began using him as a skeletal mold: the old man loved to make papier-mâché masks and upon discovering Benjamin's perfect features could use no one else as a model. Hannah, on the other hand, could not resist feeding him: whether clear skinned or birthmarked, he was a child under her roof, and as far as she was concerned he was a little thin. As for the others, they accepted him as a brother, which meant that Abel confided in him, Herschel showed off for him, Henni was rude to him, Hilda ignored him, and Sara-Hilda followed him wherever he went. After being so intensely focused upon in his life with Jean Pierre Michel, Benjamin found it a relief to be suddenly part of the crowd.

As for the sewing, Benjamin took to it quite quickly. It was mostly a matter of mending ripped seams, yet the costumes were so threadbare that Benjamin's stitches had little to cling to. He soon began to find himself mending his own mendings, and he could often tell, as he sewed things together, that his work would not last through the day. In the evenings, however, after the others had gone to sleep, Sara-Hilda would sneak up to his room to help him. She taught him how to tighten the joining of a sleeve, how to reinforce a collar, how to keep his stitches tiny and even. And though Benjamin realized that the sewing was not why she came, he never discouraged her visits. There was something strangely affecting about Sara-Hilda. He found himself looking forward to being near her at the end of the day—intrigued by her hair, which went off in all directions, and the odd, fragile sweetness of her presence.

For those first few weeks, while the others were off performing at the Vondelpark, Benjamin remained at home, exploring his new use of his gift. He found that he could consistently use his powers to fuel his playing and that he could even experience that moment of dissolving. The only problem was that when the music began to soar, he would find himself whisked away. Sometimes it was to the sitting room or to the street beneath his window, while other times it was as far off as Volendam or Leiden, and once, when he hit a particularly rapturous high C, he wound up on the west coast of Norway. His only recourse was to moderate his playing—to allow his gift to enliven his music, but hold back its full power for fear that he might disappear.

As soon as he was certain he had things under control, Benjamin began to play with the Family Guildenstern. He was careful, of course, to try not to offend Hilda: Abram made certain that she always played first, and the others took turns privately whispering to her that they liked her playing better. But the truth was that Benjamin's playing was superb, and despite its strangeness and unconventionality, it soon became the highlight of the act. The sparse, straggly audience began to fill out into a crowd. The scattering of coins in the oversize soup tureen began to thicken into a generous stew.

One evening, about six weeks after Benjamin had begun playing, he was lying across his bed when he heard the familiar sound of Sara-Hilda's tapping at his door. He had not expected her that night; it was well past midnight, and as the evening was warm, he was lying in his underwear, exploring a few chord changes and enjoying the gentle breeze that blew in through his small attic window. As the knocking continued, it was accompanied by a voice —

"Benjamin! Ik ben Sara-Hilda!"

— so he threw on his clothes and went to the door. When he opened it, however, he was startled by what he found: there was Sara-Hilda, smiling as ever, but her crisp blue diamond and her neat green triangle were carefully scrubbed away and in their place was an exact reproduction of his birthmark. How she had managed to do this without Benjamin standing before her was a testament to how meticulously she had studied him: each curve of the border was perfectly delineated, each subtle variation in color precisely observed.

The evening sessions were not the same after that. Benjamin could not concentrate with this fey doppelgänger beside him or pretend any longer that her attentions were merely sisterly. He only hoped that with the sewing, and the saxophoning—and perhaps a little soap—his life would soon return to what he was gradually beginning to think of as normal.

12 / An Upside-Down World

flying eggs

s SARA-HILDA'S infatuation with Benjamin grew more and more obvious, so did Henni's dislike and disdain. At first it expressed itself in a coolness of manner, but it quickly developed into a series of scowls, and then an overt rudeness, until it finally boiled over into actual aggression. Benjamin would discover slugs in his *erwtensoep* or marbles on the stairway that led up to his room, and whenever she could Henni would jab him a little or shove him to one side or "accidentally" step on his toes. Benjamin could not figure out why she hated him so. Was it his smile? Was it his birthmark? Had he done something to offend her bird? Or was it simply the fact that his presence in the house had offset the balance of the family? He would have better understood such behavior had it come from Hilda, to whom his saxophone playing was obviously a threat. From Henni, however, it was a streak of ill nature as unfathomable as it was malignant.

Despite the vehemence of Henni's antipathy, it was nothing compared with the rancor and venom that were sweeping across Europe that summer. Yet the Family Guildenstern never said a word about it and seemed almost unaware of the danger, at that time, of being Jews in Europe. To be fair, they were not alone in the belief that the Netherlands was safe; even as late as the summer of 1939 there was a sense throughout Holland that the horrors that were happening elsewhere would never penetrate their borders. In early September that feeling was shaken when the Nazis invaded Poland, and England and France declared war on Germany. The Family Guildenstern, however, went right on clowning, convinced that their city was in need of a good laugh now more than ever.

One afternoon toward the beginning of November, something happened to change their thinking. It was an unusually cold day for so early in the season; the air seemed peppered with tiny particles of glass, and the leaves that remained on the trees in the Vonderpark seemed flattened into two dimensions. The family's performance was quite altered by the coldness: Abel and Hershel were like a pair of overwound toys, speeding through their movements in an effort to increase their blood circulation; Benjamin had to wear fur-lined gloves, which made his playing a disaster, and Sara-Hilda had to refrain from doing cartwheels, as the patches of ice that had formed on the ground sent her careening into the trees. By twelve o'-clock there were only three guilders in the soup tureen. By half-past one Henni had begun to cry, which made Stella begin to squawk, which made Hilda begin to grumble. Hannah quickly dispatched the latter to play some music, and it was while she was struggling through the solo parts of Mozart's Clarinet Concerto that the strange thing happened. The rest of the family was huddled behind the blanket, hugging themselves and stamping up and down and not really listening to the music. Only when the clarinet began to squawk like Henni's bird did they look out from behind the curtain to see a small man in a large overcoat throwing a series of eggs at Hilda. His face was fixed in grave determination, yet his body remained calm and relaxed. The family could only watch in amazement as egg after egg sailed gracefully through the air to break over the astonished girl.

"*Joden!*" he shouted. "*Smerige Joden!*"

When the shock of it subsided, the family took action. Abram began hurling apples at the fellow; when he started to run away, Abel began to chase him, and Hannah followed after on her unicycle. Only by flinging his remaining eggs at the unicycle—which made Hannah falter and Abel turn back to help her—did the villain finally manage to escape.

It took the Family Guildenstern several weeks to recover from the incident. By the time they did, however, they had discovered that such things were occurring throughout the city. The Zuckerman family, who ran the bakery on the Raamgracht, had a brick thrown through their window. Naomi Adler, who lived across from the Zuiderkerk, found a slaughtered pig on her doorstep. A number of Jewish families simply packed up and left; those who did not found their homes smeared with mud and their businesses boycotted. Fear became a part of the daily diet, laid out beside the *frikadellen* and chased with a bottle of beer.

For Benjamin these incidents had a sobering effect—for after years of trying to avoid it, he finally felt pressed to examine what it meant to be a Jew. On the one hand, he did not consider himself to be Jewish at all; their guilt notwithstanding, Edward and Lavinia had been about as Jewish as a Sunday tea towel. On the other hand, however, there was his life with Jean Pierre Michel, not to mention the sacred vows of his Bar Mitzvah. Even if he gave back all of his presents—that vast compendium of holy knives he'd never wanted in the first place—he could never give back the imprint of Judaism that came with them.

But what, he asked himself, did it mean to be a Jew? He knew by now that it had as little to do with Jean Pierre Michel's need to acquire things as with Abram's need to toss things in the air. Was there some hidden quality that made a Jew a Jew? Some secret characteristic that compelled the man with the little mustache to hunt them down like a pack of disease-infested animals? He watched the anti-Jewish slogans appear on bridges and monuments, he heard the anti-Jewish grumblings at the butcher's and the brown café, yet it all seemed as senseless as hating people with freckles or people with limps or people with strawberry birthmarks.

The deeper question, as Benjamin came to see it, was whether or not, in such a climate of hatred, he should keep his adoptive Judaism a secret. There was nothing in his passport to identify him as a Jew, and with his dark blond hair and porcelain features, the Germans were not likely to take him for one. For weeks he wandered along the banks of the Herengracht, and the Keizersgracht, and the Prinsengracht, trying to make up his mind. Until finally he decided that it made no sense whatsoever to claim an identity that could only bring him *tsuris*.

It was a painful decision. And it might have stuck — or at least lasted longer — had he not come to it on a Friday just a few hours before the Sabbath. For when Benjamin returned to the house on the Groenburgwal, he found Sara-Hilda lighting a series of tapers, and Henni placing grapes and pinecones on the mantel, and Abel and Herschel carrying chairs in from the kitchen, and Hilda laying the cloth over the challah, and Abram tending the logs upon the fire. By the time Hannah entered with the roast chicken and vegetables, their *gezelligheid* fragrances pouring out into the room, Benjamin was utterly vanquished.

He couldn't do it. No matter how angry he was at Jean Pierre Michel, no matter how justified he might seem in choosing his own safety. If the Family Guildenstern could not cast off their Jewishness, then he would not, either. He would simply have to accept it and — God help him — whatever came with it.

the splendor of a good pot roast

THE ANTI-JEWISH sentiment continued to rise throughout the winter. Hannah's best coat was slashed with a razor blade while she was waiting at the Zuckermans' to buy a loaf of rye bread. A fire was set on the steps of the Neuwe Synagogue, although they managed to contain it before any damage was done. As a result, a feeling of uneasiness began to creep over the household. Abram started sleeping in the hallway. Hannah could not stop rearranging the furniture. Herschel began copying out passages from Leviticus and taping them to the sitting room walls. Finally, in May, the situation came to a head when the Germans attacked Holland and Holland—like Denmark and Norway and Belgium—capitulated. Within weeks the Nazis began isolating the Jews, and it became impossible to leave the country. The Family Guildenstern had to give up performing: eggs led to crispbread, which led to *bitterballen*, which led to stones, at which point the hoops and the horns were packed away and the circus was officially closed.

As the pressure mounted, Benjamin gave in more and more to his craving to eat sand. Borrowing one of the purple bicycles, he headed out to the *Ijmeer*, filled up his pockets with as much as they would hold, and carried it back to his small attic room, where he placed it in a pair of cigar boxes under his bed. He did not eat it often—and when he did it was generally just a couple of grains—yet knowing that it was there somehow helped him to face the oppression.

Despite the collapse of their entire way of living, the Family Guildenstern did not *dray* their *kops* about their circumstances. Instead they cleared a space amid the chaos of their sitting room and established their home as the nucleus of an underground Resistance movement. The form was simple: Three times a week a group of neighboring Jews would climb the steep, sloping stairs to convene beneath the seven purple bicycles: Leo Lipson, the waxyheaded man who ran the laundry on the Verversstraat; Mendy Fischelberg, the broad-shouldered butcher who smelled of garlic and salt beef; Arthur Himmelfarb, the neighborhood zealot who liked to rant about "the reckoning"; Mimi Manheim, the zaftig blonde who always brought along a pot roast or a kugel. If it was Mendy Fischelberg's unflagging optimism that inspired the group, it was Mimi Manheim's pot roasts that kept them going. Where she got the provisions to make them, and how she managed to smuggle them through the streets without anyone seeing, was a mystery to everyone. Once they were heated and sliced, however, and served with a nice glass of beer, they made the specter of the Nazis float off on a warm sea of gravy.

Despite the splendor of a good pot roast, food was not the reason for the gatherings. Mendy Fischelberg explained it best at the very first meeting.

"There are groups like this one gathering all across Europe," he said. "People who refuse to just lay down in the street and be kicked in the kishkes."

"But what do you expect to accomplish?" asked Leo Lipson.

"We can create a network," said Hannah. "Establish communication."

"If we remain isolated," said Mendy Fischelberg, "we increase their power. If we band together, if we know what's happening in Belgium, in France, we stand a chance."

"A chance for what?" said Mimi Manheim.

"A chance to protect ourselves," said Mendy Fischelberg. "A chance, just maybe, to help a few people escape."

"Who can escape?" said Leo Lipson. "They're like a giant foot that crushes everything in its path."

"People are escaping," said Mimi Manheim. "The Vanderberg family got out just last week."

"If we can help people escape," said Arthur Himmelfarb, "it'll be worth schlepping up those steps for these
fakakta meetings."

Everyone agreed, so the house on the Groenburgwal
was swiftly transformed from a clown's paradise into the
makeshift headquarters of a secret intelligence operation.
Enormous maps with crisp, bold lettering and brightly colored borders were taped to the walls; Hannah donated a
variety of hat pins to mark the foreign headquarters and to
chart the progression of the Nazis. A filing system was established in the large painted cabinet that had formerly
housed Abram's juggling equipment (which was shuffled
beneath his bed); it contained the names of over a thousand Dutch Jews, plus a list of those in England and
America who would shelter them should they manage to
escape. All that remained of the clowning was the seven
purple bicycles, which began to seem symbolic: an eccen-
tric fleet of upside-down vehicles for escape from an upside-
down world.

Benjamin quickly found himself swept up into the tide
of activity. Each Tuesday he would assist Mendy Fischelberg in wrapping up parcels of food to be taken to
families that had gone into hiding. Each Friday he would
accompany Leo Lipson to the Mandelbaums' market to
retrieve the coded documents that were smuggled in
weekly with the lox. Most significant, however, Benjamin's Dutch was now good enough to allow him to participate in the thrice weekly meetings, which had settled
into a clear pattern: first Mendy Fischelberg would introduce an idea; then Arthur Himmelfarb would attempt
to tear it apart; then Abel would attempt to tear Arthur
Himmelfarb apart; then Benjamin, Abram, Henni, and

Mimi Manheim would endeavor to explore what Mendy Fischelberg had suggested in the first place. Herschel and Hilda tended to remain in their rooms, and Sara-Hilda, though she sat in on the discussions, rarely said a word. At seven-thirty Hannah would serve the food. Then Leo Lipson would rise and solemnly repeat what everyone else had already said, as if it were a stream of new ideas just come to him.

By the middle of June the operation had helped eight people to flee the country. By the end of August that number had increased to twenty-three. Then, in late September, around the time of the High Holy Days, Mendy Fischelberg came up with a plan that would allow more than thirty Jewish children to escape to England. It involved, among other things, an a cappella choir, a secret benefactor in Enkhuizen, and a passenger ferry called the *Acacia*. Mendy Fischelberg was able to do most of the groundwork himself: the briefing of the children's parents, the forging of the identity papers, the series of communications between Amsterdam and Enkhuizen. As the mission approached, however, he began to recognize that certain aspects of the operation required a more sophisticated hand. And that was when he decided to call in "the Calculator."

In the underground circles of the war Resistance, "the Calculator" was a near mythic figure. He was named for his ability to calculate virtually anything in his head, from the farthest distance a piece of shrapnel might travel during the explosion of a Nazi outpost to the number of minutes it would take a bakery truck loaded with Jews to cross a border during a very bad electrical storm. It was said that he had a platinum-plated device inside his head.

It was said that he could calculate even in his sleep, answering questions whispered at his bedside with a speed and precision that were astonishing. Even more intriguing than such abilities, however, was the variation in reports on what he looked like. Some people claimed that he was a very old man, twisted with arthritis, missing all his front teeth. Others insisted that he was a woman, or a child. Jewish, not Jewish, Italian, French—Leo Lipson even heard that he was a dog.

"That's how he slips across the border so easy. The Germans don't even notice."

The others found this theory a bit difficult to swallow. What seemed clear, however, was that "the Calculator" was able to produce a series of bizarre effects that could consistently baffle the Nazis.

For over two weeks there was no response to the elaborately coded telegram that Mendy Fischelberg sent out through the underground channels. Reluctantly the group began to let go of the idea and to resume their efforts to move forward with the Enkhuizen mission without him. Then, one evening toward the beginning of October, Mendy Fischelberg suddenly hurried into the house with a crumpled piece of paper in his hand.

The mission was approved. Instructions would follow.

And "the Calculator" was coming to visit.

a trick of memory

SOMETIMES, between the pot roasts and the secret maneuvers, amid the growing fear and the deepening sense of danger, Benjamin's old life would rise up over him.

As he climbed the stairs of the house on the Groenburg-wal, he would see the white marble banister of the stairs of the Fifth Avenue mansion. As he lowered his spoon into his earthenware bowl, he would see the glint of silver or the thin blue line that ran about the rim of the Sevres. What surprised him, however, was not so much the apparition of these objects, but the torrent of feeling that came with them. For beneath the braided drapery sash and the crystal chandelier was neither the woman he had made love with nor the man who had betrayed him, but those two magnificent, larger-than-life figures from his childhood.

It was a trick of memory, a game played in the mind to draw him back to what he did not wish to think of. And it functioned most cruelly when it conjured up Lorna O'Shaughnassy. Her face would suddenly appear at his window as he gazed out over the rooftops. Her body would materialize in the narrow bed beside him, a ghost that evaporated even as he reached out to hold it.

Benjamin was always aware that he could have reached for Sara-Hilda, the quirky reality that countered the ghostly visions, the live heart beating inches away that mocked the false, elusive one formed by memory. She still beamed at him with her lopsided smile, still followed him around with her penitent look of devotion, and she still wore the replica of his birthmark on her cheek, though that cheek was less girlish now, as her body was more like a woman's.

Sara-Hilda was now sixteen years old. And what had seemed odd and sweet only a brief year earlier was suddenly strangely alluring. Whenever Benjamin considered moving toward her, however, the clock or the chair or the desk would intercede and trip up his path with memories.

The Calculator

"IF HE COMES," said Arthur Himmelfarb, "he'll want to get down to business, not eat and drink and carry on like a *schlemazel*."

"If he comes," said Mimi Manheim, "he'll want to take off his clothes and pass out from the heat like the rest of us."

On the evening "the Calculator" was to arrive there was a heavy rainstorm, and with the windows closed, and the fireplace going, and an extra-large pot roast basting in the oven, the house was like a kosher Turkish sauna. Abram and Leo Lipson kept pacing from room to room, while the others sat waiting to see what age, sex, or species was going to walk through the door. The tension had been building for several days, ever since the moment that Mendy Fischelberg had announced that "the Calculator" was coming to visit. Hannah had insisted that the entire house be aired out, so one by one each cup, chair, book, plate, sofa, table, candlestick, ashtray, mirror, cushion, doily, and lamp was carried down the stairs, along the canal, and then one full turn around the block. Henni argued that carting objects of glass and wood through the streets would not alter them in any way, but Hannah was adamant: it was not every day that a celebrated spy came to visit, and she was determined that the house be immaculate. In the meantime, Hilda prepared a performance on the French horn, Herschel touched up the paint on the purple bicycles, Leo Lipson composed a brief welcoming address, and Mimi Manheim began preparations for a pot roast to end all pot roasts.

"Black peppercorns," she whispered to Benjamin, "with a dash of *jonge jeniver.*"

In short, the entire household was in a fever of anticipation, and no one was more excited than Benjamin. "The Calculator" was situated at the heart of the war; his exploits were legendary; he was a world-renowned hero. Perhaps he would help Benjamin find a way to be more useful than bundling stale loaves of bread and smuggling papers that stank of smoked salmon.

As the evening wore on, however, Benjamin began to wonder whether "the Calculator" was even coming. By eight o'clock the pot roast had begun to sizzle, and Hannah had to remove it from the oven. By nine o'clock the skylight had begun to leak, and Abel had to fetch a ladder and some caulking putty and seal it while the rain was seeping in. By ten o'clock the pot roast had been eaten, and Abram, Mimi Manheim, Mendy Fischelberg, and Leo Lipson had begun a game of five-card stud at the table. By eleven o'clock Arthur Himmelfarb had decided that "the Calculator" had been intercepted and had given their names to the Nazis and that they would soon be tracked down—while Benjamin had begun to wonder whether "the Calculator" existed at all.

At four minutes to midnight, just as Mimi Manheim was winning her fifth round of poker, there came a sharp rapping at the door. For a moment there was a perfect stillness in the room—that weightless space that hovers between anticipation and fulfillment—then Abel hurried down the long flight of stairs to return a moment later with their guest. At first, as he stood dripping upon the large towel that Hannah had placed in the doorway, it was difficult to tell much about him; the hood of his rain slick obscured his face, and though it was clear that he was not a dog, the rest was still a rain-soaked mystery. Then he drew back the hood, lowered his glasses, removed a dark wig, peeled off his mustache, and it was revealed that he was a small, if most decidedly peculiar-looking, young man.

The group was fascinated, but only Benjamin was stunned. For though nine years had passed and they were both now adults, there was not a doubt in his mind that the fellow standing before him, "the Calculator" himself, was his old friend and playmate, his partner in crime, the one-and-only Petrie Woolrich.

13/The Shadow of an Eclipse

a feast of flesh and reason

S INSTANTLY AS Benjamin recognized Petrie, Petrie recognized Benjamin. The birthmark, of course, was a dead give-away; no matter how dramatically the rest of him might have changed, there was no mistaking that bold purple red insignia. What differentiated Petrie's recognition of Benjamin from Benjamin's recognition of Petrie, however, was that there was not the slightest trace of surprise in it.

"Good to see you, Benjamin," he said as he stepped out of his galoshes. "I was afraid you might be missing the entire war."

Benjamin did not know what to say. He had thought about Petrie so often—had imagined them talking, laughing, scheming—he found it difficult to believe that he was standing there with him now.

"Petrie?" he finally managed. "Is it really you?"

"It's me all right," said Petrie. "I've just gotten into some faster circles."

The others, of course, were astonished to discover that Benjamin and "the Calculator" were friends. Petrie therefore launched into an elaborate description, in perfect Dutch, of how they'd met as children during a train derailment in Venezuela, when Benjamin, in a moment of bravery, had leapt into the burning wreckage to pull him to safety. The story, of course, was a complete fabrication, yet it managed to startle the entire group into silence, so that Petrie could draw their attention back to the business at hand. After seating himself at the table, he drew a series of papers from his inside breast pocket and began laying them out in a grid; then Mendy Fischelberg produced his own set of documents: sales receipts, nautical timetables, bits of butcher paper scribbled over with scraps of conversation; then, while Hannah heated up the few slices of leftover pot roast and Abram poured a warm glass of beer, "the Calculator" calculated: eyes darting swiftly from side to side, shoulders twitching, mouth contorting, faint grumbling noises emerging from the depths of his being. He was like a machine sleekly camouflaged as a small human being, his rodentlike features a mask to the clockworks inside.

Petrie continued on in this way for close to an hour. Then he put down his pencil, pushed back his chair, and stood. "That's enough for tonight," he said. "We can continue in the morning."

By this time Herschel and Hilda and Leo Lipson had already fallen asleep; now Abel and Henni and Sara-Hilda followed suit, while Mimi Manheim and Mendy Fischelberg and Arthur Himmelfarb stumbled off to their various dwellings. Benjamin was about to head off to sleep, too, when Petrie turned to him and suggested that they sit by the fire.

"I think we have a bit of catching up to do," he said.

Benjamin, who had remained somewhat flabbergasted since the moment of his friend's arrival, now followed him across the room to the small sofa that sat before the hearth. Then, while Abram threw a log upon the fire and Hannah brought in some bread and cheese and a bottle of schnapps, Petrie asked Benjamin to tell him what had happened after they'd gone their separate ways in Rome.

"I want to know everything," he insisted. "From start to finish."

Benjamin was not sure if it was either possible or desirable to tell Petrie everything, but he did his best to describe the trajectory that he had followed from his visit to Alma Esther to his love affair with Lorna O'Shaughnassy. He did not mention how that love affair had ended or how he had come to be living in Amsterdam with a family of Jewish clowns, but Petrie did not press him on either issue. Instead he began an account of his own passage from street-corner pickpocket to infamous underground spy. It turned out that his career as a thief had lasted only a few weeks beyond Benjamin's departure, as one afternoon, while attempting to remove a platinum-and-diamond bracelet from the wrist of a widowed Englishwoman in the lobby of the Villa Fonseca, he was arrested by the hotel security and taken to jail. To his great surprise, he was released within the hour by the woman he had accosted, who told the police that he was actually her lover and that the supposed theft had been part of an elaborate game they liked to play to stimulate their sex life. When he accompanied the woman back to the hotel, they proceeded to spin the lie into truth, and for the next three years Petrie traveled the continent with her, mastering the language of each place they visited and studying mathematics.

"You have no idea how many hotels there are in Europe," said Petrie. "The amount of bed linen that has to be changed, on a daily basis, is staggering."

One day, while he was lying on a chaise longue at a thermal bath in Wiesbaden, Petrie began reading a volume on probability that so astounded him, he left the spa and headed to Munich to track down the man who had written it. When he found him, in a run-down rooming house near the outskirts of the city, this man proceeded to change Petrie's life. In the first place he demonstrated that there was a vast field of unexplored territory at the cross-junction between pure mathematics and applied mathematics and that the future of the field lay more in engineering than in science. In the second place he demonstrated that there was a vast field of unexplored territory in the realm of sexuality, thus altering Petrie's inclination forever.

"I hope it doesn't disturb you, Benjamin," said Petrie. "But the fact is, I'm a poof."

Benjamin, once again, did not know what to say. It was not something he'd really thought about before, and he was not entirely certain that he wanted to think about it now. "The idea doesn't appeal to me much personally," he said. "But otherwise I guess it doesn't matter."

Petrie went on to explain that his new lover, whom he referred to as "Der Schwann," was in the process of building a machine that combined the power of mathematics with the marvels of electricity.

"When he discovered my ability to calculate almost anything," said Petrie, "he decided that our relationship was a product of fate."

The collaboration between Petrie and Der Schwann soon developed into a feast of flesh and reason. By the end of their first year together they had solved most of the problems that Der Schwann had been grappling with since the late 1930s. By the end of their second they had succeeded in constructing the practical prototype for an electromechanical computing machine. By this time, however, the situation in Germany made it impossible for them to continue. So Der Schwann accepted an offer to teach mathematics at Princeton, and Petrie went to join the Resistance. By combining his astonishing powers of computation with the slipperiness that he'd acquired as a pickpocket, "the Calculator" was born. The rest was merely a series of death-defying encounters and hairbreadth escapes leading up to his arrival in Amsterdam.

"I'd like to tell you that it's not as exciting as it sounds," said Petrie. "But the fact is, it is."

At this point Petrie paused for a moment, and Benjamin sat forward and yawned. As he looked at the table he saw that somewhere during the telling of their tales he and Petrie had eaten all the bread and cheese and drunk a good portion of the schnapps. He could not, however, remember tasting a single thing. A part of him wanted Petrie to go on and on, regaling him with the details of his every adventure. Another part, however, wanted only to go to sleep—which Petrie seemed to recognize.

"I think we'd better leave it for now," he said. "We've got a war to fight in the morning."

They rose then and found a couple of blankets and made up the couch for "the Calculator." Then, his head swimming with diamond bracelets and thermal baths and swans, Benjamin stumbled up the stairs to the attic and went to bed.

deadly daffodils

PETRIE REMAINED with the Family Guildenstern for the next six weeks, overseeing the details of the Enkhuizen mission and becoming reacquainted with Benjamin. By the light of day he was less peculiar than at midnight, yet his looks were still startling: what had made him seem old beyond his years when Benjamin had first met him now made him seem almost like a child. If people stared at him in the street, however, it was mostly because he was with Benjamin; only when juxtaposed against that red-speckled beauty did his pin-sharp visage truly shock. No matter how intense the stares were, however, no one—from the rabbi at the Obbene shul to the head of the Dutch-German regiment—would ever have guessed that this slight, strange creature was "the Calculator."

To Benjamin it was almost as if he and Petrie had never been separated; they roamed the streets of Amsterdam as if it were the next logical stop after Rome. Benjamin told Petrie about his history with the saxophone: how he'd followed up his discovery of it with years of futile struggling, how he'd only just learned how his powers could transform his playing. Petrie, in turn, regaled Benjamin with further stories of his adventures: how he'd spent four months in a lunatic asylum in Frieburg disguised as a female orderly, how he'd had to parachute from a biplane after being shot down over a mustard field near Reims.

Eventually Benjamin lighted upon the idea of using his gift to become a spy himself.

"Think about it," he said. "No borders to penetrate. No guards to bribe. I could communicate messages the instant they were finished being formulated."

"There are too many variables," said Petrie.

"What do you mean?"

"You have to look at things scientifically, Benjamin. You have to consider what might go wrong."

"For example?"

"Who's going to guarantee you'll end up where you intend to? How do we control who's going to be there when you do?"

Benjamin thought about this for a moment. "I guess I'll just have to take the chances."

Petrie shook his head. "You can't take those kinds of chances, Benjamin. There are too many people involved. You have to trust me—you're just not spy material."

Benjamin didn't agree, but for the moment he did not press it. "We'll see, Petrie," he said. "We'll see."

Toward the end of November the Enkhuizen mission was set into motion, and with the exception of a girl named Liesl Goudsbloem, who refused to board the ferry at the very last moment and had to be hidden in a cheese cellar in Hoorn, the operation was a tremendous success, effecting the passage of twenty-three children to Lowestoft, near Norwich, and fourteen to Kingston-upon-Hull. The following morning Petrie announced that he was leaving immediately for Bialystok, Poland, where he was organizing medical provisions for the members of the ghetto. He assured Benjamin, however, that he would return on a regular basis if it was all right with the Family Guildenstern.

"I'd like to think of this as a home away from home," he said. "Although there's not actually any home that it would be away from."

Hannah insisted that he would always be welcome, so "the Calculator" departed, and the house on the Groen-burgwal returned to the lively chaos that it had known before his visit.

As Hanukkah approached, the bombs began to drop, which made Sara-Hilda thrust her arms up into the air and clasp her hands together tightly overhead. Hilda, on the other hand, started to crawl on all fours, while Henni came to the conclusion that Benjamin was to blame and began sketching skulls and crossbones on his door. Benjamin could not help thinking of Cassandra Nutt's dream or keep from noting that the explosions seemed to be getting closer.

The Resistance operation continued to make efforts, but nothing approached the excitement of the Enkhuizen mission. Then, one evening toward the end of January, Arthur Himmelfarb came puffing up the stairs with news.

"There's going to be a strike!" he cried as he collapsed into a fit of wheezing.

"A strike?" said Leo Lipson. "How can there be a strike when we're all out of work?"

Arthur Himmelfarb waved his hand about frantically as Hannah fetched him a glass of water. "Not that kind of strike," he gasped. "A protest against the pogroms."

"It's about time," said Mimi Manheim, crossing to Arthur Himmelfarb and giving him a good *zets* on the back.

"It's going to make history," said Abel. "Someone finally has the guts to stand up to these bastards."

"It's going to make *tsuris*," said Mendy Fischelberg. "You don't walk up to a bully and spit in his face. He only hits you harder the next time."

The event that Arthur Himmelfarb was referring to took place on the following Tuesday, and both Abel and Mendy Fischelberg proved to be right: as the first anti-pogrom strike in Europe it made history, and as a way of irritating the Nazis it made an incredible amount of *tsuris*. Signs were posted in shop windows, saying Jews could not enter; a curfew was established requiring Jews to be off the streets by eight o'clock in the evening; Jews owning bicycles were "strongly requested" to turn them over to the authorities. In addition, the Germans began cracking down on all forms of resistance, forcing the activities of the operation in the house on the Groenburgwal to become even more circumspect than before.

The following months were like living beneath the shadow of an eclipse. In April Mimi Manheim's apartment was ransacked. In August Leo Lipson was arrested for approaching a non-Jewish woman in the street. Throughout this time, Petrie continued to come and go, yet Benjamin began to notice that with each of his visits he seemed smaller and wearier. Finally, in December, when the Japanese bombed Pearl Harbor and America joined the war, Petrie announced that he would not be returning for a very long while. He said that it was because it was becoming too difficult to cross the Dutch-German border. When he was alone with Benjamin, however, he told him the truth. "They've built these camps, Benjamin. Terrible, horrible places. The Jews go in and they don't come out. I have to focus my efforts in a new direction."

He gave Benjamin an address in Munich where he promised that he could always be reached. Then "the Calculator" vanished into the dark, bloody seams of the war.

The winter of 1942 was lean and grueling. Benjamin celebrated his twentieth birthday with an extra egg and a piece of dusty chocolate that Abel had managed to steal for him. Toward the beginning of March, rumors began to circulate about the deportation of Jews. Then, in April, the Nazis suddenly announced that henceforth all Jews would be required to wear the yellow Star of David, and in a matter of days, like a crop of deadly daffodils, they began sprouting across the city. While the others were busily stitching them onto their jackets and blouses and coats, however, Sara-Hilda came up with a better idea: she finally removed Benjamin's birthmark from her cheek and replaced it with a yellow star.

The Family Guildenstern tried to ignore the implications of this new form of fascism. They got out the hoops and the banners and the balls and began entertaining one another in the sitting room. They made endless jokes about the stupidity of the Nazis, laughing just enough to ease the hunger in their bellies. Yet no matter how they tried, they could not help feeling that they were being sorted, and branded, and herded toward the gate, and that something unspeakable was waiting for them on the other side.

strawberries and Little Sidney Lowenthal

"A TRANSIT CAMP?" said Abram. "What do you do in a transit camp?"

"You wait," said Mendy Fischelberg. "You live like some kind of farm animal and you wait."

"We've been doing that in Amsterdam for two years now," said Mimi Manheim. "Suddenly we need a special facility?"

At the beginning of June the Germans announced that they would be sending all Jews to a transit camp in the Drenthe province, where they would remain for a short period before being transferred to a work camp in Poland. There were countless rumors as to what actually went on in these places, but for most people it was impossible to believe that such stories could be true. The best they could do was prepare themselves for another exodus and cling to the belief that God would see them through.

Mimi Manheim was the first to receive her orders. Two weeks later Arthur Himmelfarb received his, and the week after that Mendy Fischelberg went into hiding. By the time the Family Guildenstern were called up, toward the middle of August, they were more or less ready. What they were totally unprepared for was Benjamin's announcement that he was going with them.

"It's *meshugge*," said Abram. "You're not a Guildenstern. You don't have to go."

Benjamin, however, would not be dissuaded. The order was for all members of the house on the Groenburgwal, and the shipping out, in the end, was for all Jews.

"I've already lost two families," he said. "I don't intend to lose a third."

The family quickly began to make preparations for their journey. According to their orders, they were each allowed to bring a small rucksack containing a specified list of clothing and a handful of toilet articles. When it came time to prepare these, however, each insisted upon adding a personal treasure: Hannah took a pair of tortoiseshell hair combs that Abram had given her on their wedding night; Abram took the key to his juggling box, which he hid beneath the floorboards of his room; Abel took the pocket watch that he'd bought with the money he'd saved from three consecutive birthdays; Herschel took the smooth piece of flint that he'd found on the trip he'd taken to Rotterdam when he was eleven; Henni took a photograph of Stella; Hilda took a photograph of Leslie Howard; Sara-Hilda took a copy of Shakespeare's sonnets; Benjamin took the black Brillhart mouthpiece from his sax, which he wrapped in a piece of yellow felt and placed inside an empty breath-mint tin. They knew it was likely that these things would be confiscated once they arrived, yet they could not bear the thought of venturing into the unknown without a book or a bead or a pin to remind them who they were.

On the fourth of September they boarded the train for Westerbork, the small camp that clung like a filthy beetle to the edge of the Dutch-German border. When they arrived, however, they were greeted by a prison, with countless rows of cramped wooden barracks, surrounded by endless tracts of sand, surrounded by barbed-wire fencing. After filling out registration forms, the women were placed in a hut beside the washing facility, the men in one beside a building that was known as the "punishment block." Then they were given some turnips and a hunk of stale bread and sent to join the rats in their beds.

Over the next few weeks their hearts grew heavy as the horror of the place began to penetrate. Hannah and Henni were sent to work in the laundry, while Hilda was made to clean the floors of the sick ward (along with Mimi Man-heim) and Sara-Hilda was made to clean the latrines. The men, on the other hand, had their heads shaven and were forced to push wheelbarrows loaded with gravel around the camp. At mealtimes they were crowded into a dark, smelly mess hall, three times a week they were forced to "take exercise," and everywhere they looked there were children crying and parents bickering and old folks shuf-fling about in a daze. And every so often they would shud-der with fear as an alarm bell sounded and the next group was loaded onto a goods wagon and taken to Poland.

The members of the Family Guildenstern exhibited a variety of reactions to the experience of being held in the camp. Henni began whispering to an imaginary Stella, convinced that her beloved bird was still with her. Abram, who was outraged by the shaving of his head, stopped talking entirely, except to cry out occasionally, "I am an egg! An egg cannot speak!" Hershel, who was troubled by the lack of formal prayer, developed a private ritual, which he performed twice a day, of banging two stones sharply together three times in a row, convinced that God would know what he meant.

Benjamin tried not to think about God, but to concen-trate instead on not cracking up. There was so much ugli-ness that he could hardly breathe, such meanness and cruelty that he could hardly believe he was still living upon the earth. The camp guards, unable to process the contra-diction of his beauty and his birthmark, called him "Feber Geschicte" and jabbed him between the shoulder blades with the butts of their guns. He was surrounded on all sides by a vast sea of sand, but without a moment of pri-vacy he was unable to taste a grain. And though he knew that he could always try to transfer himself away, he could not bring himself to go and leave the Family Guildenstern behind.

The answer finally came from Sara-Hilda. She, like the others, found the transit camp unbearable, so whenever she could she would stand by the fence and imagine that she was eating strawberries. Sara-Hilda loved strawberries. She had loved them even before Benjamin had arrived with his lavish strawberry birthmark. Now she discovered that if she stood close to the fence and gazed out into the distance—beyond the bits of scrub, beyond the stinking ditch—she could feast, in her imagination, upon an endless supply. Then the barbed-wire fence would become a latticework grill covered over with freesia, the smoke from the canteen would become chicken with rosemary roasting on a spit, and the terrible feeling that she was being crushed between two planks would recede for a moment or two.

Day after day Benjamin watched Sara-Hilda as she stood beside the fence. He did not know what she was thinking about, but he knew that, whatever it was, it helped her deal with the anguish of being trapped inside the transit camp. So one evening, as the sun was setting and the others were preparing for bed, he decided to approach her and find out.

"What are you looking at, Sara-Hilda?" he said. "What do you see?"

Sara-Hilda did not answer, so he turned to leave. As he started away, however, he heard her whisper softly, "Strawberries."

Benjamin turned back to her in the fading light, and for the first time he noticed how gaunt she had become. The camp officials had insisted that she remove the yellow star from her cheek, and without any markings her face seemed incredibly vulnerable. "If I could leave this place," said Benjamin, "I'd get you some strawberries, Sara-Hilda. I'd bring you baskets and baskets of the most delicious strawberries you ever tasted."

Sara-Hilda stood there with her pristine cheeks and her chaotic hair and her dark, glistening eyes. "If you could leave this place," she said, "you'd take me with you."

Benjamin was startled by Sara-Hilda's words. For though he knew that she could not possibly know about his powers, he could not help but hear what she'd said as a challenge. And what surprised him most was that he had not thought of it before: that he might be able to use his powers to help his friends escape as well as himself.

Benjamin did not know if this was remotely possible, but he knew that he had to find out. And just as it was Sara-Hilda who had led him to the idea, it was Little Sidney Lowenthal who allowed him to test it out. Six weeks earlier, in a moment of confusion, Little Sidney's parents had been loaded onto the transport wagon and shipped off to Poland without him. As a result, Little Sidney had become the transit camp waif. No matter how dirty the other children were, Little Sidney was always dirtier. No matter how flimsy or ill fitting their clothes, Little Sidney's were always worse. Little Sidney, however, never complained and for a kind word would give you the broadest, most gap-toothed grin you had ever seen in your life. Besides scratching, and coughing, and occasionally spitting, grinning was Little Sidney's specialty.

Benjamin decided that Little Sidney was the ideal subject for his experiment. He couldn't have weighed more than thirty-five pounds, he was sweetly naive enough to do almost anything, and no one was likely to notice if he went missing for a while. So on the morning after his conversation with Sara-Hilda, Benjamin searched the camp until he found him, seated in a wheelbarrow, playing with a cluster of twigs and a rotten potato.

"Hello, Little Sidney," he said.

Little Sidney looked up. "Did God paint your face like that?"

Benjamin thought about this for a moment. "Yes," he said. "I guess He did."

"Oh," said Little Sidney, returning to his twigs and potato.

"What are you playing?" said Benjamin.

Little Sidney held up a twig. "These are the Jews." He held up the potato. "And this is the transport wagon."

Benjamin nodded. "Very nice."

Little Sidney began to move the potato along the edge of the wheelbarrow, stopping every few inches to plunge in a twig. Benjamin watched him for a moment and then knelt before the grimy wheelbarrow. "How would you like to go on an adventure with me?"

"An adventure?" said Little Sidney.

"A trip somewhere. Just for a quick visit."

Little Sidney paused to pick something out of his nose. "Where to?"

"Wherever you like," said Benjamin.

Little Sidney thought about this for a moment. Then his face exploded into its fabulous grin and he said, "Zanzibar."

"Zanzibar," said Benjamin.

Little Sidney nodded.

"You're sure you wouldn't like to try someplace closer?" said Benjamin. "Like Utrecht, perhaps? Or maybe Brussels?"

Little Sidney shook his head. *"Zanzibar."*

Benjamin rose and wiped the dirt from his pants. The whole thing, he reasoned, was a crapshoot anyway, so why not a crapshoot to Zanzibar? "Let's see what happens," he said, reaching out his hand to the child.

Little Sidney took Benjamin's hand and climbed down from the wheelbarrow. Then Benjamin closed his eyes and told Little Sidney to close his, and without thinking about what would happen if they were discovered, and without thinking what would happen if they failed, he concentrated on willing both himself and Little Sidney to Zanzibar.

Little Sidney never doubted. He closed his eyes and held on tight and waited to be swept away. But even after so many trips, to so many places, over such a number of years, Benjamin was surprised to find that it actually worked.

14/(How He Did It This Time)

HIS IS HOW he did it this time:

Focusing his mind inward, he freed himself as before—not the birthmark, not the body, not the anything-recognizable-as or in-any-way-considered-to-be-Benjamin. Where it had been sufficient for his own transference, however, to travel in the manner of a scent or a sound, for the transfer of others it was necessary to imitate light. Holding on tightly to Little Sidney's hand, he imagined a white-hot sun burning fiercely inside him—a light source that expanded until it saturated his body—until it encompassed Little Sidney—then reality melted, the camp fell away, and they found themselves swept off to Zanzibar.

For a thousandth of an instant, just before they vanished, Benjamin felt the light inside him illuminate the camp—the huts and the paths—the dirt and the gravel—the stray cats, the moldy bread, the Jews, the Nazis, the sadness, the sickness, the suffering. Like an X ray exposing the truth beneath the illusion. Like a flash of compassion that yielded an extraordinary understanding.

Then, like a ghost at the window, it was gone.

And so were Little Sidney and Benjamin.

15/Ghosts

Purim in January

ESPITE THE LUXURY of being freed from the transit camp, Benjamin and Little Sidney did not linger in Zanzibar. They visited the port and caught a glimpse of the sultan's palace; they shared some fried maize and a bowl of cassava; then Benjamin transferred them back to the camp, where he swore Little Sidney to absolute secrecy and then tried to embrace the significance of what had just occurred.

He had used his powers to transport another. And if one was possible, then two, or ten, or a hundred were possible. In the midst of the war, with so many held prisoner, the implications of such a discovery were astounding. He still wasn't certain that he could do a one-way transfer, but he remembered Petrie's words:

Maybe if the need to escape is strong enough, a one-way transfer is possible. Maybe if you have no intention of ever returning to the place you started, you cancel out the time factor.

Benjamin realized that it was only a theory, but if he was going to test it, he could not think of anyplace that inspired those conditions better than Westerbork.

Before he could attempt to save the entire world, however, he had to figure out how to free the Family Guildenstern. He decided that he would have to do it at night, for there was hardly a moment during the day when they were not being watched. And he decided, after investigating a variety of locales, that he would take them to an abandoned farmhouse on the island of Gotland off the southeast coast of Sweden, as it seemed as unlikely a place as any to search for a family of Jewish clowns. What concerned him most, however, was how to tell the Family Guildenstern about his powers without convincing them that he had gone mad. He decided that he would simply have to take the plunge, so on the following afternoon, toward the end of the lunch break, he went up to Hannah and told her about his gift.

"You can disappear," she said.

"I know it sounds crazy," said Benjamin, "but I swear to you it's true."

"And you can make us disappear."

"I took Little Sidney to Zanzibar."

"Zanzibar," said Hannah.

Benjamin shrugged. "That's where he wanted to go."

Hannah paused for a moment, folding a spindly carrot into her handkerchief and then slipping it into the pocket of her apron. "I've seen a lot of strange things in my life, Benjamin. But nothing has been stranger than what I've seen inside this camp." She looked into Benjamin's eyes. "If you say you can disappear, then I believe you. If you say you can get us out, then I believe that, too."

Abram, however, was not so easy to convince. He listened attentively while Benjamin described his powers, but when he was finished talking he demanded a demonstration. Benjamin was reluctant, but when he saw that Abram would have it no other way, he took him to a quiet corner behind the sick ward, spirited them both to Hoogeveen, and then returned them securely to the camp. At first Abram was utterly silent. Then he shook his head and said, "All this time you've been the circus act of the century and you never bothered to tell us?"

Both Hannah and Abram ultimately agreed to go along with Benjamin's plan. They decided, however, to not try to explain Benjamin's powers to the others but merely to tell them that he'd come up with a way to help them escape from the camp and then fill them in on the voodoo once it had been accomplished. Benjamin, meanwhile, began getting himself ready, taking quick trips to Gotland to build up his stamina and studying the exact location of each of their beds, plus those of Mimi Manheim, Arthur Himmelfarb, and Little Sidney, whom he'd decided to take as well. Then on Friday night, when everyone was asleep, he transferred himself to the various bedsides and, like an avenging angel, escorted his friends to safety.

For the most part, they hardly knew what was happening. Only Herschel and Hannah were roused by his approach, while the others woke only after they'd arrived at the farmhouse in Gotland. Once they were all there, Benjamin tried to present them with an explanation of what he'd done, yet even three or four tries could not convince them that what he was saying was true. All they knew was that they were out of the transit camp and that, however it had happened, it demanded a celebration. So while Abel and Herschel gathered wood to build a fire, Hannah found some flat bread on a shelf above the sink, Henni some wildberry preserves in a corner of the pantry, and Hilda a string of dried marjoram sausages hanging from a beam above the stove. They laid these out on the large oak table, which they garnished with spruce twigs and a scattering of stones; then they shared out the contents of a bottle of aquavit and raised their glasses as if it were Purim in January.

"To Benjamin!" cried Abel.

"To Benjamin!" cried the others.

Benjamin looked around the table at the faces of his friends: the exalted face of Hannah, the grateful face of Abel, the sparkling, open, clean-washed face of Sara-Hilda. He wanted to bask in them—bathed by the candlelight, flushed with their joy—but before he could do so, Henni began to go a bit fuzzy about the edges and then slowly fade away. One by one the others followed suit—Hannah and Abram—Herschel and Hilda—Arthur Himmelfarb and Mimi Manheim and Abel and Sara-Hilda—until all that were left were Benjamin and Little Sidney. Curled up in his chair with a bowl of wildberry preserves, Little Sidney had not even noticed what was happening until he raised a handful of jam to his mouth and he suddenly saw his fingers begin to flicker and go transparent. Then the bowl crashed to the floor—Little Sidney disappeared—and Benjamin was left alone.

sand

BENJAMIN STOOD at the edge of the water with his hands on his knees and his head bent over as his vomit washed away on the sea. There was a clenching inside him and a ringing in his ears and a harsh, bitter burning in his throat—while outside, the stark Swedish landscape looked on with a quiet, perfect detachment.

For the first time in his life, Benjamin had given himself over to his craving to eat sand. Like a strange inversion of the dry man in the desert, he began hungrily gulping great mouthfuls of the stuff. This, in turn, had led to the vomiting: no sooner had the rough grains bombarded his stomach than they triggered the reflex that sent them violently coursing up out of him. Benjamin continued on, however—gulping and retching, battering his insides, performing a ritual that barely stroked the surface of his pain.

There were occasional moments when the tightness in his stomach and the rawness of his throat were superseded by a shimmering lightness in his head, and Benjamin nearly lost consciousness. Then he could almost feel the sea come inside him and cleanse him and carry him away. When he came to, however, he was right back on the beach—his hands on his knees, his head bent over, his eyes on the wrenched-up contents of his guts as they gently floated off on the current.

smoke

"IT'S NOT YOUR FAULT, Benjamin."

"You're wrong."

"You were trying to help."

"But I only made things worse. Who knows where they wound up when they were transferred back. I probably sent them straight to the punishment block."

Benjamin looked around the cramped, smoky bar where he and Petrie were huddled over a pair of *weissbiere*. There was a bright, animated energy in the room—as if nothing existed outside its limits, as if the war were not happening, as if the world were at peace.

"The punishment block is nothing compared with what they'll find in Poland," said Petrie.

"Why wasn't I sent back?" said Benjamin. "Or why didn't 'the Cinderella factor' blow me to bits?"

"It's hard to say. I mean, it's not exactly a science. But we have the example of your transfer into the car when you were a child. Apparently, if the need is great enough, it works." Petrie took a sip of his beer. "At least for you, that is." He took another sip of his beer and looked up at Benjamin. "It's not your fault."

Benjamin looked into Petrie's eyes. "Then whose fault is it?"

Petrie shook his head. "I don't know," he said. "The whole thing stinks like a barrel of shit, and even Hitler can't take all the blame. It's something about the nature of things. About the nature of us all." A burst of laughter came from the next table. "It's a barrel of shit, Benjamin. A great big barrel of shit."

While Benjamin's attempt to free the Family Guildenstern had failed, he'd tried to transfer himself back to the transit camp to check on the safety of his friends. He found, however, that he was unable to do so—so he left the farmhouse and walked to a nearby village, where a fisherman and his wife gave him food and lodging in return for his help cleaning fish. That was when Benjamin had begun eating sand, an experience that lasted exactly twenty-seven days. On the twenty-eighth he raised a handful to his mouth and could no longer consume it, and on the twenty-ninth he decided to contact Petrie. He'd had no idea whether the letter he wrote to him would actually reach him, but six weeks later, toward the end of March, he received a telegram instructing him to meet Petrie in a bar on the outskirts of Karlsruhe, which was where they were sitting now.

"So what do we do next?" said Benjamin.

Petrie took a long, pensive drag from his cigarette and blew the smoke up toward the ceiling fan. "I'm going back to the States," he said.

"You're joking," said Benjamin.

"I leave in three weeks. A cargo carrier will take me from Marseilles."

A barmaid came by to empty the ashtray. She was wearing a tight red dress and black fishnet stockings, and she made Benjamin think of Lorna. He had not thought of her in a very long time, and it saddened him to realize it. As the barmaid removed the ashtray and replaced it with a clean one, Petrie ordered another pair of beers. She halted for a moment, as if seeing him for the first time; then she took up their glasses and made her way back to the bar.

"You can't just give up," said Benjamin.

"Who said anything about giving up?" said Petrie. "I'm going back to work on a project with Der Schwann." He looked around for a moment and then leaned in closer. "I can't say too much about it except that it involves the U.S. Navy. And that it has the potential to completely redefine the war."

"You're going to New Jersey to redefine the war?"

"He's at Harvard now, not Princeton," said Petrie. "And don't be a smartass."

The barmaid returned with another pair of *weissbiere* and a bowl of peanuts. Petrie took a handful of these and stuffed them into his small, ratlike mouth.

"Why don't you come with me?" he said.

"What good can I do at Harvard?"

"You can help us," said Petrie. "You're bound to be more useful than you will be staying here."

"I don't agree."

"You can't mean you're going to use your powers again—"

"I'm done with my powers," said Benjamin. "They only cause trouble."

Petrie leaned forward again. "Then come with me to Boston. If you knew how exciting this thing was, you'd want to be a part of it."

Benjamin shook his head. "The war's in Europe, Petrie. There are thousands of people helping here who don't have any special powers. I can do it, too."

Petrie leaned back and lit another cigarette. Across the room there was a scuffle at the bar; voices flared; a rough-looking man was escorted outside.

"If you'll come with me to Marseilles," said Petrie, "I'll give you a list of people who can help you." He blew a stream of smoke into the air. "I think you'll be wasting yourself. But it's your life, Benjamin. Not mine."

As Benjamin watched the smoke curl away, he was reminded again of Lorna. He did not wish to think of her, any more than he wished to think of Jean Pierre Michel or Cassandra Nutt or the ill-fated family of clowns. He saw, however, that the bar—like the war—was inhabited by ghosts. And that not even his gift had the power to make them disappear.

what was hidden inside the breath-mint tin

A FEW DAYS LATER Benjamin and Petrie traveled to Mannheim, where they arranged to be smuggled across the French-German border beneath a layer of bratwurst in the back of a Nazi vehicle headed for Strasbourg. From there they continued, via Besançon and Lyons, to the rough port city where the ship was waiting to take Petrie back to America. Before boarding, Petrie once again tried to convince Benjamin to go with him. When Benjamin again refused, Petrie handed him a list of thirty-seven names, in fifteen different cities, of people he could contact for help. Then, just as he'd done in Rome a decade before, "the Calculator" disappeared.

Benjamin did not wish to remain in Marseilles. So he contacted the first person on Petrie's list, who provided him with a new set of identity papers under the pseudonym "Bertrand Tabordeau." Then he headed to Toulon to join the French Resistance. His ability to communicate was limited by his French, but that restriction was balanced by his willingness to go anywhere, do anything, to take his mind off what had happened to the Family Guildenstern. Over the following year he bounced like a pinball from one city to the next, doing an assortment of activities. No matter where he went, however, the war always seemed to be happening somewhere else. In April, for example, while the members of the Warsaw ghetto were rebelling, Benjamin was in Villefranche-de-Rouergue, manning a wireless unit that helped smuggle pork in from Spain. In October, while the Danish underground was helping seven thousand Jews escape to Sweden, Benjamin was in Clermont-Ferrand, delousing bedding in an underground shelter. And the following June, when the first of the Allied troops touched down on the occupied beaches of Normandy, Benjamin was in Montceau-les-Mines, standing guard, under the code name "Visages des Fraises," outside a *fromagerie* that was a front for an Allied hideout.

It was not easy to be relegated to the nooks and crannies of the war. And though Benjamin drowned his sorrows in the occasional woman—a shopgirl in Nîmes, a nurse in Épinal—for the most part he kept to himself. No matter how lifeless the time seemed, however, he would not use his powers to enliven it. His gift couldn't be trusted, so he locked it away—beneath the piece of yellow felt, beside the black Brillhart mouthpiece, in the breath-mint tin he'd carried throughout the war.

There were hundreds of times when Benjamin yearned to open that tin, to remove the mouthpiece, to find a saxophone and play. But he couldn't do it. No matter how much it might have soothed his anguish or tempered the harsh thunder of the dropping bombs, he could not conceive of making music in the midst of so much suffering.

So he traveled to Poitiers and Tours and Le Mans. He traveled to Vichy and Arles and Figeac, doing an assortment of odd jobs as the Allies swept in and systematically drove back the Nazis. By the winter of 1945 the tide had clearly turned: the Allies began to evacuate the death camps, and the end of the war seemed at hand. Benjamin, however, could not help feeling that his efforts had been meaningless, that Petrie had been right, that he'd wasted himself after all.

One day in early March, as he was washing out bandages in an alley behind a patisserie in Chatillon-sur-

Seine, a small boy came up to him with a huge grin on his face.

"*Bonjour,*" said the little boy.

"*Bonjour,*" said Benjamin.

"*Que fait-tu?*"

"*Je lave les bandeaux.*"

The little boy nodded, and though he was not quite as dirty, Benjamin could not help being reminded of Little Sidney Lowenthal. When the boy reached into his pocket, however, and drew out a packet of Pablito's Spearmint Chewing Gum and offered him a stick, Benjamin understood that no matter where he traveled, no matter what he did, he was doomed to be followed by specters from the past. So he carried the bandages into the patisserie, gathered up his things, and headed back to New York.

16/Whoopee

HEN WORD FINALLY came that the fighting had ceased, that there was "victory in Europe," the streets of the Allied cities went insane. Thousands upon thousands thronged the parks, squares, *places*, piazzas, courtyards, avenues, boulevards, and waterways as the long years of anxiety and deprivation exploded in a burst of celebration. In the West End of London traffic came to a standstill, while the crowds converged on Buckingham Palace, shouting and clamoring for the king. On the Left Bank of Paris loudspeakers were installed, as bodies crammed the boulevard Saint-Germain from the Sorbonne to the Jardin du Luxembourg. In Oslo the bands marched for hours through the streets. In Rome the bells of St. Peter's rang on without stopping.

Nowhere, however, was the pandemonium greater than in New York City. In Times Square there were sailors dancing and champagne parties in the backs of open convertibles and people being passed, like loose sacks of candy, from shoulder to shoulder above the crowd. In Harlem there was a bonfire lit outside the R.K.O. Alhambra. In west Greenwich Village the sound of honking horns was drowned out only by the sirens off the Hudson.

In Murray Hill a pharmacist filled his pockets with quarters and scattered them along East Thirty-seventh Street.

In Washington Square a nurse tore off her clothes and danced naked, to Glenn Miller, in the moonlight.

In a certain mansion, however, on the Upper East Side, there was not a drop of music or a drip of wine or the slightest sign of celebration. In the first place, nearly all of the rooms had been closed, the curtains drawn, the furniture covered with sheets. All that remained was a portion of the master bedroom, where an elderly gentleman sat by the window in a crisp set of flowing white robes. In the street outside that window there were flags waving, corks popping, voices cheering, confetti flying. To the old man, however, all that existed was the photograph, in his left hand, of a magnificent woman playing tag with a laughing boy, and the rough pumice moon that he turned over and over in the dry, bony palm of his right.

17/A Farewell to Clam Sauce

Brenda Ribenski's announcements

ENJAMIN WAS STANDING in the kitchen of Mario and Luigi's Spaghetti House on West Twenty-fourth Street, immersed to his elbows in a sink of dirty dishes, when Brenda Ribenski rushed in to announce that the Germans had finally surrendered. Sandro Sabatelli was seated on the counter, eating a package of *grissini,* and as Brenda babbled on he punctuated each sentence with a vigorous and resounding crunch. Benjamin noted the ecstasy on Brenda's plump face, yet he could not be certain that the joy that rose within him to meet it was anything more than relief at the thought of being released, for a few hours, from his apron.

Benjamin had returned to New York ten weeks earlier, having managed to steal passage in the belly of a freighter sailing from Brest. Upon arriving in Manhattan, he took a small room in Chelsea and with only thirty-seven dollars left to his name (plus a few stray francs left to Bertrand

Tabordeau) got a job washing dishes at Mario and Luigi's Spaghetti House. The job was pure drudgery, the kitchen always noisy and steamy, the standing hell on his back. But he could work when he wanted and eat what he liked, and for the first time in as long as he could remember things seemed to have slowed down. When Brenda rushed in with news of the surrender, it was like a stamp coming down to finalize a document: everything he knew of as his life up to now was over.

What was next, however, Benjamin couldn't say. As he walked through the city everyone he encountered seemed to be in a state of hypnosis; the war was over, there was euphoria in the air, yet people went right on shouting at one another and smacking their children and worrying about the price of eggs. Before he'd gone to Europe he'd always believed that people created their own destinies. Now he began to feel that things merely happened, that life was just a machine rolling hard along a track, impersonal and completely unalterable.

It was a lonely summer. Benjamin worked long hours at the restaurant and spent his days off at the movies or sitting in Central Park. Occasionally he would accompany Sandro Sabatelli to see his mother in Astoria, where she would make him cannelloni verde or veal parmigiana or her own special eight-layered lasagna. He made certain, however, to steer clear of the Upper East Side or anything that might evoke Jean Pierre Michel. For the most part this was easy, for New York seemed quite different from the city he'd known before the war, with a host of enticements to tantalize him. It was not until August, however, and another announcement by Brenda Ribenski, that Benjamin decided to take advantage of the city's charms. This time he was seated in the corner of the dining room, eating linguini with red clam sauce and listening to Dinah Shore, when Brenda rushed in with the news.

"They blew it up," she said.

"They blew what up?" said Benjamin.

"Japan," said Brenda. "They blew up Japan."

Benjamin sat there, his fork in midair, clam sauce dripping in tiny drops to the table. "The whole thing?"

Brenda thought for a moment. "I think so," she said. "They just blew it right out of the water."

For the remainder of his life, Benjamin would lose his appetite whenever he was confronted with either linguini with red clam sauce or the singing of Dinah Shore. That afternoon, however, all he could register was that things seemed to keep exploding—and that maybe it made no difference, in the end, what anyone did or didn't do.

It was a dangerous proposition. For if everything was equal, where did conscience or morality or responsibility come in?

Benjamin didn't know. But as a twenty-three-year-old, alone in New York, the opportunities to take his mind off the question were endless.

Spiros Creopolis and the girls of Flo's

THE FIRST THING Benjamin did on the night of Brenda Ribenski's second announcement was get very, very drunk. He started out with Sandro Sabatelli in a bar on Eighth Avenue, where he had three rum and Cokes and a shot of Jack Daniel's. Then he continued on to a bar on West Fourteenth Street, and then a bar on Bank Street, and then a bar on

Charles Street, until he finally passed out in a bar on Mac-Dougal near Houston. Somewhere along the way he lost Sandro Sabatelli, but he acquired, in his place, a dark, swarthy creature named Spiros Creopolis, who was built like a refrigerator, who spent the entire night singing "Ciribiribin," and who was waiting beside him with a metaxa espresso when he woke the following morning between the ice machine and an enormous German shepherd.

Spiros Creopolis, as Benjamin soon learned, was a twenty-seven-year-old boxer-cum-bookie whose dream was to open a string of expensive pet hotels and who proceeded, over the following weeks, to show Benjamin a completely new world. He took him to a strip show that operated from a Greek orthodox church in the East Village. He took him to a crap game that floated from a bakery in Astoria to a gas station in the Bronx. He taught him to wear dark clothing and buckets of cologne, and he guided him through the purchase of a large gold pinky ring engraved with a naked woman.

"Style," said Spiros Creopolis, "is a man's best calling card."

Most significant of all, however, he introduced Benjamin to the girls of Flo's Whorehouse, on the corner of East Twenty-Seventh Street. Benjamin had assured Spiros that he was not a virgin, yet Spiros could tell that he knew almost nothing about women. Over the following months he was therefore initiated into the delights of Ella, who smelled of lemons; Gretchen, who tasted of figs; Suzy, who was a natural redhead; Franny, who wore men's underwear; Vicki, who squealed; Verna, who screamed; and Maude, who did things with her legs that seemed anatomically impossible. At first Flo was hesitant to let Benjamin in, as she feared that his birthmark was the sign of some unknown venereal disease. Eventually, however, Benjamin gained her confidence by bringing her take-out Chinese food and helping her with the daily crossword. By February she had lowered her prices for him by half, and by the following spring he was practically a member of the family.

The rest of the time Benjamin spent wandering through the city, trying to make sense of his life. He had not used his gift in over three and a half years, and though he knew that this was partly why he felt so lost, he could not bring himself to reactivate it. He felt that by now his elusive powers should have revealed their meaning, should have yielded up insights and precise lessons that demonstrated how to live. As the months passed, however, he became more and more certain that he understood nothing at all.

Spiros Creopolis tried to rouse Benjamin's spirits with everything from reefers to retsina. The only thing that interested Benjamin, however, was sand. He kept a small vial of it in his pocket at all times, bought boxes and containers to stash it around his room. And though he still carried the breath-mint tin wherever he went, he could not seem to open it or even think about playing the saxophone.

It was not the worst life that anyone had ever lived. But it did not seem, to Benjamin, that it was Benjamin's life. It was more like a holding pattern—a period of waiting—until whatever it was that was to come next decided to appear.

clown dreams

THROUGHOUT THIS TIME Benjamin made countless efforts to try to find the Family Guildenstern, buoyed by reports that there were thousands of Jews who managed to survive the death camps. But no matter how many dozens of letters he wrote—to the Dutch government, to the house on the Groenburgwal, to Mimi Manheim and Mendy Fischelberg—they were always sent back to him unopened. He realized that they might have chosen not to return to Holland. He realized that they might have decided to change their names, or been taken into hospital, or developed amnesia. Eventually, however, he came to accept that, in all likelihood, he would never see them again.

It was then that Benjamin began to have a series of dark dreams, which came, just before morning, like a variety of scenes in a sideshow. Sara-Hilda walking slowly across a tightrope over a pit of naked bodies. Abel and Herschel doing back flips and leaps amid a spray of Nazi bullets. Abram juggling the bloody, severed heads of the other six members of the family.

They were horrible dreams that filled Benjamin with terror and made his sleeping blood run cold. But what disturbed him most was the underlying knowledge that, unlike Cassandra Nutt's dreams, these were not so much predictive of the future as suggestive of the brutal events that had already occurred.

slings and arrows

BENJAMIN'S LIFE might have continued on this way much longer had it not been for the startling accident that occurred in the spring of 1947. He'd stopped on the way to Flo's that evening to fetch her and the girls their supper; Flo had complained of a "ravenary" hunger, so in addition to the spareribs and the chow mein and the rice, he got half a dozen egg rolls, an order of fried wontons, and a double portion of moo goo gai pan. While he was waiting for the cashier to get his fortune cookies, however, the gas range exploded in the apartment beneath Flo's and the entire building went up in flames. Through the aid of the local fire department — many of whom were regular customers — the girls managed to escape unharmed. The incident, however, convinced Benjamin that he was cursed, that those associated with him were doomed to disaster, that sooner or later Cassandra Nutt's dream was destined to become a reality. So he moved into a room on West Forty-Ninth Street, got a job selling tickets at a nearby cinema, and proceeded to bear the slings and arrows of his outrageous life alone. He wore dark glasses. He grew a thick beard, which obscured his birthmark. And he followed along as the newspapers told of an explosion in a coal mine in Centralia, Illinois, an explosion in an ammunition factory in Cádiz, Spain, an explosion in a chemical factory in Ludwigshafen, West Germany. His only comfort came from the women he picked up: Joan at the Automat, Gwen in Central Park, Elaine outside Grand Central Station. He'd learned well at Flo's — he'd become a deft and accomplished lover — yet his heart remained out of it, a casualty to the hunger of his body.

Who was this Benjamin Chernovsky? Was he the lean frame? The extraordinary face? The splattered stain upon it? Was he the orphaned child — the betrayed son — the spurned lover — the escaped Jew? Was he the generous Benjamin or the selfish Benjamin? The idealist or the scoundrel? The prodigy or the fool?

As the months slipped by, Benjamin's looks began to change: there was less yearning in his jawbone, more knowing in his eyes. He did not really see it for himself, however, until one morning, just before Christmas, as he was standing on the sidewalk waiting for the Seventh Avenue bus. It was a damp morning, the streets slick and glistening from a recent shower, the people around him burdened by raincoats and umbrellas. Benjamin was on his way home from the Village, where he'd gone to do some shopping, and his thoughts were mostly on what he was going to prepare for lunch. As he stood there, however, he suddenly became aware of a fierce-looking young man who was glaring at him from across the street. For a moment he felt his blood rise—his body tense with danger—and then he realized that he was looking at his own reflection.

As Benjamin gazed into his burnt-out eyes he saw anger and confusion and pain. What he did not see, however, was how much he was beginning to resemble the very fellow he'd set out to escape from in the first place.

18/The Power of Bop

the Sister's strange hand gesture

T WAS SISTER E. BERRY who finally turned things around. Benjamin came upon her one cool, breezy morning in the spring of 1948, seated on a beer crate on the corner of Forty-first Street and Eighth Avenue. She looked to be about seventy years old, though her eyes still beamed with a giddy sort of youth and her chocolate-colored skin was drawn tight across the bones of her eager face. She wore a loose white dress and an oversize sweater patterned over with daisies and a little paper boat upon her head. At her side was a large sign that read—

> *Don't stop*
> *The Power of Bop —*
> *Be brave*
> *Sister E. Berry saves!*

—and in her mouth was a Buescher Aristocrat Alto in E-flat saxophone.

It wasn't the first time that Benjamin had heard a saxophone since he'd returned from Europe; in the crazy, postwar streets of Manhattan, it would have been almost impossible to have avoided it. What Sister E. Berry was playing, however—or seemed to be playing, for as Benjamin soon realized, the sounds were actually coming from an amplified recording that the Sister was miming—as much resembled what he'd heard before the war as a soufflé resembled a rice pudding. It was taut and idiosyncratic and totally unsentimental, and it was as close to the crazy music that he made himself as anything he had ever heard.

When the song was over, the Sister lowered her saxophone, drew a monogrammed handkerchief from the pocket of her sweater, and began to clean her teeth. Benjamin stepped forward and threw a quarter in her case; then he leaned in and asked her who was making those sounds on the recording. The Sister flashed an enormous smile, linked both thumbs together, and made her hands rise like a sparrow taking fight. Then she placed the saxophone back in her mouth and returned to her crazy bliss.

Benjamin had no idea what the Sister's strange hand gesture was meant to signify. Her spiritedness, however, inspired the sudden urge in him to venture uptown to Harlem. He hadn't been there since just before the war, when he and Lorna had frequented the jazz scene, but as he headed toward the subway he realized that what he longed for was the Harlem he'd visited when he was still a child, that faraway place where Cassandra Nutt would take him when the days were long and hot and dreamy and Jean Pierre Michel was not around. He knew that it was not possible to go back in time, but he boarded the Broadway local and headed out to see what he could find.

When he exited the subway station at 125th and Lenox, he could immediately feel the changes that had taken place; in the eight and a half years since he'd been there with Lorna, Harlem seemed to have reinvented itself. As he headed north, he glimpsed a few of the old haunts—the Chicken Coop, Logan Hill's, Rudy's All-Nite Rib Joint— yet he doubted that Lazy Joe's would still be there. When he reached the corner of 138th Street, however, he saw the old neon sign with its bright cursive lettering, and when he climbed down the stairs and opened the door, he found himself plunged into the past. There was the cloakroom with its honey-wood counter and its green velvet curtains and its gleaming brass hooks. There was the bar with its smoked-glass ashtrays and its bevel-edged mirror lined with photos. There was T-Bone Sanders and Ed "Caesar" Robinson. There was Loolie Jones behind the bar. But what startled him most was that there at piano, shining like a beacon, exuding her fabulous clove-orange fragrance, was the wonderful, the incomparable, the irreplaceable Cassandra Nutt.

a sea change

WHEN THEIR EYES MET, the jolt was substantial, and for a moment nearly anything seemed possible. Then Cassandra Nutt rose, adjusted her shawl, and started across the room. Benjamin could feel himself tremble at her approach, for though her gait was slower and her hair streaked with white, her body seemed even more voluptuous than before: acres of dark flesh cascading from a sheath of white satin. When she reached him she paused for a moment, the brief space between them crackling with uncertainty. Then she threw back her head in a great burst of laughter, flung her arms open wide, and crushed Benjamin to her in a maternal embrace that washed back over the confusion of their last encounter to the far deeper heart of their relationship.

"Damn if you ain't a sight for sore eyes," she said, stepping back to look at him. "I can hardly keep my heart from jumpin' out on the floor and doin' a little dance. Loolie!" she cried. "This here's my boy! The one I used to bring in for them lemon-lime sodas! Ed Caesar! T-Bone! This here's my Benjamin!"

Loolie Jones slapped his rag down on the bar. "Go 'way, Cassandra! This here's little Benjamin?"

"Render unto Caesar, baby," said Ed "Caesar" Robinson.

"I knew he looked familiar," said T-Bone Sanders. "Even with that rug on his face."

"How 'bout a drink?" said Cassandra Nutt. "How 'bout a sloe gin fizz? Loolie don't make 'em like Joe used to do, but there's still nothin' like 'em when you got somethin' to celebrate. Loolie! Make us a pitcher of sloe gin fizz!"

Loolie Jones nodded and began pouring the gin into a tall glass shaker. Then Cassandra Nutt led Benjamin to a table in the corner and, with the help of Ed "Caesar" Robinson and T-Bone Sanders, began to explain how she'd found her way back to Harlem.

"Rock Hill was like a rest cure," she said, "after working for Monsieur C. I got a nice little apartment, and for the first time in thirty-five years I was spared having to listen to that old man complain." She went on to explain how, after a year or so of concentrating mostly on herself, she began doing some catering and some interior decorating and a bit of legal footwork for the mayor. "I even bought me a little Esso station. Just for the fun of it." She paused to take a sip of her sloe gin fizz, which Loolie had brought to the table while she was talking. "Then Joe went and died."

"Right there at the bar," said Ed "Caesar" Robinson.

"While we was playin' 'Perdido,'" said T-Bone Sanders.

Cassandra Nutt went on to explain that when they found Lazy Joe's will, in a Four Roses bottle at the back of his sock drawer, it was revealed that he had left both the club and the rooms above it to Cassandra Nutt and Loolie Jones. Loolie wired Rock Hill, and the next day Cassandra Nutt sailed into town, spruced up the joint, and settled in behind the white baby grand.

"We ain't the Cotton Club," she said, "or even Sneaky Pete's. But we sure do have ourselves some fun."

At this point the others began to join in, describing how the club had flourished after Cassandra Nutt's arrival and revealing a few things about themselves. Benjamin tried to keep up with the story, but the more they talked, the more he found himself studying the storytellers: Ed "Caesar" Robinson, a light-skinned fellow with a tiny brush mustache who painted "jazz landscapes" and whose name came from his propensity for saying, "Render unto Caesar, baby"; T-Bone Sanders, a bantam-weight drummer with slightly crossed eyes who was always working his teeth over with a gold-plated toothpick; and Cassandra Nutt herself, who, though she was every bit as vibrant as she had been in the past, must by now be nearing sixty. They spoke in a giddy counterpoint, finishing each other's sentences and arguing about dates. And only when they were sure that their story was finished did they turn their attention to Benjamin.

"What about you?" said Ed "Caesar" Robinson.

"What brings a white boy up to a hundred and thirty-eighth Street," said T-Bone Sanders, "on some plain-ass Tuesday in March?"

Benjamin felt that he could not begin to speak about either his time in Europe or what he'd experienced since the war, so he decided to take the question quite literally and focus on what had happened that morning. Slowly and carefully he described his encounter with Sister E. Berry, beginning with a description of the strange, compelling music that she was playing along with and culminating in an imitation of her flying fingers. He still had no idea what the hand gesture meant, but from the reaction of the others it was clear that it made sense to them.

"Yardbird," said T-Bone Sanders.

Ed "Caesar" Robinson nodded in agreement. "Has to be Bird."

Cassandra Nutt went on to explain how jazz had undergone a sea change while Benjamin was in Europe, how the focus of things had shifted down to Fifty-second Street, how people like Charlie Parker—otherwise known as "Bird"—were making a music of ideas, radical and improvisatory, that had turned the world of jazz upside-down.

"Those boys," Cassandra Nutt, "got a fever inside 'em ain't nothin' can calm down."

Benjamin tilted his straw toward his mouth and took a few sips of his sloe gin fizz. "I can play like that," he said.

The others just stared at him, not saying a word.

"This music you're describing. What I heard in the

street. That's what I've been trying to do since the day I first picked up the saxophone."

Cassandra Nutt took her own straw and stirred up her ice. "That racket you used to make?" she said. "You call that bop?"

"Back then I could only hear it in my head," said Benjamin. "But now I can play it." He paused for a moment. "Or at least I could before the war." He paused again. "By using my powers. My gift."

Cassandra Nutt stared at Benjamin in perfect silence, while Ed "Caesar" Robinson and T-Bone Sanders tried to fathom what he was talking about. Then Cassandra Nutt spoke. "T-Bone," she said, "go up to Loolie's room. In the closet, behind the cowboy boots, is Sonny Carter's sax. Bring it on down here."

"You got it," said T-Bone, rising from the table and bounding out of the room.

"But I haven't played in almost five years," said Benjamin. "I don't know if I can still do it."

Cassandra Nutt shrugged. "Can't see much harm in findin' out."

Benjamin was about to protest when T-Bone ran in with Sonny Carter's saxophone. It was a 1943 Conn in fourteen-karat-gold plate with mother-of-pearl touch pieces, and as it sailed toward him Benjamin felt a ringing in his ears and a sucker punch to his abdomen, and he knew that he was going to play. T-Bone laid the instrument upon the table, where it glittered like a golden serpent. Then Benjamin reached his hand into the breast pocket of his jacket, drew out the breath-mint tin, and laid it down gently beside the sax. He sat there for a moment and stared at the two objects: bright metal and dull, the foreign and the fa-

miliar. Then he opened the tin, folded back the felt, removed the mouthpiece from Sonny Carter's sax, replaced
it with his own mouthpiece, rose from the table, walked up
to the bandstand, and played.

At first he could barely even manage a sound: his lips were
like granite, and the instrument felt hard and heavy in his
hands. But he closed his eyes—and breathed in deeply—and
concentrated his energy—and then once again he sent his
gift through the saxophone and organized it into sound. Joyful and antic. Spasmodic and raw. Bold, hot licks that issued
deep from the center of his being.

Benjamin had no idea how long he played, but when he
lowered the saxophone and looked about the room, the
others were in a state of amazement.

"Render unto Caesar, baby," said Ed "Caesar" Robinson.

"We got us here a white boy," said T-Bone Sanders,
"who could give Bird a run for his money."

Cassandra Nutt just smiled and shook her head and
leaned back in the booth, while Benjamin closed his eyes
again and steadied himself on the bandstand. He felt a
lightness in his head and a stiffness in his fingers and a tingling sensation in his lips. But most of all he felt that the
gift he'd buried inside the breath-mint tin—beside the
black Brillhart mouthpiece, between the piece of yellow
felt—was finally soaring free again.

Strawberry Delight

ON THE BASIS of Benjamin's impromptu performance, Cassandra Nutt and Loolie offered him a gig at Lazy Joe's. Benjamin wasn't certain that he was ready for this, but on the

following morning he quit his job, gathered up his things, and moved into one of the rooms above the club. Cassandra Nutt had decorated these with her usual panache, hiring Ed "Caesar" Robinson to paint a variety of colorful, Gauguin-like scenes upon the bureaus and the nightstands and the walls. Benjamin had to spend the first week moving his bed about the room, until he finally found a spot that was tranquil enough to allow him to sleep.

Once Benjamin had settled in, he began the tender process of acquainting himself with Sonny Carter's sax. Cassandra Nutt assured him that Sonny Carter would not be returning for it anytime soon, as he was wanted for armed robbery in New York, New Jersey, Connecticut, Massachusetts, and Pennsylvania. So day after day Benjamin raised it to his lips and tried to get back the feel of playing. It was rough going at first: moments of rapture were immediately followed by passages of earsplitting torture. He was convinced, however, that if he practiced and practiced, he would figure out a way to use his gift to fuel his playing without having to hold back any of its power.

Benjamin's desire to work the kinks out of his playing was not the only reason he decided to wait to take his place on the Lazy Joe bandstand. For now that he'd found that this music had a name, he wanted to study the rudiments of bop. He bought dozens of recordings—on Dial and Decca, on Savoy and Prestige—and several nights a week he went down to Fifty-second Street to listen to Bird and Dex and Diz. Most important of all, however, he began his apprenticeship with the illustrious Fever Fredericks.

Fever Fredericks was a small, grizzled fellow with a gap-toothed smile and a laugh like a sackful of rocks. He hailed from New Orleans and, according to legend, had been present at the birth of jazz. Whether or not this was either possible or true, he was undeniably a genius: everyone who was anyone had studied with Fever Fredericks, and though he himself only ever played the mouth organ, he was considered to be responsible for virtually every new style that made an impact in the last thirty years. What kept Fever down, however—and almost eradicated him—was his addiction to drugs: over the course of his life he'd tried everything possible until he finally settled in, during the years of the war, to a long-term relationship with heroin. As a result, he had begun to fade from the scene, and it was only at the urging of Cassandra Nutt, whom he loved like a daughter, that he agreed to take on a new student, and a white boy at that. Soon Benjamin was studying with him five times a week, polishing his fingering and fashioning his instincts into craft.

The rest of the time, when he wasn't working on perfecting his playing, Benjamin was finding his way into the world of Lazy Joe's. The fact that he was white gave the place a frisson; to the women he was a lick of vanilla ice cream, to the men a cool splash of bay rum after a vigorous rubdown. He bought a pinstriped suit with an impressive lapel and a double-breasted sharkskin jacket with a serious crease; then he slicked back his hair, shaved off his beard, and began to settle down to business. At first he was content to be a part of the decor: slipping between the tables, laughing with the customers, lounging like a cat against the bar. As time passed, however, he began to organize the bookings and order the liquor and oversee the upkeep of the carpets and the linens. Bunty LeRoi, who was a jockey up at the racetrack, called him "Fireworks Face," while Mavis Johnson, who was first manicurist at

Lula B. Cooper's French Beauty Salon, called him "Strawberry Delight"—which inspired Loolie Jones to name a cocktail after him consisting of a teaspoon of sugar, a jigger of light rum, and a generous helping of strawberries soaked overnight in Benedictine.

By the winter of 1949 Benjamin's life had turned completely around, and though a part of him kept waiting for the cash register to explode, or the ceiling to cave in, another part tried to accept the fact that he'd entered a period of harmony. With the painful example of Fever's addiction, and the childlike groveling that it reduced him to, he even gave up his strange habit for sand. The final stroke of glory, however, arrived just before midnight on the sixteenth of February while he was playing gin rummy with Slim Betts and Ed "Caesar" Robinson.

"It was fate," said Loolie Jones. "As sure as I'm alive. When somethin's fated, ain't nothin' can stop it."

Benjamin himself had no theories about it, for as he would later philosophize, such moments of sweetness could be neither predicted nor explained. He could only observe that, once again, it was Cassandra Nutt who had ushered it into his life.

Cassandra Nutt had a great deal to occupy her in addition to managing Lazy Joe's. There was chairing the Council for the Beautification of Harlem. There was redecorating the Manhattan Temple Bible Club Lunchroom. There was playing the organ for the Sunday morning service at the Abyssinian Baptist Church. What mattered to her most, however, was a project that she'd created by herself. Cassandra Nutt had realized, once the dust had finally settled in her new life in Rock Hill, that when she'd traveled to New York as a girl of sixteen and taken up employment with Jean Pierre

Michel, she'd actually stepped into a new form of slavery. She therefore decided, when she found herself transported back to New York, to dedicate herself to helping others avoid the same situation. It was not possible, of course, to remove every colored woman in the city from a position of service, and many would have insisted that their jobs were just fine. So Cassandra Nutt focused upon a strip of Broadway, just north of 180th Street, that was commonly referred to as the Bronx Slave Market. Having sprouted up during the years of the Depression, it was a place where colored girls who could find no other work could offer themselves to clean white ladies' apartments. The wages they received were ridiculously low, yet day after day they stood shivering on the sidewalk, averting their eyes as they were picked over like a parcel of packhorses.

Cassandra Nutt found it disgusting and degrading. So whenever she could she would steal away one of the girls herself and install her at Lazy Joe's. She developed a kind of revolving door policy: she'd buy the girl some clothes, allow her to gain a bit of professional experience (as coat check girl, cocktail waitress, souvenir photographer), and then help her to secure a more long-term employment somewhere else. The customers appreciated the stream of changing faces, and the girls appreciated Cassandra Nutt's care: they were never allowed to be ogled or handled, and though they were generally reluctant to wear their costumes—a series of bizarre creations Cassandra Nutt designed herself—they always managed to get used to them in the end.

There was Almaline Carter, who had a voice like a trash mixer, and Nancy Duquesne, who liked to whistle off-key, and Francette Williams, whose breasts were so large that they kept knocking over the table lamps, and Rosalind

Dexter, who spent most of her time hiding behind the large standing oven in the kitchen. They came and they went, and dozens of others like them, gracing the landscape for a week or a month and then vanishing to make room for someone new.

Except for Charlene.

The club was closed on the night she arrived. Cassandra Nutt felt Wednesdays fell too smack and dull in the center of the week, so she used them to give the place a chance to breathe and herself a night out on the town. Benjamin and the others usually stayed in to play cards, which was just what they were doing on that particular evening when the door suddenly swung open, a few minutes before midnight, and a strong gust of air blew into the room. As Benjamin turned he saw the sharp silhouette of a figure in the doorway, but what sent a chill through his body was neither the figure nor the cold, but the impression, in the lamplight, of hundreds of flakes of snow falling up.

For a moment the figure paused and removed a shawl from its shoulders and shook it out lightly over the threshold. Then it moved into the nightclub and the light fell upon it and the air plumped like a wine-soaked raisin. It wasn't simply that she was beautiful, though she was: her face like carved rosewood, her hair like spun satin, her body a set of mathematical principles refigured in flesh and bone. It was that there in the late night glow of the empty club—as she undid the top two buttons of her coat, and straightened her left earring, and leaned into the bar to ask Loolie for some water—she was the perfect picture of what Cassandra Nutt must have looked like as a girl.

Even if he'd wanted to, and at the moment he did not, Benjamin could never have saved himself from this.

19/Snow Falling Up

shadows in the desert

HEN CASSANDRA NUTT entered a moment later, she announced to the room that the girl was Charlene Wilkins and that she was replacing Annette Voovray as their new cocktail waitress. It was not until the following morning, however, over fried eggs, banana fritters, and a pot of black coffee, that Benjamin found out that she was twenty years old, that she hailed from Athens, Georgia, and that her ambition was to someday become a nuclear physicist.

"That girl's got a brain on her the size of a watermelon," said Cassandra Nutt.

Benjamin did not mention the fact that at that moment he was not particularly interested in the size of Charlene's brain. Over the next few days, however, it became painfully obvious that he could not take his mind off the rest of her. He asked Loolie Jones, who had known Cassandra Nutt for thirty-six years, if Charlene looked as much like the old girl as a young girl as he suspected she did.

"Down to the ankles," said Loolie with a grin. "Except for a bit of poundage. And the hue."

This last observation was not really necessary, for when the two women actually stood side by side it was obvious that they were not the same color. Where Cassandra Nutt's skin was like a fresh *pain d'epices*, Charlene's was like a rich loaf of pumpernickel. Where Cassandra Nutt was "high-toned" or "dark-skinned" or "colored," Charlene was, without question, black. To Benjamin she was devastatingly beautiful, and the only thing he wanted was to touch her.

His interest, of course, did not go unnoticed by the others.

"The coast looks clear," said T-Bone Sanders. "Though I don't 'spect it'll stay that way for long."

"If I was you," whispered Ed "Caesar" Robinson, "I'd get in there as quick as I could."

Benjamin soon discovered that it was sound advice—for the moment that Charlene began to work at the club, the men were lining up for her charms. Her costume didn't help: there was more of her showing than there was concealed, and even Loolie, who had given up women in the spring of 1933, had to admit that the sight of her was better than a triple martini. Benjamin therefore came to the conclusion that in order not to repeat the mistake he'd made with Lorna O'Shaughnassy, he would have to make certain that Charlene knew exactly how he felt. So he bought her French perfume and long-stemmed roses. He bought her bags of oranges and dark Belgian chocolates. He had Cassandra Nutt play "Salt Peanuts," her favorite song, whenever she entered the room. Charlene, however, did not make the slightest response, leaving Benjamin in a constant state of yearning.

It went on like this for the next several months. But what Benjamin didn't realize was that, for all her aloofness, Charlene was as attracted to him as he was to her. The difference was that Charlene understood the dangers involved in a colored girl responding to a white boy's attentions. She tried to rationalize it. She told Yolanda Martin, who was coat check girl during the month of May, that in his own way, with that birthmark on his face, Benjamin was as "colored" as she was.

"You can't just call him white," said Charlene. "It's not a fitting description."

Yolanda Martin just raised her eyebrows, trusting that Charlene knew better than to enter such waters.

It was not until August, however, on a warm, sultry evening toward the end of the month, that the dynamic between Charlene and Benjamin finally changed. For it was on this night, after more than a year of waiting, that Benjamin at last made his debut at Lazy Joe's. Benjamin had worked hard to prepare himself for this moment. He'd studied with Fever for several hours a day, and in a matter of months his technique was as smooth as satin. What took such a long time was to learn how to use his gift to power his playing without suddenly finding himself transported to a village in Zagreb. And what he eventually came to was that in order to do the one thing, he could no longer do the other: either he transcended space or he made transcendent music on the saxophone.

It was not much of a contest, for after all the trouble his gift had caused him, he was glad to finally be rid of the more exaggerated aspects of its power. What he was not prepared for was the difference it made when he gave that power completely to his music. He made a sound so penetrating, it stopped all thought—and instead of being transported to some distant locale, he found himself neatly dropped into that place of dissolving. For the duration of a set—which, keeping "the Cinderella factor" in mind, always lasted exactly forty-five minutes—he was thrust into a state of unimaginable sweetness where he was as separate from Benjamin as he was from the tables or the ashtrays or the other musicians.

It was this, more than anything, that Benjamin looked forward to when he stepped onto the bandstand that warm August evening, accompanied by Cassandra Nutt on piano, Spider Perkins on bass, and T-Bone Sanders on drums. They began with a cool rendering of "How High the Moon," then slipped gently into "I Found a New Baby," "I Can't Get Started" and a pair of compositions Benjamin had written himself, "Snow Falling Up" and "Charlene." And though Benjamin had not expected anything out of the ordinary, the Saturday evening crowd went wild. By the end of the second set they were pounding on the tables, and by the end of the evening the white boy on sax was a star.

Over the following months Benjamin found himself the unexpected focus of a renaissance at Lazy Joe's. Tables began booking up three weeks in advance. Cadillacs and Packards began lining 138th Street. The newspapers crowed about the new jazz discovery, this "White Bird" who was wailing up in Harlem. What thrilled Benjamin, however, was that Charlene finally began to respond to his attentions. As she slid between the tables she would brush her hip against his shoulder. As she hoisted a tray of drinks she would brush her breast against his arm. And gradually, almost imperceptibly, Benjamin began brushing back. His hand against her forearm. His thigh against her thigh. Until their evenings together became a strange sort of mating dance, a ritual hidden in plain sight.

There were many things that Benjamin and Charlene would have liked to say to one another. They both knew, however, that the wrong word at the wrong time might stop the whole thing in its tracks. So they just went on brushing—and brushing—and brushing—until finally one evening, as Charlene stood in the kitchen, slicing lemons, Benjamin slipped past her so that the swell of his groin grazed the curve of her bottom and she turned, placed the lemon down and the sharp knife beside it, led Benjamin out into the narrow alley, undid the buttons of her tight cotton blouse, and offered herself up to the night.

Benjamin stood there and drank in her beauty, the splashes of moonlight on the contours of her body like inverted shadows in the desert. And though he was fully aware that in New York City, in 1949, a white man did not make love to a black girl in a back alley in Harlem, at that particular moment—with the breeze against his cheek, and the music from the nightclub, and the smell of gardenias and garlic in the air—Benjamin was not white and Charlene was not black, and love was the only game in town.

a tropical period

CASSANDRA NUTT listened to the crackle of the ice as she poured the pineapple juice into the tall, frosted glass. She was alone in the nightclub, as she wanted to be; each Friday she made certain that Loolie went down to Jimmy Clarke's to play billiards, that Charlene went to Lula B. Cooper's to get her hair done, and that Benjamin went over to Fever Fredericks's to practice his horn. Cassandra Nutt needed a few hours to be alone—to catch up on her newspapers—to hear herself think. So she sent the others off, slipped into a muumuu, and reveled in her momentary solitude.

Cassandra Nutt was in her tropical period, which found her feasting on guava and passion fruit and mango, poring over travel guides to Bali and Tahiti, and wearing an assortment of boldly patterned, loose-fitting clothes. She'd finally given up on the world of high fashion, having grown impatient with tight waists and form-fitting bustlines and skirts that articulated her bottom like a large loaf of bread. Age and experience had brought size to Cassandra Nutt, and rather than try to cinch it all in, she preferred to let it flow beneath brightly colored caftans and other forms of nonbinding attire. In the evenings, when the customers came, she added long dangling earrings or a silk-fringed turban or a necklace made of painted glass beads. On Fridays, however, there was nothing but her, with a loose tent of color on top.

When Cassandra Nutt had finished pouring her pineapple juice, she reached for a swizzle stick, slipped it in her glass, and then carried it across the nightclub to table number eight, where she proceeded to paint her toenails Calypso orange and to contemplate the sweetness of her life. She could not remember a time that had seemed more harmonious, with so much laughter and so many loved ones around her. The only thing that stopped her from floating away completely was the nagging persistence of her dreams. From her passage to Rock Hill through her journey back to Harlem, Cassandra Nutt's dreams had never ceased for a single night.

There were dreams about taxis and chickens and cheese. There were dreams about egg crates and weather vanes and wolves. There were dreams that recurred at periodic intervals and dreams that came once and then vanished from sight, leaving a lush trail of images to decipher.

There was one dream, however, that Cassandra Nutt could not fathom. She was alone in it, on a barren landscape, with the sun beating down, traveling across a sea of dry bones. She had no idea where she was going, but as she continued forward the bones began to soften into a powdery dust, which eventually began to swirl into clouds about her head, obstructing her vision and preventing her from continuing on.

Cassandra Nutt had this dream at least once a month. And though she knew that it might turn out to mean something quite trivial—that T-Bone was going on a trip to Nevada or she was allergic to that new brand of talcum powder she'd bought—what troubled her about it was the presence of herself at its center. For Cassandra Nutt was always absent from Cassandra Nutt's dreams, and she could not help feeling, from her presence in this one, that something bad was on its way.

interactions among nuclei

CHARLENE HAD NO DREAMS of impending disaster, but from the time she was ten, when her uncle had visited the World's Fair in Chicago and had returned home with books about the various exhibitions, she'd been convinced that the only way to confront the future was to become a nuclear scientist.

"The world is hurtling in a new direction," she said. "And you can't have much say about it if you don't learn to speak the jive."

Benjamin was not certain that he was cut out to "speak the jive," but over the following months Charlene did her best to explain the properties of the atomic nucleus, the equivalence of mass and energy, and the range of forces, beyond the gravitational and the electromagnetic, that govern interactions among nuclei. Benjamin listened attentively, and even took notes, but in the end he did not find a word of it as intriguing as the slope of Charlene's neck, the slant of Charlene's eyes, or the lilt of Charlene's voice as she explained it.

It was obvious to everyone who frequented Lazy Joe's that Benjamin and Charlene were a couple. And in the small world of the nightclub, where black mixed with white like the keys on a piano, no one seemed bothered by it at all. What was troubling was what happened when they stepped outside that world. If they went down to Fifty-second Street, for example, they had to travel separately, and when it was time to return home, Benjamin had to hail a taxi by himself and then bring it back to pick up Charlene. If they went to a restaurant, they had to take Ed "Caesar" with them, or T-Bone, or Spider. They could not go to the park together. Or the museum. Or the movies. They could not walk down the street holding hands.

To Benjamin these circumstances were utterly baffling: he could not see how anyone could be offended by what he felt for Charlene. To Charlene, however, they were enraging, and the only thing that saved her from breaking either the furniture or somebody's head was her decision to put the energy of that rage into improving things at Lazy Joe's. Over the next few months she increased the seating capacity by twenty percent; she revamped the sound system so that speakers could be distributed throughout the room; she framed the photos that were taped above the bar and mounted a history of the nightclub on the wall just opposite the cloakroom. Eventually, however, she came to realize that for all her anger at the narrow-minded whites who felt that she and Benjamin were a threat to their sense of order, and all her anger at the narrow-minded blacks who felt that she and Benjamin were a threat to their sense of pride, she was angriest at herself for having gotten into the situation in the first place.

She could not fight it, however. The attraction was too strong. And neither the pressures of society nor plain common sense could seem to do a thing to cool the heat.

the Book of Genesis

"IF YOU WANTED pork chops," said Ed "Caesar" Robinson, "we should've gone to Lola's."

"Nobody makes pork chops like Lola," said T-Bone Sanders.

"Cassandra Nutt don't like pork chops," said Mavis Johnson.

"Cassandra Nutt likes chicken salad," said Loolie Jones. "I sure hope Willette remembered to make Cassandra Nutt some chicken salad."

Ed "Caesar" Robinson, T-Bone Sanders, Mavis Johnson, and Loolie Jones were seated at a table, set up on the bandstand, for a small celebration of Cassandra Nutt's sixty-second birthday. They'd had a big blowout the previous year, with buckets of champagne and a huge cake in the shape of a baby grand. This year, however, the party was to be intimate—as well as a surprise—with just Willette Walker, who worked the jewelry counter at McCrory's, Benjamin, Charlene, and the four now seated around the table. As the day fell on a Wednesday, Lazy Joe's was closed, so Benjamin and Charlene took Cassandra Nutt to a movie, while the others prepared for the event. Willette was in charge of the food, which consisted of smothered catfish, red beans and rice, black-eyed peas, fried codfish balls, and Cassandra Nutt's beloved chicken salad, made with white grapes, almonds, and a 64-ounce jar of mayonnaise. Mavis and T-Bone were in charge of the decorations, while Ed "Caesar" Robinson was in charge of creating Cassandra Nutt out of cake frosting on top of the cake.

"Did you hear the chicken salad at the luncheonette is up to thirty-five cents?" said Mavis.

"Thirty-five cents!" said T-Bone. "I can get me a *steak* for thirty-five cents!"

"At Bibby's," said Loolie, "you can get three hot dogs for a dime."

"That's 'cause Bibby's hot dogs taste like shit," said T-Bone.

"Shit soaked in grease," said Ed "Caesar" Robinson.

The door to the kitchen swung open and Willette entered with a great steaming platter of red beans and rice. "You better not be talkin' about my cookin'," she said, "or you gonna find somethin' else soaked in grease."

"Willette," said Loolie, "that smells like paradise."

"Render unto Caesar, baby," said Ed "Caesar" Robinson.

Willette laid the platter on the table and wiped her hands on her dress. "Mattie Clarke just phoned to say they passed by her window."

"T-Bone," said Mavis, "help Willette with the food. They'll be here any minute."

T-Bone accompanied Willette to the kitchen, and then, platter by platter, they brought out the food. Then they switched off the lights and waited for the trio to arrive. After a few moments there came a fumbling at the door.

"Dang that Loolie," came the voice of Cassandra Nutt. "I told him to stop tryin' to save on electricity."

Whether this was really a reaction to the darkness or a line she'd made up to go along with the ruse, Cassandra Nutt's words were greeted instantly by shouts of "Surprise!" and a flurry of embraces and even a few renegade tears. Then they went to the table, and while Willette Walker began to dish out the food, Ed "Caesar" Robinson raised his glass into the air.

"There are those who claim to have had some sort of lives before they met Cassandra Nutt. But the truth is none of us can remember a single day without her that amounts to more than a dirt speck on the side of a pork chop."

"You still harpin' on them pork chops?" said T-Bone.

"So we'd like to thank you, Cassandra Nutt. For bein' born. And for livenin' up our lives."

There was a round of applause as Cassandra Nutt raised her hand. "Thank you, Ed 'Caesar.' That's a beautiful tribute. But if we don't start eatin', Willette's gonna have a coronary."

Ed "Caesar" Robinson lowered his glass, and as the feasting began, the guests took turns telling stories about Cassandra Nutt. Then the plates were cleared away and she opened her presents: T-Bone and Loolie gave her a gold-plated wristwatch, Ed "Caesar" Robinson gave her a heat rack for her towels, Mavis and Willette gave her some honeysuckle bath salts, and Benjamin and Charlene gave her a blue silk kimono with a white bird embroidered on the back. Cassandra Nutt was delighted by everything she received, and as the cake was being sliced and passed around, she decided that it had been the nicest birthday she could remember. Just as it seemed to be ending, however, the door flew open and Rabbi Marcus Hazleton Jerome hurried in.

"I do hope I haven't arrived too late," said the rabbi.

Willette Walker scanned the length of the table. "We still got some coffee," she said. "An' a bitty piece o' cake. That is if you don't mind eatin'—what is that, Ed 'Caesar'?"

Ed "Caesar" Robinson tried to evaluate what remained of his cake-frosting portrait. "I do believe that's an ear," he said.

"I'll decline on the refreshments," said Rabbi Jerome. "But I would be most grateful for a moment of Cassandra Nutt's time."

Rabbi Jerome was head of the large congregation of Negro Jews who lived and worshiped in Harlem. Claiming to be direct descendants of Abraham and Isaac (by way of King Solomon's son, Menelik I, who was said to have married the queen of Sheba), they gathered in a small synagogue in a red-brick tenement on the corner of 128th Street. They were noted for the conservative clothing they wore, for their strict adherence to Jewish dietary laws, and for their general tendency to keep to themselves. Rabbi Jerome was especially sober—always dressing in black, always wearing a yarmulke, always speaking as if he were addressing a conference on the advancement of the urban Negro. His only known weakness was a particular fondness for the talents of Cassandra Nutt. As far as Rabbi Jerome was concerned, the way she fingered the

keys of the piano was rivaled only by the mysteries of the
Talmud. When Benjamin appeared, it seemed a sign from
God: what harm could there be in frequenting a nightclub
where the saxophone player had been Bar Mitzvahed?

"I do not mean to interrupt the festivities," said Rabbi
Jerome, "but I have a little present for the birthday hon-
oree."

"Well, you got me curious," said Ed "Caesar" Robinson.

"Give it to her quick," said Loolie Jones, "before I wet
myself from the suspense."

Rabbi Jerome pulled a chair up to the table, seated himself, and then turned to Cassandra Nutt. "I don't know if
you recollect my cousin Delmont," he said.

Cassandra Nutt thought for a moment. "Chubby little
fellow? With the big, bulgy eyes?"

"An excellent description," said Rabbi Jerome. "Well,
Cousin Delmont happens to work as a domestic for a fine
Jewish gentleman by the name of Mr. Stanley F. Harburg.
And Mr. Stanley F. Harburg happens to be vice president
in charge of programming for the National Broadcasting
Company. And the National Broadcasting Company happens to be in the process of creating a series of new enter-
tainments for a rapidly growing national television
audience."

"Cut to the chase, man!" said T-Bone Sanders.

"We ain't got time," said Ed "Caesar" Robinson, "for the
entire Book of Genesis."

"Well, it seems that Mr. Harburg has been developing a
new program for a certain young singer. And it seems that
this singer has a few, shall we say, 'unsavory' connections
that are not disposed towards the contract that he has
signed. And it seems that these connections have decided

against this singer's participation, leaving the National Broadcasting Company, shall we say, in the lurch."

"And?" said Mavis Johnson.

"For the love of Jesus," said Loolie Jones, "get to the point!"

"Well, at my suggestion," said Rabbi Jerome, "Cousin Delmont invited Mr. Stanley F. Harburg and his lovely wife, Lorraine, to visit Lazy Joe's. And Mr. Harburg, my friends, was considerably impressed. So impressed, he would like to offer Miss Nutt here a thirteen-week contract to host her very own television program, featuring Mr. Chernovsky on the saxophone. Fifteen minutes of music and variety, each and every Thursday evening."

A hush fell over the room as everyone turned toward Cassandra Nutt and Benjamin.

"What do you say, Miss Nutt?" said Rabbi Jerome.

Cassandra Nutt sat quietly in her chair and studied the remains of Ed "Caesar" Robinson's cake-frosting portrait: a bite of eye, a bit of ear, a smudge she judged to have been her chin. "What do you think, Benjamin?" she said. "Should we give it a whirl?"

Benjamin shrugged. "I don't see how we can say no."

The table erupted into a series of cheers; then T-Bone went to the bar to get a bottle of champagne, Willette went to the kitchen to get a fresh set of glasses, and the others began to contemplate the curious notion that Cassandra Nutt and Benjamin were about to become television stars.

20/The Black-and-White Blues

the smudged fingerprint

HE FOLLOWING MONDAY a white limou-
sine pulled up to Lazy Joe's and whisked
Cassandra Nutt and Benjamin down to
Rockefeller Center, where they met with
Mr. Harburg to discuss the proposal for
their show. The idea was to have Cassan-
dra Nutt begin at the piano, where she'd play a few songs,
and then move to a pair of stools, where she'd introduce
the week's "special guest." They'd chat for a few minutes,
and then the guest—who was likely to be either a top-forty
crooner or some borscht-belt comedian—would perform.
Then Cassandra Nutt would return to the piano to play
again, this time featuring Benjamin on the saxophone. Mr.
Harburg stressed that the talk was to be simple and the
music strictly mainstream.

"Television has to please Mrs. Smith in Cedar Rapids,"
he said with great seriousness, "at the same time as Mrs.
Jones in New York."

Despite the restrictions, Cassandra Nutt and Benjamin agreed to the format, convinced that the idea of allowing a colored woman to enter Mrs. Smith's living room at all — to laugh and make music rather than vacuum the carpet — was remarkable, and radical, enough. Before they were willing to sign the contracts, however, they added a few stipulations: first, that Cassandra Nutt would be provided with her own costume designer, who would fashion a new outfit for each week's show; second, that she would be allowed to choose her own songs; third, that once a month she might present a new artist in a segment entitled "Cassandra's Hot Spotlight"; and last, that Charlene would be hired to be her personal assistant. Mr. Harburg agreed, so they drew up the contracts and they signed them and they broke out the champagne and they celebrated. Then the limousine whisked Cassandra Nutt and Benjamin back to Lazy Joe's, where Loolie mixed up a few pitchers of sloe gin fizz and they celebrated all over again.

"To our future celebrities!" said Ed "Caesar" Robinson.

"Eat your heart out, Uncle Miltie!" said Loolie Jones.

When the excitement died down, the hard work began, for as the program was scheduled to begin airing in September, there were only a few weeks in which to find a sponsor, build the sets, compose the theme song, arrange the publicity, schedule the guests, and teach Cassandra Nutt the basics of performing on television: how to relax in front of the camera, how to work with a hidden microphone, how to keep from squinting beneath the glare of the heavy lights. There was some discussion about airing the show in the new color process, but when it was pointed out that it might be awkward to announce that Cassandra

225

Nutt would be appearing "in color," they decided to abandon the idea.

From Charlene's point of view, it was not much of an improvement to say that *The Cassandra Nutt Show* would be "in black and white." In fact, as things developed, she became convinced that the entire thing was a mistake.

"They're trying to 'Uncle Tom' you," she said. "They don't just want you to be *in* black and white, they want you to *be* black and white.'"

"Nobody's gonna make me anything other than what I am," said Cassandra Nutt.

"Puttin' a colored woman on television," said Loolie Jones, "is a step forward no matter how you slice it."

Charlene disagreed, but as the preparations accelerated she found herself far too busy to continue stressing the point. Over the following weeks she saw to it that the legs on Cassandra Nutt's piano were sawed down to a more suitable playing height, that the cameras were repositioned so that they did not prevent contact with the studio audience, that the air-conditioning on the soundstage was kept to a minimum, as Cassandra Nutt was allergic to the coolants. Toward the end of August, however, the show faced a pair of technical crises that caused a personal crisis for Charlene.

The first of these was what Ed "Caesar" Robinson referred to as "the black-and-white blues," for it was discovered, during the test runs, that when Cassandra Nutt shared the television screen with a light-skinned guest, the cameraman could work the contrast so that either Cassandra Nutt was visible, in which case the guest looked like a marshmallow in a wig, or the guest was visible, in which case Cassandra Nutt looked like a slightly smudged fingerprint. After a good deal of panic, one of the technicians figured out that by adding a layer of "Pale Hibiscus" to Cassandra Nutt's makeup and a layer of "Egyptian Bronze" to the makeup of her guest, an acceptable balance could be achieved. This solution, however, utterly infuriated Charlene.

"Next they'll be straightenin' your hair!" she insisted. "Then they'll decide that your eyes oughta be blue!"

It was the second technical crisis, however, that finally pushed Charlene over the edge. A few weeks before the show was to premiere it was suddenly discovered that whenever Benjamin was on camera the signal became scrambled, so that instead of *The Cassandra Nutt Show* the network would begin transmitting *The Ford Television Theatre* or the finals at Wimbledon or whatever else was coasting the airwaves. The technical staff tried everything they could think of, but the only thing that seemed to solve the problem was the removal of Benjamin. So with some loopy excuse about the sound frequency of his saxophone, Mr. Harburg sadly informed him that his spot on *The Cassandra Nutt Show* was ending before it had begun.

Benjamin, of course, knew that the problem was his gift: his powers were obviously too volatile for this new medium; if he wasn't careful, he might short-circuit the entire network. At first he was disappointed; his dreams of fame had burst like a soap bubble. It was not long, however, before he began to feel relieved, for he still had his place on the Lazy Joe bandstand, and he knew, in his heart, that Cassandra Nutt was more suited to stardom than he was. Everything would have been fine had Charlene not decided to find out what had actually happened.

Though she still kept a room on 134th Street, over Jimmy Clarke's Pool Hall, Charlene spent most of her nights now with Benjamin over the club. They felt safe there together; in the velvety darkness, surrounded by Ed "Caesar" Robinson's rich, earthy images, all sense of division between them vanished. It therefore seemed natural, on the night after Benjamin had been taken off the show, when Charlene rolled over and gently insisted that he explain what was going on, that Benjamin suddenly found himself recounting the entire history of his gift. Charlene listened closely—never interrupting—never once challenging the remarkable thesis that Benjamin was presenting. When he'd finished, however, the coldness in her voice was clear.

"That's it?" she said.

"What do you mean?" said Benjamin.

"You've got a gift like this and that's what you do with it?"

Benjamin turned over and placed his hand on her shoulder. "I told you what happened when I tried to save the Family Guildenstern. It was a complete disaster."

"Then you try again. You keep on trying until you figure it out." She paused for a moment to let her words sink in. "You think God gave you powers of biblical proportions just so you could play 'Stormy Weather'?"

Benjamin wanted to explain himself, but Charlene had only reinforced his own hidden fears that he had failed to actualize the magical powers that he'd been given. So he rolled back over and lay there in the darkness, listening to the rise and fall of Charlene's breathing as she gradually found her way back to sleep.

When Charlene had chastised Benjamin, the rebuke had been clear—yet Benjamin trusted that in a day, or a week, the distance between them would evaporate. He never dreamed that on the following morning she would march right out of both Lazy Joe's and his life.

It was partly due to the whitening of Cassandra Nutt. It was partly due to Benjamin's wasting of his gift. But more than anything else it was due to the fact that in all the time she and Benjamin had been together, he had never thought to share with her the most intimate secret of his life.

postcards from Petrie

THROUGHOUT THIS TIME, at varying intervals, Benjamin would periodically receive postcards from Petrie. He'd tried to make contact with him when he'd first returned from Europe; mixed in with the letters he wrote in search of the Family Guildenstern were a series of letters trying to locate his elusive friend. It was not until he moved up to Harlem, however, that he finally received a response: a postcard from New Mexico saying that Petrie was working on a top-secret project and that he would be sure to come see him the next time he visited New York.

The postcards continued for the next several years. Sometimes they came from as near as New Hampshire, other times they came from as far off as Spain. Sometimes they conveyed a detailed description of the place where they were written, other times they merely said "hello." They never actually explained what Petrie was doing, however, or said that he was coming to visit.

As time passed, the Petrie of the war years became as distant and shadowy as the Petrie of his youth. Benjamin saved the postcards, however, convinced that he and his friend were still connected and that there was still another chapter to come.

high stakes

GOLD CRESCENT SOAP presents The Cassandra Nutt Show premiered on September 11,1950, in an evening lineup that included *The Americana Quiz, Be Grateful You're Stupid!* and *World-Wide Boxing Tonight. The New York Times* ignored it completely, but *Variety* called it "jaunty" and the *Herald-Tribune* said that it was "a lively addition to the box." What no one could have predicted, however, was the overwhelming manner in which the American viewing public clutched its jovial star to their hearts. It didn't happen immediately, for with so few people actually owning TVs, even a lion's share of the audience represented a fairly small segment of the population. By the third or fourth program, however, word had got out that on Thursday nights, at nine eastern standard time, this wonderful new creature was appearing on the tiny home screen. All across the nation people began crowding into their local taprooms or pressing against the windows of their furniture and appliance stores to watch Cassandra Nutt as she plied the eighty-eights and chatted with her assortment of guests. By November she had become a household name; by December caftans had become the latest fashion; by January dinner parties were being cancelled and movie attendance was plummeting as Thursday nights became reserved for Cassandra Nutt.

When spring arrived the show was extended to half an hour, and Cassandra Nutt began to settle in to her season of fame. She'd been around too long to let the attention go to her head; mostly she enjoyed the chance to work with the other performers, to eat at the best restaurants, and, best of all, to meet her fans. Cassandra Nutt was always delighted to make contact with the people who waited for her at the stage door and lined the streets when she made a personal appearance and wrote her thousands upon thousands of letters. At first she attempted to answer her mail herself; when this became too difficult she hired Ed "Caesar" Robinson to assist with the overflow, and eventually he took on the entire operation himself. His letters were so warm and effusive, the recipients often wrote back three or four times, creating a chain of correspondence that required three full-time postmen to deliver.

With the incredible success of *The Cassandra Nutt Show*, life changed dramatically at Lazy Joe's. In the first place, Cassandra Nutt was hardly ever there, and when she was the place was a madhouse packed with people desperate to see her. She therefore decided, at the beginning of March —with Loolie Jones's approval—to turn the whole thing over to Benjamin.

Outwardly, the change made little difference. Benjamin already had a substantial following, and he saw no reason to alter things for the sake of novelty. Personally, however, it turned out to be a lifeline, for it provided him with a set of clear responsibilities that helped him take his mind off himself. Benjamin had suffered terribly after Charlene had gone away; while Cassandra Nutt's star was rising rapidly, his heart was fighting not to cave in. He was determined, however, that he would not fall into the kind of hopeless despair that had consumed him when he'd come back from Europe. So despite Charlene's charge that it was a waste

231

of his gift, he poured his pain and anguish over losing her into his saxophone. His playing, as a result, became lighter and leaner, and by the beginning of the second season of *The Cassandra Nutt Show*, Lazy Joe's, even without Cassandra Nutt, was a bigger success than ever before.

It was during this time that Benjamin found himself thrust into a situation that would ultimately test his powers more than anything had ever tested them before. He had just completed the final set on a quiet Tuesday night; while the customers shuffled out, he sat at the bar, sharing a beer with Spider Perkins. Loolie had not been in all evening, yet no one seemed concerned. The old man had a habit of wandering off sometimes—to a boxing match or a midtown double feature—and Slim Betts was always happy to slip on his apron and stand in for him at the bar.

Benjamin loved this time of the night. There was a sweetness in the air that was a mixture of cigarettes and faded music and a creeping feeling of fatigue. He would often sit there until T-Bone had finished closing up the bandstand and Loolie had finished wiping down the bar and the lights were turned off and everybody had gone. Then he'd carefully go over that evening's sets, searching for those places where his breath had seemed just a bit constricted, his fingers, or his pickup, just a bit too slow— those moments where a glitch in the mechanics of his playing had interrupted his flight through that sweet, abstract space he entered when he used his gift.

On this night, however, he did not get that far, for as the last few customers were saying their good-byes, Ed "Caesar" suddenly tore into the nightclub with a look of panic on his face.

"It's Loolie," he whispered as he sidled up to Benjamin. "He's got himself in a shitload of trouble."

Benjamin turned to Spider and told him to fetch T-Bone and then turned back to Ed "Caesar" and told him to grab Slim from behind the bar. Then he made his way over to booth number four and, when the others had all gathered, asked Ed "Caesar" to explain the situation.

"Y'all know Loolie likes to gamble," said Ed "Caesar."

"That ain't no news," said T-Bone.

"Well, it seems like he's finally got in over his head. Loolie's been playin' poker over at Billy Morton's—"

"Billy Morton's!" cried Slim Betts.

"That's high stakes for Loolie!" said Spider.

"Damned high stakes. Well, apparently Loolie's been on a losing streak since last April. And in order to stay in the game he started to borrow from Tiger Knolls. A whole lotta money, at Tiger's goin' rate. Now, he didn't say a word to Billy about the fact that he was borrowin'. And he told Tiger Knolls that his sister down in North Carolina was fixin' to hand him over his share of their inheritance from the passin' of their mama, and that he'd be able to pay him back by the first of August."

"Loolie's mama done died forty years ago," said Spider.

"At a Labor Day picnic," said T-Bone, "out in Queens."

"So August comes and goes and there ain't no inheritance money. Same with September. Then two days ago Billy Morton bumps into Tiger Knolls and finds out that Loolie's been borrowin'. And so they go to Loolie and give him forty-eight hours to come up with the money. And the upshot is they got him locked up in the basement of Joe Tyler's Boarding House and they's fixin' to hurt him good."

"They gonna hurt Loolie?" said Spider.

Slim shook his head. "That's like whuppin' your grandma."

"That ain't all," said Ed "Caesar." "Billy and Tiger say that if they don't get the money, they's gonna take Lazy Joe's in exchange."

"They can't do that!" said Spider.

"You gonna try and stop 'em?" said Ed "Caesar."

T-Bone leaned closer. "So what do we do?"

"Don't know," said Ed "Caesar." "But if we don't do it fast, it's gonna be bad for Loolie."

"Mighty bad," said Slim.

Benjamin reached out his hand and ran his finger across a small cigarette burn in the starched linen tablecloth. He pictured Billy Morton burning holes in Loolie Jones or breaking his legs or his ribs or his fingers, or worse. "I'll save Loolie," he said.

"How the hell you figure on doin' that?" said Spider Perkins.

"I can't say," said Benjamin. "You just have to trust me. And do what I say."

Ed "Caesar" turned to T-Bone, who turned to Spider, who turned to Slim, who turned back to Ed "Caesar" with a shrug.

"Somebody got a better idea?" said Ed "Caesar."

"Looks like we're in your hands," said T-Bone.

As Benjamin looked at the others he tried not to reveal that, as yet, he had no idea what to do. He only knew that he would have to use his gift—and that he had very little time to figure it out.

21/Home Before Midnight

like a stone on water

T TOOK BENJAMIN approximately forty-five minutes to sketch out a plan, and he wondered afterward, considering the length of time, if he had somehow used his gift to figure out how to use his gift to save Loolie. The first thing he'd had to do was find out the conditions of the room where he was being held. This was accomplished by way of Velma Johnson, an ex-girlfriend of T-Bone's who had once lived at Joe Tyler's and who was able, although she'd been awakened in the night, to describe the entire place in detail. According to Velma there was only one door to the basement and a single window, high above a wash sink, that led to an alley that ran along the back of the building. One man alone— especially Loolie—could never have reached it, but two men, one standing on the shoulders of the other, who was standing on the sink, might succeed. Benjamin therefore reasoned that if he could transfer himself to Joe Tyler's,

235

help Loolie up to and out of the window, and then transfer himself back, he might save the old fellow without
causing any major catastrophes. In the meantime, perhaps
Loolie would provide him with some information that
would help him to save Lazy Joe's.

Once he'd devised a plan he wasted no time, for he
knew that it stood the best chance of succeeding if he put
it into action while it was still the middle of the night. He
therefore instructed T-Bone to drive Ed "Caesar" and Spider over to Nick Carter's bar, which was two blocks from
Joe Tyler's, and then make his way out to the window in
the alley and to wait there, while the others waited in the
car, from two forty-five to three-thirty. Then—while Slim
Betts held down the fort at Lazy Joe's—Benjamin prepared to work his magic.

In truth, he wasn't certain that he could do it anymore,
for he hadn't used his gift, except to play the saxophone,
since he'd tried to free the Family Guildenstern. In spite of
his doubts, however, he went to his room, closed the door,
and tried to recontact the first use of his powers. He closed
his eyes; he breathed in deeply; he concentrated. And
though his lips kept waiting for the feel of the mouthpiece
and his fingers kept tingling for the touch of the keys, he
was eventually able to make use of the energy to transfer
himself to Joe Tyler's basement.

Loolie was wide awake when Benjamin materialized.
Seated on a cot in a corner of the room, he was convinced
that Benjamin's sudden appearance was the product of
some desperate dream. Only when Benjamin placed his
finger to his lips and moved through the clutter to where
Loolie was sitting did the old man realize that he was not
hallucinating—at which point he became so emotional, he

started gasping for air. Benjamin quickly cupped his hand over his mouth and then took him in his arms and rocked him like a child. "It's all right," he whispered. "I'm going to get you out of here."

"Jesus Lord," said Loolie. "I sure is glad to see you. But how'd you get in here? They got Whitey Parker on the door."

Benjamin leaned back and looked Loolie in the eye. "No questions," he said. "We don't have the time. Now, I can get you out of here. But I need your help if we're going to save Lazy Joe's."

"But I got the money, Benjamin—I told that to Tiger. It's my mama's inheritance."

"Spider says your mama died in 1921."

"She did," said Loolie. "But my sister, Sugar Henderson, held on to the money. I don't got no head for money, Benjamin. So me and Sugar agreed she'd keep it safe for me till I decided I needed it."

"Then what's the problem?"

"Don't know," said Loolie. "I wrote her in August and told her to send it. Since then I been callin' her damn near every single day. But I don't get no answer. I was just about to go down there myself when Billy goes crazy. He locks me up in here and says if I don't get the money by mornin', he's gonna take over the club. Well, I can't get that money by tomorrow mornin', Benjamin! It ain't possible!"

Benjamin closed his eyes and took a deep, long breath. "I'll get it, Loolie."

"What you mean, you'll get it?"

"If I try to explain it to you," said Benjamin, "I won't have time to do it. Now will you go along with me?"

Loolie thought for a moment. "All right, Benjamin. Whatever you say."

"Good. Now where does this sister of yours live?"

"North Carolina. She got a nice little house just south o' Winston-Salem. Place called South Dillon."

"Can you describe the house, Loolie? So there's no mistaking it?"

Loolie rubbed his forehead. "Don't know," he said. "There's a porch swing. And a flagstone path. But that ain't so special." He closed his eyes and rocked a little, searching his mind for something specific. "Simon's igloo!"

"What's that?"

"Sugar's daughter, Sal, lived with her for 'while. And Sal's boy, Simon, built an igloo in the backyard out o' motor oil jugs. Strangest thing you ever seen. Nobody else in South Dillon got an igloo in their backyard."

Benjamin tried to picture this. "I guess that'll do," he said. "Now if I was to show up at your sister's house and tell her you needed your share of that money, would she give it to me?"

"That part's easy," said Loolie. "All you got to do is say 'lemon-water ice.'"

"Lemon-water ice?"

"That's our signal. See, when me and Sugar was kids we used to lie on the roof and eat lemon-water ice. Make our lips all puckery. So we agreed that'd be our signal. Just say, 'Loolie wants his money—lemon-water ice.' She'll hand it right over."

Benjamin looked at his watch and saw that, though there was still enough time to get Loolie to safety before he'd have to start worrying about "the Cinderella factor," the pressure was mounting. "We'll see if it works," he said.

"Now let's get you out of here." He took Loolie by the hand and led him through the quiet sea of empty bottles and broken lamps until they reached the large sink with the standing base, and Benjamin mouthed the words "Climb up." Loolie was skeptical, but he made his way up and clung to the wall while Benjamin scrambled up beside him. Then Benjamin squatted down—and Loolie climbed onto his shoulders—and then slowly, gently, Benjamin raised him up to the window.

Fortunately it was easy to open—a slight push outward from the bottom of the pane—and fortunately T-Bone was right there, waiting to lend a hand. Loolie thrust his arms through the window, and T-Bone grabbed them and began pulling him through, but as Loolie's body grazed the edge of the frame, his mouth organ suddenly sailed out of his pocket and hit the sink and went skipping, like a stone on water, across the floor. Benjamin, Loolie, and T-Bone froze.

"What's goin' on in there?" shouted Whitey Parker. " 'Tain't no hour to be messin' 'round."

Loolie started to answer, but as he was already halfway out in the alley, Benjamin knew that a response would give them away. So he squeezed Loolie's ankles and, imitating his high-pitched, crenulated voice, responded to Whitey himself.

"Had to piss," he shouted back. "When nature calls, you got to respond."

After he'd said this, Benjamin patted Loolie's left leg and indicated that they should continue with the escape. So T-Bone gave one last vigorous yank, and Loolie went flying to freedom.

"A'right," said Whitey. "But don't be makin' so much noise. It's three o'clock in th' mornin'!"

Benjamin listened as T-Bone and Loolie padded off down the alley. He knew that if he stayed, he was courting danger, but he also knew that if Whitey discovered that Loolie was gone, and alerted the others before he'd had time to get away, things would go a good deal worse for Loolie than if he'd never tried to help him at all. He imagined Loolie then as the last of the Family Guildenstern: with his crooked smile and his twinkling spirit, he would have fit right into the act. So he climbed down from the sink, seated himself on an old stack of *Photoplay* magazines, and waited until he was certain that Loolie was well away. Then he transferred himself back to his room at Lazy Joe's and prepared himself to pay a visit to Sugar Henderson.

like a pat of butter on a piece of peach pie

THE MOMENT that Benjamin materialized on the doorstep, he knew that he'd managed to find the right house, even without seeing Simon's motor-oil igloo in the backyard. At three-thirty in the morning the streets of South Dillon were shrouded in sleep, and except for a faulty street lamp that kept twitching on and off, there was hardly a sign of life. Benjamin only hoped that Sugar Henderson was inside — and that when he woke her up she did not call the police, or unleash the dogs, or greet him with an upraised frying pan.

Benjamin took a deep breath and pressed the doorbell. When there was no response, he pressed it a second time, and then a light came on in a second-floor window, and then, after what seemed like a century, he heard footsteps and a raspy-wispy voice came through the door.

"Who the hell is it?"

Benjamin leaned closer. "Loolie sent me," he said.

There was a long pause. "Loolie?"

"Your brother, Loolie Jones."

"I dang well know who Loolie is," snapped the voice. "The question is, who are you? And what are you doin' on my doorstep in the middle o' the night?" Benjamin began to answer, but the voice cut him off. "You ain't drunk, are you? Loolie knows how I feel about liquor."

"I'm not drunk," said Benjamin. "But Loolie's in trouble. If you'll let me in, I can explain."

There was another pause that seemed to last for several days; then a chain rattled, and the door swung open to reveal a tiny creature in a padded robe and a crocheted cap, with the squashed little face of a lapdog in between. That face was fixed in prideful indignation until it suddenly caught sight of Benjamin's face, at which instant the glorious contradictions, etched out in the moonlight, cast a spell over Sugar Henderson.

"Come in!" she suddenly crooned. "It's cold out there at this time o' night!"

Benjamin had seen this dazed, dazzled look on many a face, yet it had never seemed quite as incongruous as it did on Sugar Henderson. He nevertheless stepped into her wallpapered foyer and waited while she closed the door behind him. There was a smell of meatloaf and gravy in the walls, fried potatoes in the carpets, blackberry cobbler on the stairs—all laced with the faded jasmine that poured off this woman who was now smiling at him as if he were Jesus.

"I 'spect you must be hungry," said Sugar. "How 'bout a slice o' applesauce cake?"

"I don't have much time," said Benjamin. "I need to speak with you."

241

"Well, come into the parlor," said Sugar, cocking her head slightly and reaching out her hand. "You might as well take a load off."

Benjamin followed Sugar down the dark, narrow hall to an open doorway; then Sugar switched on the light, and he was confronted with a vast room with a green flowered sofa, an upright piano, and a surprising number of chairs. Glancing at his watch, he saw that eighteen minutes had now passed since he'd left Lazy Joe's, so he turned to his host and said, "Please, Mrs. Henderson, I need you to listen."

Sugar Henderson smiled and slipped her tongue through the generous gap where a cluster of teeth were missing. "You children got no patience these days," she said. "You got to learn to relax—to let your mind go free and your body melt down like a pat o' butter on a piece o' peach pie."

Benjamin thought that this was excellent advice, and he would have been glad to try it had it not been for the fact that he could hear the ticking of "the Cinderella factor" like a bomb gently placed on a doily on Sugar Henderson's piano. "I'm here, Mrs. Henderson, because Loolie needs his money."

The old woman kept right on smiling. "What money?" she said.

"The money you've been keeping for him since your mother died. His share of the inheritance."

Sugar Henderson cocked her head again. "You want a piece o' cold chicken? I got some legs in the icebox that'd do you just right."

"Mrs. Henderson, you're not listening!"

"Oh, I'm listenin'," said Sugar. "I just can't figure out why I should give Loolie's money to some white boy I never seen before in my life." She smiled. "Even if you *is* pretty as a Christmas tree."

"Because Loolie needs it. Because his life may depend on it." Benjamin rubbed his temples, which were beginning to throb. "Didn't you get Loolie's letter?"

"Of course I did. But I was savin' it for one of my 'dark days.' They come over me now and then, and when they do, ain't nothin' can cheer me up like a letter from Loolie."

"But he's been trying to phone you for weeks."

Sugar scrunched her face up like she'd just tasted a bad bite of sweet potato pudding. "Don't answer it no more," she said. "Anybody important want to reach me"—her face lit up as she looked at Benjamin—"they just got to knock on my door!" She paused for a moment, her expression turning serious. "Loolie don't need that money. Loolie works hard."

Benjamin leaned forward. "Lemon-water ice," he said.

Sugar Henderson's tongue froze in the absence of teeth. "What you say?"

"Loolie told me to tell you 'lemon-water ice.'"

The old woman sat there for a moment, the levers and gears whirring madly in her head. Then she sprang up, smoothed out her dress, and said, "Be right back."

Benjamin closed his eyes and sank down on the couch—if not like a pat of melting butter, at least with considerable fatigue. He had never done back-to-back transfers before, and at four o'clock in the morning he felt woozy and sore. He could feel his strength gradually draining away, but even more he could feel the minutes slipping by, bringing him closer and closer to danger.

Benjamin waited. And waited. And waited. Then, just when he'd decided that he could wait no longer, Sugar

Henderson swept into the room with a large wooden tray piled with food.

"A good day don't happen without a good breakfast!" she sang. "So eat up, honey, and enjoy!"

Benjamin stared at the tray of delights that Sugar placed down on the polished oak table: fresh-squeezed orange juice, steaming black coffee, fried eggs, bacon, and grits. But all he could manage was a strangulated whisper: "The money—," he sputtered.

"What did you say?" said Sugar.

Benjamin felt his heart pound like a drum inside his chest. "The money!" he shouted. "You have to get the money!"

Sugar Henderson stared at him, stunned; then her face caved in like an overdone soufflé. "No manners," she said as she turned on her heels. "No manners at all." Then she sauntered out of the room.

Benjamin did not know if she had gone to get the money, but he knew, from the pain and pressure in his head, that he could not chance staying any longer. Just as he was about to transfer himself back, however, that vague, burning smell began to rise up in the air—then the room began to spin—then suddenly everything went black.

unlike Alice

UNLIKE ALICE, whose passage through the rabbit hole was straightforward and down, Benjamin found himself, upon losing consciousness, spiraling forward along a tunnel of disconnected memories. At first he thought he was seeing his life flash before him, but it would be truer to say that he was seeing himself flash before his life, and not so much the events as the chief individuals, who were not so much showing him what he had lived as reminding him what he had lost. He saw his mother and father, he saw Lorna O'Shaughnassy, he saw the Family Guildenstern, he saw the girls of Flo's: they rose up and vanished, one after the next, a series of bright scarves whipping madly in the wind as Benjamin journeyed on through the tunnel. He saw Jean Pierre Michel surrounded by a sea of weapons. He saw Charlene floating on a sea of light.

As he continued along, visions of himself began to rise up: the boy with the birthmark, the eager young man with the war at his heels, the fellow in the striped suit with the high-polished horn in his hand. He saw himself grappling with the gift he'd been given—trying to understand what he was meant to do with it—and coming up empty again and again and again.

Benjamin began to sense that the end was truly near, that he had crossed over the line, that Cassandra Nutt's dream was about to happen. He pictured the roof blowing off Sugar Henderson's house. He pictured Sugar Henderson being tossed into the air amid bricks and beams and bits of broken glass. He pictured himself being shattered and scattered, a million fragments of Benjamin shooting off in every direction. Then the tunnel went dark, and all sense of motion was suddenly interrupted. And then Benjamin became conscious of nothing, nothing at all.

snow on the screen

WHAT WOULD HAVE happened to Benjamin—not to mention Sugar Henderson and a good portion of South Dillon—had

Sugar not returned in time to find him sprawled out on the floor, and not reached for the glass of orange juice, and not splashed it in his face—is anybody's guess. She did it, however, in just enough time for Benjamin to awaken, and reach out for the envelope of money in her hand, and whisk himself back to safety, and Lazy Joe's. Sugar thought the orange juice had made Benjamin disappear, but in the morning she decided that the entire thing had just been an unruly dream. Upon returning, Benjamin gave the money to Ed "Caesar," who gave it to Tiger Knolls, who informed Billy Morton that they would not be taking over Lazy Joe's. Billy was furious, however, to learn of Loolie's escape, and although Benjamin and the others swore that they'd had nothing to do with it, they decided that it was not safe for Loolie to remain in New York City. So the following evening, just after sundown, Mavis's brother Arthur drove Loolie to South Dillon, where he moved in with Sugar, changed his name to Snooky Cartwright, and opened a little bar in the empty building next door to the local bowling alley.

Benjamin had had a good deal of explaining to do when he'd returned from his double mission. Yet despite his attempt to disclose the secret of his gift, the gang at Lazy Joe's would have none of it.

"Say what you like," said Ed "Caesar," "but I know voodoo when I see it."

The others were less certain how to categorize what they'd seen, but in the end they decided that it was best not to think about it—or, as Slim Betts put it, "not to question the ways of Providence." Benjamin, however, did not leave the incident unscathed, for though he'd managed to make it "home before midnight"—without turning into a pumpkin or exploding into smithereens—the burning that had begun left a numbness in his left leg that produced a distinct limp. Benjamin, however, could not regret what he'd done. He'd finally faced the danger inherent in his powers—he'd used his gift to save Loolie as well as Lazy Joe's—and he was sure that, had she known of it, Charlene would have been extremely proud.

As a result of Loolie's departure, Benjamin was left to run Lazy Joe's alone. What followed, however, was one of the quietest periods in the history of the nightclub that anyone could ever remember. It wasn't that nothing occurred during this time: the following winter Slim Betts (who'd taken over behind the bar) lost his vision; the winter after that T-Bone and Mavis suddenly got married; the winter after that Ed "Caesar" began an enormous mural for Rabbi Jerome's synagogue that depicted the reception of the Ten Commandments with a Negro Moses. It was that Benjamin stopped waiting for that moment of illumination—that flash of insight—that sweeping explanation of who he was and what he was supposed to accomplish. He was a guy who played the saxophone at a smoky club in Harlem, and finally that seemed enough.

The Cassandra Nutt Show, meanwhile, rolled on and on. As Eisenhower was elected president. As Salk discovered a vaccine against polio. As Mount Everest was climbed and the Rosenbergs were executed and Balenciaga introduced the tunic dress. By the beginning of the third season there was a six-month waiting list to appear on the show. By the beginning of the fourth season sixty-eight percent of America's televisions were tuned in regularly, each Thursday evening, to the one-and-only Cassandra Nutt.

Throughout this time the world of television was changing rapidly; what at first seemed no more than an extravagant joke had now captured the nation's attention. Dozens of new programs were foisted upon the airwaves, while the number of televisions skyrocketed to over thirty-five million. The most significant change, however, was the gradual conversion of nearly all "live" programming to prerecorded taping. The producers of *The Cassandra Nutt Show* tried to resist this trend; they argued that a good deal of the show's effervescence was a result of their star's spontaneity. Toward the end of the fifth season, however, they reluctantly announced that for the sixth season *The Cassandra Nutt Show* would be taped just like everything else.

Cassandra Nutt was not certain there was going to be a sixth season, for despite the fact that she was now the idol of millions, she was beginning to grow tired of the whole thing. She was too old, she insisted, to keep smiling like an idiot. She was too fat to be an arbiter of taste. And though she hated to admit it, she was becoming too weary to grind out a new program each week. When she tried to explain this to Mr. Harburg, however, he got down on his knees to beg her to stay. So after eliciting his promise to fund a scholarship for young Negro college students in her name, she agreed to go on with the shenanigans for a little while longer.

It was decided that a special show would be created for the last "live" telecast, an hour-long program featuring Cassandra Nutt's favorites out of the performers who had appeared with her over the years. Benjamin and the rest of the gang were invited to be a part of the audience, but they decided instead to remain at Lazy Joe's, where it had become a Thursday night ritual to crowd around the bar and watch *The Cassandra Nutt Show* on Slim Betts's fourteen-inch Admiral.

On the night of the telecast, the nightclub was packed. T-Bone had raised the television onto a shelf over the cash register, Slim Betts had mixed up half a dozen pitchers of sloe gin fizz, and Mavis had decked out the walls and the ceiling with ribbons and banners and balloons. A few minutes before nine Benjamin went to the bar to turn on the set. When he did so, however, he found that there was a problem with the reception.

"What's wrong?" said Slim Betts.

"It's the picture," shouted Mavis.

"You don't have to shout. I lost my eyes, not my ears."

"There's snow on the screen," said Ed "Caesar."

"Is it a winter theme?" said Slim.

"It's static," said T-Bone. "Somethin's wrong with the reception."

For the next few minutes Benjamin played with the dials and fiddled with the antenna and adjusted the position of the television set, until he finally accepted that there would be lousy reception for Cassandra Nutt's last "live" broadcast.

"Must be time to get rid of that Admiral," said T-Bone.

"That's my *new* Admiral," said Slim.

"I hear Emerson makes a good model," said Rabbi Jerome.

"I ain't sellin' my new Admiral!" cried Slim. "I don't care if the whole damn screen is a blizzard! I can't see it anyway!"

"Hush up!" said Mavis. "It's starting!"

The nine o'clock hush quickly descended over the club as the theme song began and Cassandra Nutt appeared on the tiny screen. Because of the special nature of the show, she did not go immediately to the piano, but talked instead about the fun of airing "live," recounting a few of the more unexpected moments that had occurred over the course of the show. Despite her lightness, however, and her usual gaiety, Benjamin could tell that something was wrong.

"Something's the matter," he said.

"What do you mean?" said T-Bone.

"With Cassandra Nutt. Look into her eyes."

"I can't see her eyes," said Mavis. "The screen's too small."

"I can't even see the TV," said Ed "Caesar."

"Well, join the club," said Slim.

Benjamin did not press the issue, but as the show continued a feeling of panic rose over him, for despite the fact that the others could not see it, he was certain that Cassandra Nutt was unwell. There was a hesitancy to her movements, a glaze over her eyes, a strained quality to her voice. Yet it was not until the show was nearly over that Benjamin's fears were realized. For just as she began to launch into a rousing version of "Sweet Georgia Brown," Cassandra Nutt suddenly cried out, "Sweet Jesus!" and collapsed, on "live" television, upon the keys of her white baby grand.

22/Time Folds

an unforeseen hurricane

EAN PIERRE MICHEL sat in his Carrara marble bathtub in his twenty-seven-room Fifth Avenue mansion and stared at the delicate ribbons of steam that rose from the surface of the water. The bath was a mixture of ylang-ylang, eucalyptus, and salt from the Dead Sea, and its rich, palliative properties removed the tender aching from Jean Pierre Michel's ninety-seven-year-old body. Perhaps when he was finished he would have a nice cup of tea—a crisp Darjeeling or a dark, smoky Assam—and then a brief walk about the garden before taking his late morning nap. He hadn't been out of the house in several days; a walk in the garden was bound to be pleasant and revivifying.

Jean Pierre Michel had been through a great many things in the more than sixteen years that had passed since both Benjamin and Cassandra Nutt had disappeared from his life. At first he'd tried to pretend that nothing had happened: he barreled through his days with his usual self-absorption, this time turning his attention to the collection of antique humidors. His affair with Lorna O'Shaughnassy had ended as swiftly as it had begun, for when the act of defiance that he had lured her into revealed itself to be an act of betrayal, she ran from the mansion never to be seen again. This did not prevent Jean Pierre Michel from continuing to take lovers or, perhaps more remarkably, from continuing to please them. What he found, however, was that it was becoming more and more difficult to convince anyone to go along for the ride. He enticed them, as ever, with silk camisoles and jade bracelets and ruby-encrusted cigarette boxes. When the war broke out, however, the country grew sober, and he found himself, increasingly, alone. He gradually began to close off rooms in the mansion. He went through an endless chain of domestics, each less competent than the one who had come before. Until he could no longer pretend that the loss of Benjamin and the loss of Cassandra Nutt had not left him utterly devastated.

For the next few years Jean Pierre Michel went numb; even the end of the war and the nation's euphoria could not shake him out of his stupor. He stayed in his room. He stared at old photos. He drifted in and out of a dreamlike state in which the past was indistinguishable from the present. Then, one morning in the winter of 1947, he felt a pain like the crack of a whip down his spine, and a terrible sobbing tore through him like an unforeseen hurricane. For the next few years he sobbed and he sobbed, going through twenty-seven servants and an endless stream of handkerchiefs in the process. Until eventually he could tell when an attack was coming on and could stop and bend over, so that his tears fell directly to the carpet or the pavement and neither streaked his face nor required him to change his clothes.

The tears that Jean Pierre Michel shed over the loss of Cassandra Nutt were searing, yet they were not half so painful as the tears that he shed over Benjamin. For while the former were in mourning for a wealth of cherished memories, acquired over a period of almost thirty-five years, the latter were in mourning for those memories that had never occurred. The geography lessons he had never thought to help with. The bedtime stories he had never paused to read. The walks not taken, the explanation of the birds and bees not given, the complex journey from adolescence to manhood not counseled in any way. It stunned him to realize that for all his determination to procure himself a son, he had never really allowed himself to become a father.

As the sobbing went on, it drew into its field each loss, betrayal, longing, rejection, disappointment, and frustration that the now nonagenarian had ever experienced in his life. Until finally it was nothing but sobbing itself, free of associations or any specific object or cause. At this point Jean Pierre Michel actually began to look forward to its coming, in part for the lightness that it left in its wake and in part for his conviction that it would finally bring an end to his life. Jean Pierre Michel was ready to die. He'd been ready, in fact, for a long, long time, and although longevity ran in his family (Alma Esther had lived to one hundred and five, dying peacefully in her bed in those last sweet days before war had gripped Europe), he could not quite grasp, with the degree of wear and tear that he'd incurred, why he continued to go on and on. Go on, however, he did, through extravagance, through abstinence, and, ultimately, through his season of sobbing. Until one day, in November of 1950, at the tremulous beginning of yet another decade, he stopped, bent over, and not a single teardrop came. So he had no choice — with a heart purged of sorrow and death playing hide-and-seek — but to take one last stab at living.

This wasn't as easy as he'd thought it would be, for though the sobbing had softened some of the hardness of his spirit, it had taken quite a toll on his body. Even channel-set diamonds could not lure in the women, and though his penis was somehow as eager as ever, the rest of his frame was as fragile as an overbaked matzo. It was at this point, however, that Bruno Goetz came into his life. At six feet four inches and two hundred and eighty pounds, Bruno Goetz had been hired by Jean Pierre Michel in order to carry him when his own body failed him. What Jean Pierre Michel had not known, however, was that, although outwardly quite virile, Bruno Goetz was possessed of a penis that, when fully erect, was approximately two and a half inches long. As a result he restricted himself to the custom of prostitutes (who were well trained to neither comment nor complain), and it was by the hiring of these that he was able to resolve Jean Pierre Michel's sexual dilemma. At first Jean Pierre Michel resisted the idea of love as commerce, but he eventually began to see that where he had been previously paying with bracelets and furs, he was now simply dealing in hard cash. In addition, Bruno addressed the problem of his fragility by constructing an elaborate harness that would raise him into the air and then slowly lower him down upon his lover. Jean Pierre Michel complained that he felt less like a Don Juan than a Flying Wallenda, but the truth was that he was deeply grateful.

If Jean Pierre Michel remained troubled by anything after his season of sobbing, it was the concept of time: here at the end of a somewhat convoluted life he was convinced the entire thing was a clever swindle. Years seemed to have passed with the swiftness of seconds, while days trailed with the torpor of decades. Incidents from childhood would rise up more clearly than things that had occurred the previous week. By all outward signs he had little time left, yet the more Jean Pierre Michel thought about it, the more he became convinced that if he could penetrate its illusions, time would yield him plenty of time. He therefore decided, at the close of the summer of his ninety-fifth year, to devote himself to the contemplation, and collection, of clocks.

He began with an assortment of English chronometers, strong, solid objects whose form was clearly secondary to their function. He soon moved on, however, to more exotic specimens: banjo-cased tavern clocks, gilt-and-marble lyre clocks, bell-mounted French striking-skeletons. In the winter of 1953 he decided to go large, amassing Viennese brackets and American tallcases. In the summer of 1954 he decided to go small, gathering miniature mechanisms carefully set into cameos and pendants and rings. He had a grand time with musical clocks, acquiring a Ceylonese satinwood seven-tune carillon and a tortoiseshell-and-ormulu eight-tune Turkish bell, and he had a field day with automatons, acquiring a turn-of-the-century Phalibois with a pair of spinning cupids and a late Mastongris with a tightrope walker and six dancing elephants. He found clocks set into books, lamps, bowling balls, candlesticks, salt-and-pepper shakers, snuffboxes, and skulls. He even found one set into the belly of a black jade Jesus that was nailed to a cut-crystal cross.

Jean Pierre Michel loved his clocks. They made time seem more tangible, and they helped him to avoid thinking about the development of the hydrogen bomb and the findings of *The Kinsey Report* and the advent of this thing called television. Jean Pierre Michel did not own a television himself, yet he was aware of its influence and of the tremendous popularity of a certain black Thursday night performer. Each week an assortment of chimes and bells would signal the commencement of her program, and though he never actually saw it, for those fifteen minutes (and later that half an hour), his entire body would tingle with her remembered presence. No matter how strong the feeling, however, he could not bring himself to contact her. She was imprisoned in the past, as remote and unapproachable as a shimmering Sunday from childhood.

There were days when this circumstance—the simultaneous nearness and farness of Cassandra Nutt—brought Jean Pierre Michel to the brink of a fresh episode of sobbing. Today, however, was not one of those days—for he was about to receive a visit from a gentleman from Cartier, who was bringing him a 1928 Jaegar diamond-and-platinum watch, which was bound to amuse him for at least the remainder of the morning.

Jean Pierre Michel turned his eyes toward the slim jade mystery clock that sat on the ledge of the bathtub. According to its hands, it would be another eight minutes before Bruno came to help him from the water. Just as he was about to slide beneath the surface, however, the door suddenly opened and Bruno walked in.

"You're early," said Jean Pierre Michel.

"There is a visitor," said Bruno.

"He's not supposed to be here until half-past ten. I haven't had my tea yet, or my walk, or my nap. I haven't even finished my bath—"

"But—"

"I'm going under!"

"—it's *not* the man from Cartier," said Bruno.

Jean Pierre Michel paused, his head just visible above the surface of the water. "Then who is it?"

"He wouldn't tell me," said Bruno. "But he says you know him. He has a strange mark on his face. Like someone puts a hot iron down while he's sleeping."

Jean Pierre Michel closed his eyes for a moment and breathed in deeply. Then he opened them again and drew himself up to a sitting position. "Help me out of here."

Bruno reached for one of the large towels that were stacked on the crystal stand by the sink and draped it over his shoulder. Then he went to the tub and, in a swift movement that had been perfected over time, raised the old man up from the herb-scented water, laid him down gently over his massive shoulder, and wrapped him up like a tiny baby. Then he lowered him to the floor, where he was able to grasp the sink for support, and gently dried him off.

Jean Pierre Michel did not ask him to hurry. For though he had never been inclined to keep a visitor waiting, he was convinced that if that visitor was truly Benjamin, time had somehow folded back upon itself, and a few more minutes were not going to make any difference.

welcoming back the spring

BY THE TIME Benjamin reached Cassandra Nutt on the night she collapsed, the majority of the hospital ward to which she'd been taken was gathered around her, listening to her tell stories about her adventures in television. To this cluster of fans she seemed the picture of health; even the doctors

and nurses seemed to have lost track of the reason she was there. To Benjamin, however, it was perfectly obvious that something quite serious was wrong. So although the hospital was unable to explain her collapse, he insisted that she remain there for a comprehensive battery of tests.

The following day she was tested. And the day after that. And the day after that. And the day after that. At which point it was concluded that she needed a different series of tests. And then a different series. And then a different series. Until every test possible had been done and done again, and she was informed that she had a disease of the bone marrow for which there was not presently any cure.

"There's got to be a cure," said Ed "Caesar" when Benjamin gathered everyone to tell them the news.

"Cassandra Nutt's got out of trouble before," said T-Bone. "She's bound to find a way out of this."

"Cassandra Nutt and me's gonna take a jet plane to Lourdes," said Slim Betts. "I'll get my sight back, and Cassandra Nutt'll open up a gambling casino."

"Slim's right," said Mavis. "Cassandra Nutt needs our help. An' we ain't gonna be givin' it to her by sittin' around dreamin' up miracles."

"What do you think, Benjamin?" said Ed "Caesar." "How can we help?"

Benjamin looked from face to face, but he did not know what to say. For though he knew, more than anyone, that miracles did occur, he could not even conceptualize the miracle that might save Cassandra Nutt. When the group dispersed, he left the nightclub and began walking downtown. He reasoned that there must be doctors somewhere who were working on her disease. But how could he find them and communicate with them? He reasoned that with enough funding he might be able to speed up research. But where could he find that kind of money in such a short amount of time?

Benjamin walked for miles and miles, his damaged leg dragging but not holding him back. Down Lenox to the park. Across to Fifth. Through the Nineties and the Eighties and the Seventies and the Sixties. Until he finally understood that his subconscious was leading him to that mansion from his childhood to ask Jean Pierre Michel for help.

He was not at all certain that he could bring himself to do it, but he knew that he had to try. So he continued along until the great house appeared and then made his way over to the entrance. At first he was surprised at how small the place seemed; in his mind's eye he'd erected a vast Taj Mahal that neatly dwarfed the building that stood before him now. As he rang the bell, it suddenly occurred to him that it was unlikely the old man was still alive. The feelings this evoked, however—of guilt and sadness, of loss and regret—were swiftly replaced by a quiet trepidation when a large, shaven-headed man opened the door and, upon Benjamin's inquiry, ushered him into the east sitting room while he went to fetch "Herr Chernovsky."

The east sitting room was no longer the bastion of geometric modernity that Benjamin remembered. For just before the sobbing had begun, Jean Pierre Michel had filled it with an assortment of both Early and Native American pieces: Connecticut cupboards, Pennsylvania frakturs, Navajo transitional rugs. What surprised Benjamin more than the changes in the room, however, were the changes in the man who suddenly appeared in the doorway. The body, once vigorous, was shrunken and tentative. The face was like a death mask, pale and hollowed out. And on the right cheek and throat sat a cluster of liver spots that looked remarkably like Benjamin's birthmark.

From the stunned look on Jean Pierre Michel's face, seeing Benjamin, now grown to a man, was every bit as startling. So they simply stood there, in perfect silence, trying to comprehend the fact that over sixteen years had passed since the last time they'd been with one another. Only the gentle striking of the eighteenth-century *pendule à répétition* that stood on the mantelpiece finally prompted the old man to step forward and break the silence.

"It's Cassandra Nutt, isn't it," he said. "There's something wrong."

Benjamin noted that it was not a question. "She has some rare bone disease. As far as we know, there isn't any cure."

"Is she in pain?"

"I expect so. But you know Cassandra Nutt. She never complains about anything."

Jean Pierre Michel closed his eyes for a moment and pictured Cassandra Nutt. Then he opened them again, crossed to the large settee that was propped against the wall, and, indicating that Benjamin should take the pine bench opposite it, seated himself down at its center.

"What do we do?"

Benjamin lowered himself upon the hardwood bench. "I don't know," he said. "But if we could get her the best doctors—put the best scientists to work—I think we could save her."

Jean Pierre Michel did not move a muscle. "And that would require a great deal of money."

Benjamin nodded. "The kind of money that very few people have."

Jean Pierre Michel was silent again. Then he rose from

the settee and went to the French doors and looked out over the garden. Though it was still tended carefully, it lacked the stunning vibrancy that it had possessed when it was looked after by Cassandra Nutt. Jean Pierre Michel stood there for a long, long while. Then he raised his fingertips to the glass and spoke again. "I'll give you whatever you need," he said. "On one condition." He turned around to face Benjamin. "That you move back into the mansion. Both of you. Just like before."

Benjamin closed his eyes and felt a shiver run through him, yet he could not tell whether it was a shiver of excitement or a shiver of dread. He knew only that after the desolate winter that had descended over the mansion, Cassandra Nutt's return would be like welcoming back the spring.

Lazy Chernovsky's

WHEN BENJAMIN told Cassandra Nutt about his visit to Jean Pierre Michel—and the old man's insistence that they move back into the mansion—Cassandra Nutt responded that if she was about to enter her last days on earth, she preferred to do so in the warm, safe surroundings of Lazy Joe's. When Benjamin conveyed this to Jean Pierre Michel, he offered to move the entire nightclub to the mansion, to which Cassandra Nutt responded that she could not bear the thought of leaving the others behind. When Benjamin conveyed *this* to Jean Pierre Michel, he invited the entire lot of them to move in as well, at which point Cassandra Nutt caved in.

"Might as well settle up all my accounts," she said, "before they come and close down the bank."

In the end it was decided not to transfer the club itself, but to hire a team of carpenters and a fleet of designers to construct a perfect replica in the salon, the main dining room, and the second-floor bedrooms of the mansion. Out went the tapestries and the French chandeliers and the hand-stamped Italian silk draperies. In came the bar and the white baby grand, while Ed "Caesar" worked like a jazz Michelangelo adorning the ceilings and the walls. Jean Pierre Michel wanted to rename the mansion "Lazy Chernovsky's," but when Benjamin told this to Cassandra Nutt she said that Jean Pierre Michel had never had a lazy bone in his body and that she found it hard to believe he'd suddenly acquired one at the age of ninety-seven.

When the two old creatures were finally reunited it was not what either of them had expected. Jean Pierre Michel was seated in the dining room, overseeing the installation of the red leather bar stools, when Bruno suddenly entered and announced that the *schvartzes* had arrived. When he shuffled out to the foyer, he found Cassandra Nutt seated in an oversize wheelchair, plus Slim, in dark glasses, being led by Mavis, plus T-Bone and Ed "Caesar" carrying the luggage.

"You look like the New York delegation," said Jean Pierre Michel, "to a convention for the colored disabled."

"You look like an old Jewish matchstick," said Cassandra Nutt, "that's already been struck and blown out."

The gang from the nightclub was taken aback and thought that perhaps the idea of a "homecoming" had been a mistake. Benjamin, however, felt certain from the exchange that, despite the passing years and their respective struggles, Cassandra Nutt and Jean Pierre Michel were delighted to be together again.

23/Time Retracts

faded totems

HE FOLLOWING WEEKS were a whirlwind of activity as the final stages of the transformation of the mansion took place. A ramp was laid down over the steps to the garden to accommodate Cassandra Nutt's wheelchair. A chair lift was installed on the banister of the main staircase so that she could move between the first and second floors. Then one by one the rooms began to fill with laughter, as everyone tried their best to keep the old girl's spirits aloft. T-Bone and Spider took over the bandstand, taking turns at the piano to provide the melody. Ed "Caesar" donned a red felt beret and told World War II stories at the bar. Mavis took over the operation of the wheelchair, on which Slim Betts insisted a minibar be built so that she could always have a sloe gin fizz. Such incessant good cheer proved exhausting to maintain, yet it seemed to achieve its purpose. For though her body was growing weaker with each passing day, Cassandra Nutt's spirit was lighter than ever.

As for Jean Pierre Michel, his task was simple: to have enough money to do whatever was necessary to care for her. In concept this was easy, for with the postwar ubiquitousness of the American image—plus the advent of national television advertising—Pablito's Spearmint Chewing Gum was more successful than he could ever have dreamed. The profits from that success, however, were kept in a foreign bank, and since their sudden withdrawal might cause complete disaster for that nation's economy, Jean Pierre Michel had to transfer a little each day to an account in New York, where it was changed into dollars and then brought to the mansion, where it was placed in a safe beneath the fish tank at the foot of his bed. Overwhelmed by all the energy in the house, Bruno Goetz resigned; rather than dismay Jean Pierre Michel, however, it made him fend for himself, which caused a portion of his strength to return.

Benjamin's task was a bit more difficult, for he had to oversee the running of the imitation nightclub while at the same time making certain that Cassandra Nutt's medical needs were being met. The first thing he did was hire a fleet team of round-the-clock nurses and pay them three times their usual salary to dress up like cocktail waitresses. Then he returned to the library, where he spent hours poring over textbooks and medical journals in search of someone who could devise a cure. He found a number of people who were willing to try, illustrious physicians from the Harvard Medical School and the Swedish Institute who took up his offer to come to New York and study Cassandra Nutt's condition. In the end, however, his efforts did little more than exhaust him. And although it occurred to him that he might use his gift in order to save his dear friend, he could not figure out how to do it.

Both Jean Pierre Michel and Benjamin knew that time was slipping by. As the days sped, however, Jean Pierre Michel finally decided that time was a complete hoax—that if it could fold, it could retract—and that if he could gather together objects from Cassandra Nutt's past, he could lure her away from the moment when she was scheduled to die.

It was a crazy idea, but with his house full of strangers, and his world inside out, it made as much sense as anything else. So he went to the storage room on the third floor of the mansion and began sifting through boxes that were filled with things that had once belonged to Cassandra Nutt. A cut-velvet scarf that she'd worn to the opening of *George White's Scandals*. A souvenir napkin from Woodrow Wilson's second inaugural ball. An autographed photo of Ethel Waters that Benjamin had once given her for her birthday. He gathered them together and took them to her room, where he slipped them beneath her bed like a series of faded totems designed to draw her back from death.

In his heart of hearts, Jean Pierre Michel knew that a collection of hidden keepsakes could not keep Cassandra Nutt from dying. Faced with her illness, however, and the deviousness of time, he figured that it was at least worth a try.

blueberry cheesecake

DESPITE THE BEST EFFORTS of the best doctors in the world, Cassandra Nutt's health continued to deteriorate. Cassandra Nutt, however, went right on smiling—for she knew that it would help no one, and most especially not herself, to let on that she was in incredible pain. The activity at the mansion managed to distract her a bit; the music and the laughter took her mind off the bleakness of her situation. What helped her the most, however, was to turn her attention to what was happening in the outside world. She watched as the Soviets created the Warsaw Pact. She followed the conflicts that led to civil war in Sudan. But what interested her the most were the tumultuous events that were rocking the black communities of America. Earlier that year, when the great Marian Anderson had made her long-awaited debut at the Metropolitan Opera, Cassandra Nutt had hoped that the boundaries between the races were finally beginning to soften. In August, however, a boy named Emmet Till was lynched in Mississippi for allegedly whistling at a white woman. In December Rosa Parks was arrested in Alabama for refusing to give up her seat on the bus. These incidents gave birth to the American civil rights movement, and Cassandra Nutt vowed that before she laid down her head to die, she would lend her voice to the cause.

Benjamin, however, was beginning to fear that she was not going to last that long. For months now he'd been scouring the globe, yet there was still no sign of a cure for her illness. As the new year rolled in, however, it brought with it a palpable surprise. Benjamin was at the bar that morning, drinking strong black coffee and sifting through the mail, while T-Bone read the racing form to Slim. It was mostly the usual stuff: a series of medical bills for Cassandra Nutt, a brochure on hair and skin products for Mavis, a perfumed love letter for Ed "Caesar" Robinson, and an invitation to a dinner-dance from the Brotherhood of Sleeping Car Porters for Slim. At the bottom of the stack, however, like the prize in the Cracker Jack, was a bright picture postcard from Petrie.

"Where's this one from?" said T-Bone as Benjamin held it up.

"Hawaii," said Benjamin, and then came the surprise, for the inscription on the back said that Petrie was arriving in New York the following morning and that Benjamin should meet him, at ten-thirty sharp, at Lindy's.

"Lindy's got good cheesecake," said T-Bone.

"Bring us back a slice," said Slim.

The next day Benjamin took a taxi to Lindy's and seated himself at a booth by the window, and at precisely ten-thirty in walked the inimitable Petrie. He was as odd looking as ever, yet in his dark suit and his horn-rimmed glasses he drew far less attention than before.

"You look good," said Benjamin as Petrie sat down.

"Some things," said Petrie, "improve with age."

They flagged down a waitress and ordered two pieces of cheesecake, plain for Benjamin and blueberry for Petrie, and two cups of coffee with cream. Then Benjamin began an account of the intervening years, from his time in France to his struggle to find a cure for Cassandra Nutt. Petrie ate his cheesecake and listened attentively. When it was his turn to speak, however, he had very little to say.

"I've been working on various projects," he said with a shrug.

"What sort of projects?" said Benjamin.

"Oh, you know," said Petrie. "The same sort I was working on in Germany before the war."

Benjamin reached over and scooped a forkful of blueberries off Petrie's cheesecake. "Can't you say any more about it than that?"

Petrie hesitated. "Well, it's sort of confidential. And besides, I don't think it would interest you very much."

"Try me," said Benjamin.

Petrie took a few more bites of his cheesecake. "Things were really buzzing when I came back from Europe. Der Schwann was working on a dozen different projects, several of them for the government. But the thing he was most excited about was helping the army to build a more sophisticated version of the machine that he and I had built before the war." Petrie leaned closer now and began to speak more rapidly. "This baby was amazing, Benjamin. It had eighteen thousand tubes and could do over five hundred multiplications per second. The problem was that it wasn't able to remember what it had done. It had to be completely rewired for each calculation. So Der Schwann and I set out to create a program to encode the instructions in the machine itself. To create a sort of memory for it."

"Sounds complicated."

"Not nearly as complicated as the mess that ensued when we tried to claim credit for it. By the time we were finished, even Der Schwann and I had stopped speaking to each other."

Benjamin stole another spoonful of blueberries from Petrie's plate. "So you two aren't together?"

Petrie looked down. "If you wanted blueberry cheesecake, Benjamin, why didn't you order it?"

"I didn't know I wanted it until I saw yours," said Benjamin.

Petrie shook his head and took a sip of his coffee. "I've been on my own since then."

"Doing what?" said Benjamin.

"Whatever seemed most interesting. For a while I was

working on the conceptual side of things. Batch processing. Artificial intelligence. Now I'm trying to focus on the nuts and bolts again. That's why I'm in New York. We're very close to being able to shrink everything down to an incredibly small size. If we can do that, there's no end to what these machines could be capable of. But we can't seem to make it work yet—to find materials that can handle that kind of energy—to channel the kind of speed that would be required to make it cook—" He broke off. "I'm losing you, aren't I?"

Benjamin smiled. "I was just thinking about someone I used to know. She would have been fascinated by what you're talking about."

Petrie chewed on the inside of his cheek. "Lost love?" he said.

"I'd rather not talk about it."

Benjamin and Petrie finished their cheesecake. Then Petrie called the waitress over and asked for the check. While she was there, Benjamin ordered two pieces of cheesecake to go.

"So when do I get to see Cassandra Nutt?" said Petrie.

"Whenever you like," said Benjamin. "I'm sure the old man will want to see you as well."

"How nostalgic," said Petrie. "Makes me feel like going out and nipping a few bracelets."

The waitress brought the check. Benjamin and Petrie handed her some money. Then they left the restaurant and headed back home to the mansion.

the One Who Is the Sky

CASSANDRA NUTT went along with the activity at the mansion for as long as she could. Toward the beginning of February, however—just about the time of Petrie's return—she announced that she was finished with the world of the faux nightclub and that she was moving back up to her old glass garden on the roof. The others immediately began doing what they could to make the place ready. Benjamin washed the floors and the walls, then climbed a ladder to scour the glass ceiling piece, inside and out. Mavis pulled up the dead, withered plants, and laid down fresh soil, and put in hydrangeas and foxgloves and roses. T-Bone and Spider removed the divan and brought in a large bed with an adjustable back. And Ed "Caesar" painted a mural on the ceiling in homage to the goddess Nut. It was Mavis who first introduced Cassandra Nutt to the Egyptian deities, and though she was drawn to Nephtys, and taken with Neith, she could not help but feel the strongest kinship with her namesake, Nut, "the One Who Is the Sky." She therefore asked Ed "Caesar" to decorate her ceiling with the goddess and her symbols: the stars, cool water, and cows. Painted on the glass, they gave color and vibrancy to the small rooftop space, while allowing the sky, the goddess Nut's realm, to peer through.

When everything was ready Cassandra Nutt moved in, and the pattern of her final days began to emerge. In the mornings she would sift through the large stack of newspapers that T-Bone left at the foot of her bed. In the afternoons she would stare at the colors above her: the deep, rich indigos, the fiery crimsons, the shimmering, light-brimming golds. And in the evenings she would lie there and listen to Elvis Presley sing. Cassandra Nutt loved Elvis Presley. When he sang "You Ain't Nothin' but a Hound Dog" she would laugh and laugh and tell Jean

Pierre Michel that someone had finally written a song about him.

Cassandra Nutt allowed her friends to visit her rooftop sanctuary. She requested, however, that when they did they refrain from speaking. For she knew that they were afraid to admit that she was dying, and she preferred their silence to hours of hopeful small talk and chatter.

Cassandra Nutt was not afraid. She'd lived her life as fully as she'd known how, and if death was now waiting for her, what more could she offer him than a freshly laundered caftan and a clear conscience?

24/The Theater of the Gods

Thanatos and Eros

S BENJAMIN'S thirty-fourth birthday approached, he experienced a growing sense of anxiety. For shortly after Petrie had returned to his life, he'd informed him that he was in the process of completing "the year of death."

"Christ died at thirty-three," he said. "And Alexander the Great. And Eva Perón, though I wouldn't quite put her in the same category."

Petrie went on to explain that just as one went through the "terrible twos," Benjamin was now finishing up the "thanatotic thirty-threes" and that until he was done with them, death would be peering over his shoulder. Benjamin was not worried about his own mortality, but with Cassandra Nutt's health crumbling and Jean Pierre Michel nearing the century mark, he feared that these last weeks might prove Petrie's theory to be true. Before death could rear its uncompromising head, however, someone far more delightful showed up.

Perhaps the catalyst was Cassandra Nutt's illness, which the newspapers had recently trumpeted across the nation, despite everyone's efforts to keep it under wraps. Perhaps someone had finally let slip what Benjamin had done to save Lazy Joe's. Or perhaps, after five years, the strength of Benjamin's love had created a vibration so strong, it had managed to dissolve her defenses. All Benjamin knew was that one morning toward the middle of March, while he was lying in his bedroom studying the relationship between platelet levels and inconsistent cell activity, he heard the front doorbell ring—then a brief silence—then a sudden commotion—then another silence—and then finally a brisk rapping on his door. And when he went to answer it, there, like a sun-baked, southern-fried Venus, stood Charlene.

"I was wrong," she said. "It's your life. It's your gift. You should do whatever you damn well please with it." She paused for a moment, her dark eyes shining. "And I don't care if Cassandra Nutt dyes her hair blue and paints her face green."

Benjamin later found out that after she'd left Lazy Joe's, Charlene had returned to Georgia, gotten a job in the accounting department of a soft-drink manufacturing company, enrolled at the university, and finally received her degree in nuclear physics. At that moment, however, he did not care a fig where she'd been or what she'd done, as long as he could reach out and hold her.

Charlene's return was like a shot of adrenaline for virtually everyone at the mansion. T-Bone and Mavis hosted a welcome home dinner, for which Spider Perkins prepared crab-stuffed quail and at which Slim Betts played the banjo for the first time in forty-seven years. Benjamin added an oak wardrobe to his bedroom and a silk jacquard bedspread, and Ed "Caesar" painted a shower of lotus blossoms on the wall over the bed. Jean Pierre Michel, who thought that time, in its madness, had delivered the young Cassandra Nutt to the bedside of the old one, took to taking long walks through the park with Charlene at his side. But most interesting of all was the immediate bond that developed between Charlene and Petrie. Their minds seemed to be formed of the same sort of material—a dense, fibrous substance of figures and formulas—and in a matter of days it was as if they'd known each other all their lives.

Had it not been for Petrie's homosexuality, Benjamin might have been envious of this connection. What he did not realize, however, was that Charlene had begun to explore the idea that Petrie's technology might somehow be used to find a cure for Cassandra Nutt. Each morning she would travel downtown to the small research facility where Petrie was ensconced; each evening she would babble in her sleep about "temperature coefficients" and "covalent bonds." And though Benjamin could not follow a word that she was saying, he was delighted to see her so happy.

Cassandra Nutt was thrilled to have Charlene back in her life. Unlike the others, however, she did not seem startled by her return.

"People come and go," she said to Benjamin. "It's a fact of life. You never know who's gonna pop in or out next."

Benjamin had to admit that this seemed to be true. He'd

spent a good deal of his life popping in and out himself. He only hoped that there was a bit more time before Cassandra Nutt popped out for good.

Jean Pierre Michel's drool

AS THE DAYS WENT BY Cassandra Nutt grew weaker, until she could barely lift her head up from her pillow. At this point a kind of hyperawareness set in: she could hear each floorboard as it creaked throughout the mansion, she could feel each particle of bone as it disintegrated inside her. She could no longer listen to Elvis Presley sing, for it was impossible to do so without shimmying a bit, and she was riddled with pain when she moved. The only thing that soothed her was to lie there quietly while Benjamin and Charlene read her passages from *Antony and Cleopatra*. In her voluminous caftan, with the images of an Egyptian tomb upon her walls, she felt like an old Cleopatra herself, regal and ready to cross over.

With Benjamin and Charlene immersed in their separate efforts to find a cure for her illness, a good deal of Cassandra Nutt's care fell to Jean Pierre Michel. Rather than overwhelm him, however, the task seemed to ennoble him—and he could only wonder that it had taken him close to a century to discover the joys of caring for someone other than himself. For Cassandra Nutt, this was the sweetest part of dying. And though she'd never much enjoyed either one of them, she was especially delighted when he brought her toast and coffee. By the time he'd managed to carry them up the four flights of stairs, the coffee was generally cold and the toast like a piece of buttered cardboard. Cassandra Nutt, however, savored each sip and each bite, no matter how awful they tasted.

After fifty-one years of a most unorthodox relationship, there was mostly silence now when these two were together. Jean Pierre Michel would deliver the toast and coffee, or an omelet, or some soup, and then sit in a chair while Cassandra Nutt stared at the ceiling. Every so often, however, a few words would break through, and though they still had bite, they flickered with a new kind of intimacy.

"Why don't you have any wrinkles?"

"Because I'm not as old as you."

"I'm not old. I'm ancient. But you're almost seventy, and your face is as smooth as when I met you."

"Oil glands. Our faces don't wrinkle like you white folks because our glands secrete more oil. Makes a hell of a shine when you're sixteen, but it sure is nice when you're seventy."

In addition to the Shakespeare, Jean Pierre Michel would read from the Egyptian myths—*The Golden Lotus, The Book of Thoth*—and as Cassandra Nutt listened to them, over and over, a plan began to form in her mind. It centered on the cobra, that sinuous symbol of Egyptian royalty, which, according to legend, had been created by Isis from the spittle that dribbled down from the mouth of the elderly god Re. Cassandra Nutt knew that she could not forge a snake out of Jean Pierre Michel's drool, yet she was suddenly reminded of another snake with which the old man might provide her.

"What did you do with all them weapons you collected?"

"They're just where I left them. Locked away in the

first-floor gallery. They're probably a bit dusty, but they're there."

"Remember that dagger the rabbis gave Benjamin? The one with the gold snake?"

"I remember."

"Could you bring it to me?"

"Why?"

"For atmosphere. It'd fit in so nice with the whole Egyptian motif."

Jean Pierre Michel had never known Cassandra Nutt to be interested in weapons, but he agreed to find the dagger and bring it to her the following day. Cassandra Nutt thanked him and then asked if she could trouble him for a cup of jasmine tea. For the pain was coming on now. And on this tiny stage, in this vast, elemental theater of the gods, she preferred to do her wincing—and her moaning, and her groaning—alone.

a divine jump start

BENJAMIN WAS SITTING in a high-back chair, by the window of his room, trying not to feel discouraged. He'd just received a letter from a doctor in Paris, where a lead involving a research laboratory near the Port de Vincennes had proven to be a complete waste of time. Just like the letter he'd received from Leipzig the week before. And the letter, the week before that, from Rio de Janeiro. Almost a year of efforts had yielded absolutely nothing, and he was beginning to fear that it was time for him to throw in the towel.

Benjamin was tired. And he knew that he could not hide

either his fatigue or his disillusionment from Cassandra Nutt. He also knew, however, that she needed him at her side, for lately, when he went to see her, he found Jean Pierre Michel curled up in his chair, asleep. So he rose from his own chair and headed for the bathroom — to splash some cold water on his face, to change his shirt, and to prepare himself to seem optimistic. Before he could get there, however, the door suddenly flew open and Petrie and Charlene stumbled in.

"We have to talk to you —," said Petrie.

"You'd better sit down —," said Charlene.

"We'd all better sit down," said Petrie.

Benjamin laughed. "What's the matter with you two?"

Petrie crossed the room to the chair that Benjamin had been sitting in, turned it around, and pulled it in close toward the bed. Then he gestured to Benjamin to seat himself there, while he climbed onto the desk and Charlene sat on the edge of the bed.

"Charlene's had an epiphany," said Petrie.

"I think I've got the answer," said Charlene.

"The answer," said Petrie, "that might save Cassandra Nutt."

Benjamin shook his head. "I haven't got a clue what you're talking about."

"Then listen," said Petrie, thrusting his little body forward and clasping the edge of the desk. "I told you that we were close to creating a new kind of machine. A machine that could go beyond anything you've ever dreamed of."

"I know it sounds dramatic," said Charlene, "but it's true. You have no idea what this could make possible."

"But where we're stuck," said Petrie, "where we've been

stuck for a long while—is how to get the damned thing to function fast enough to do what it's meant to do."

"Only now we think we've come up with the answer," said Charlene.

They paused for a moment as Charlene turned to Petrie and Petrie turned to Charlene; then they both turned to look at Benjamin.

"It's you," said Petrie.

"You're the answer," said Charlene.

"The key to the entire thing."

Benjamin looked at them as if they'd both gone mad. "What on earth are you talking about?"

Petrie rubbed his eyes rapidly with his forefingers. "I'll try to explain it to you," he said. "Just try to stay with me." He paused for a moment to clear his throat; then his body contracted, and he began speaking rapidly. "The fundamental element of this technology we're working on is speed. The faster a machine can perform a series of calculations, the faster it can function."

"So what might take the human brain several hours to figure out," said Charlene, "our machine can do in a matter of minutes."

"The problem is that since light can only travel one foot per nanosecond—"

"Nanosecond?"

"A billionth of a second—"

"—and since electricity in circuits travels even more slowly, there are physical limitations to how fast a given unit can function."

"So for months now we've been searching for a way to ignite this thing. Kick it into the stratosphere."

"And Charlene suddenly realized that you're it."

Benjamin paused, as if waiting for the punch line. "What do you mean, 'I'm it'?"

"Your gift," said Petrie. "Your ability to come and go."

"While I was in the lab today I started thinking about your powers," said Charlene. "How you can just zip off for a little visit to somewhere halfway around the world. And it suddenly occurred to me how fast you must travel. The speed you must buzz with to get there like that."

"So we figured that if you could use your gift to go zooming around the world—"

"Imagine what would happen if you used it to power our machine."

Benjamin looked at Petrie perched upon his desk, just as he'd been perched there nearly a quarter of a century earlier, lit up by some new form of algebra. He looked at Charlene, her body alive with the fever of discovery, her eyes flashing with a sense of triumph. "I think you've both gone nuts."

"It's certainly possible," said Petrie. "But that doesn't alter the fact that what we're talking about makes sense. Or at least as much sense as something that never made sense in the first place can make." Petrie slipped down off the desk now and squatted before Benjamin's chair. "I'm a mathematician, Benjamin. My entire world is based on what I can prove with a set of equations. On logic, pure and simple. But this gift of yours goes beyond logic. It's . . . well, it's miraculous. And I think that that's precisely what we've been missing."

Charlene reached forward and tapped Petrie on the shoulder. "Tell him about the ceiling."

"Remember when we were kids, Benjamin, and we went to the Sistine Chapel? Remember that picture of

God creating man? Those fingers, just about to touch?"
He paused for a moment to let the image penetrate. "Well,
maybe our machine needs a little zap from above."

"Sort of a divine jump start," said Charlene.

"And the fact is—well, your gift might be the spark."

Benjamin was silent for a moment. Then he rose from
his chair and went to the window. In the park across the
street he saw a group of children laughing and playing,
and he thought of those times, when he was a child himself, that he had laughed and played in that same spot with
Cassandra Nutt. "Suppose it were possible," he said. "Suppose I could make this machine of yours do everything you
say." He paused to watch the children as they fell upon the
ground and covered themselves with grass. "How is that
going to help Cassandra Nutt?"

Petrie rose and moved closer to Benjamin. "Imagine if
you could access information anywhere in the world in a
matter of seconds—"

"Imagine if you could communicate with all these doctors you've been chasing after—imagine if they could communicate with each other—"

"In a matter of seconds. Imagine if you could put an
analysis of Cassandra Nutt's condition into a machine and
it could come up with a cure for her disease."

Benjamin turned around. "You're talking science fiction."

"Have you read science fiction from fifty years ago?"
said Petrie. "Most of it's now science fact."

"Airplanes, television, rocket ships," said Charlene. "A
hundred years ago any of those things would have been
considered pure fantasy."

Petrie slipped his hands into his pockets and chewed on

his lower lip. He stared at Benjamin long and hard; then he took another step toward him and spoke. "For the past two years we've been searching for a material that has the capacity to conduct energy in a particular way."

"They've experimented with a variety of things," said Charlene. "Germanium, galium arsenide —"

"But the one that we're most excited about — the one that we think might ultimately change everything — is silicon."

"Which is made," said Charlene, "out of sand."

Benjamin felt his stomach tighten. "Sand," he said.

"Sand," said Petrie.

Charlene went to Benjamin. "God works in mysterious ways," she said, then she reached into her pocket and pulled out a photograph. "This is a picture of the device we've been working on."

Benjamin held the photograph up to the window. It showed a small piece of circuitry with a variety of dots and a series of interconnected, curving lines, and it looked like nothing so much as a three-dimensional model of his birthmark.

"When we were kids," said Petrie, "you were obsessed with trying to figure out why you'd been given your gift. Well, I think we've finally done it, Benjamin. I think this is it."

Benjamin lowered the photo and looked out through the window at the children in the park. They were standing in a line now, behind a large woman in a bright red dress, and as they began to walk off he was suddenly struck by an overwhelming sense that the events of his life were all part of a larger plan. That nothing was accidental. That it had all, from his birth and his birthmark forward, been neatly and carefully orchestrated.

"The answer," said Charlene, "has been staring you in the face your entire life."

Benjamin turned back to Petrie and Charlene. "Let's say it's true," he said. "Let's say I could give my gift to this machine. Wouldn't it take years before you could use it to help Cassandra Nutt?"

"We don't know what's possible," said Petrie, "until we give it a try."

"Until we take the next step," said Charlene.

Benjamin closed his eyes and tried to think about what it would mean for him to take the next step. He might have to give up his powers completely; he might never again be able to zoom around the world or make luscious music on the saxophone. All for some machine with a few dizzy hopes of changing the world.

Benjamin opened his eyes and looked at his friends. There was such hope in their faces, such clean-washed conviction. And perhaps they were right: perhaps these strange powers had merely been lent to him—perhaps he had been meant to be a caretaker for them, to shepherd them until they could be passed on to the world. "All right," he said, taking an involuntary breath. "I'll give it a try."

Charlene and Petrie almost toppled Benjamin over with the force of their excitement. After so many years, however, of false starts and wrong turns, Benjamin would have to wait until the experiment was over before he'd let himself believe that it might work.

25/The Spirit in the Machine (How He Did It the Last Time)

HE FOLLOWING MORNING Benjamin locked the door to his room and, for the very last time, let his soul take flight on the saxophone. He played "My Funny Valentine" and "Stella by Starlight" and "Wait 'Til You See Her" and "Here's That Rainy Day." And though his bedroom had been soundproofed nearly twenty years earlier, the rich, plaintive music filled the house with an excruciating sadness. When he'd finished playing, he joined Charlene and Petrie in the downstairs library, and then they headed downtown to the small lab where the transfer was to take place. As Benjamin entered the building he was greeted by a series of large metal chambers, which led to a narrow room where a small piece of circuitry was perched on a low table beneath the glare of an overhanging lamp.

"There's our baby," said Petrie.

"We're counting on you to give it your blessing," said Charlene.

Benjamin picked up the circuit and held it in his hand. It seemed so foreign to him, so artificial and impersonal. Could it really be possible that this was the culmination of his powers?

"I need to be alone," he said.

Charlene and Petrie nodded and left the room, and Benjamin began to prepare for his task. It seemed simple enough, yet he was not sure how to start: should he stand or sit, close his eyes or keep them open, hold the brave little circuit in the palm of his hand or let his fingers, in the form of some strange incantation, wave madly over it in the air? After much deliberation, he finally decided to sit cross-legged on the floor with the circuit clasped tightly between both palms at the level of his chest. Then he closed his eyes, and breathed in deeply, and once again concentrated on disengaging that force-within-Benjamin from the hardware of Benjamin himself. As always, he felt the energy begin to build. As always, he felt the light begin to grow. But where he usually tried to focus on either his destination or his music, this time he let his force radiate out through his solar plexus into the small scrap of metal in his hands.

In the flash of light that constituted the transference — the giving up — the giving away — of what had most confused and exalted him — most plagued and pleasured him for the better part of his life — Benjamin felt an emptiness that was as simple and sweet as anything that he had ever known. It was the opposite of the yearning that had followed him most of his life. It was an absence that contained presence, a void that allowed a fresh breeze to blow through, a hole that did not require filling. And that was when he saw that, for all the excitement that his gift had brought him, all the intrigue and glory, the deepest part of its pleasure had been that space he entered in the moment before the magic took place. And that only by giving away that magic—which for so many years he had taken to be himself—would he be able to come closer to the truth of who he really was.

For a moment Benjamin felt a burning in his chest, the conflict of a simultaneous pushing and pulling. Then something snapped—there was an explosion of light—and he knew that it was over. When he opened his hands, the circuit looked just as it had looked before: the bed of silicon, the bits of metal, the squiggly wires that mocked the scarlet pattern on his face. Benjamin felt certain, however, that the transfer had succeeded—and that in one pulsating moment the future had been significantly altered.

26/The Odds Is Gone

"PROP UP MY PILLOWS," said Cassandra Nutt, "and read it to me again."

"You're too weak," said Charlene.

"It tires you out," said Benjamin.

"Oh no," said Cassandra Nutt. "It gives me pleasure. It gives me strength."

In the three weeks since Benjamin had divested himself of his powers, Cassandra Nutt's condition had taken an abrupt turn for the worse. As a result the glass garden was now outfitted with an advanced temperature control system, an air filtering mechanism, and a complex series of intravenous devices designed to relieve her pain. That pain could no longer be concealed beneath a smile, yet Cassandra Nutt refused to be taken into the hospital. If these were her last days, she wanted to spend them at home—content to ease her dolor with a few drops of morphine and the sweet, soothing words of Mr. Shakespeare.

Charlene looked at Benjamin. "All right," she said. "But just the last passage."

Benjamin lifted the large, leather-bound volume from his lap. "O! wither'd is the garland of the war," he read.

> *The soldier's pole is fall'n; young boys and girls*
> *Are level now with men; the odds is gone,*
> *And there is nothing left remarkable*
> *Beneath the visiting moon.*

Jean Pierre Michel shook his head. "I don't understand why you're so obsessed with this passage," he said. "I can accept the fact that, in the delirium of all these drugs you've been taking, you've begun to envision yourself as the queen of the Nile. I can even accept the fact that—despite our considerable efforts—you seem to be dying." Jean Pierre Michel began to sputter. "But I cannot for the life of me fathom why you wish to keep hearing this passage! It's for the death of Antony! Not the death of Cleopatra!"

"You'd better calm down," said Charlene, "or you're gonna drop before she does."

Cassandra Nutt smiled. "I just like the sound of it," she said. " 'The odds is gone.' I just like the way that sounds."

Within days of the experiment, Petrie had confirmed that the transfer of Benjamin's powers had been a success. His machine could now function at nearly ten thousand times its previous speed, and there were signs that with a bit of tinkering, it would eventually be able to work even faster than that. A world of possibilities suddenly exploded into being, and there was every sign that the exploration of these would prove to be dazzling. At the same time, however, Cassandra Nutt had begun to fade, and it was clear to Benjamin that, just as he had feared, there would not be enough time for the new technology to save her.

"I don't think I can read it again," said Benjamin. "The words are beginning to run together."

"You need to get some rest," said Charlene. "We all need to get some rest."

Cassandra Nutt closed her eyes. "Pretty soon," she said, "I'll be restin' full-time." She breathed in deeply to ease a sudden stab of pain. "Charlene, honey, why don't you take Monsieur C. for a little stroll. I'd like to spend a bit o' time alone with Benjamin."

Charlene went to Jean Pierre Michel to help him from his chair. "Let's go, handsome," she said. "Gotta get our exercise."

Jean Pierre Michel struggled to a standing position and then turned to Cassandra Nutt. "No more dying war heroes," he said. "Read some Mark Twain. Or a little Thurber."

Charlene took the old man's arm and led him from the garden. Benjamin went and sat on the edge of the bed.

"It's worse, isn't it?" he said.

"Oh, honey," said Cassandra Nutt, "I don't think it can get much worse than this."

"What can I do to help you?"

"Just stay with me for a minute. Just sit here with me."

Benjamin looked down at Cassandra Nutt's hands, which lay, like a pair of dark, delicate flowers, on the folds of the crisp white bedsheets. "I thought I could save you," he whispered.

"Benjamin honey," she said, "you saved me a million times. Every time I saw that face of yours, all speckled with sunlight."

Benjamin raised his eyes up to hers. "I gave away my powers," he said. "To a machine that Petrie and Charlene have been working on. They say it can change the world."

Cassandra Nutt smiled. "The world'll keep changin' no matter what you come up with." Another pain flashed through her. "But maybe your machine will make a difference."

Benjamin reached over and brushed a few beads of sweat off Cassandra Nutt's forehead. "Are your pillows all right?"

"You can plump 'em again. You never can have your pillows plumped up too often."

Benjamin helped Cassandra Nutt lean forward while he freshened up her pillows. Then she lay back again and stared up at the pictures on her ceiling.

"I never knew cows could be so reassurin'," she said. "I didn't like 'em at first, but they've kinda grown on me."

Benjamin looked up at the childlike images painted over his head. He knew that there were things he wished to talk about with Cassandra Nutt, things besides cows, but he could not seem to remember what they were. So he just sat there quietly, his head tilted toward the ceiling, trying his best not to cry.

"So you gave up your powers," said Cassandra Nutt.

"The whole shebang," said Benjamin.

"Then I guess," she said, "you must not need 'em anymore." She closed her eyes. "Must not need me, neither, 'cause I sure as hell seem to be checkin' out." She grimaced again as another jolt of pain passed through her. "Maybe we'd better get on with it. Before this turns into one of them Lana Turner movies."

"Get on with what?"

Cassandra Nutt ran her tongue across her lips. Then she reached her hand out to the small night table beside her bed, opened the drawer, and pulled out the dagger with the glittering snake wrapped round the handle. "I think it's time," she said, "to apply the asp."

Benjamin felt the blood drain from his face. "You can't be serious!"

"Benjamin honey, I've done my best to hold on. But it's too late in the day to start thinkin' o' life as a chore. I need you to help me with this. I need you to stand by me."

"But it's too violent," said Benjamin.

Cassandra Nutt looked up at the pictures on the ceiling. "Seems poetic to me. All them weapons you collected for Monsieur C.—all them years ago—" She turned back to Benjamin. "I thought we might finally put one of 'em to good use."

Benjamin shook his head. "I can't let you do it."

Cassandra Nutt lay there quietly for a moment. "Then how 'bout a compromise," she said. "How 'bout givin' me a bit o' that love juice over there?"

She raised her hand and pointed to the small white cabinet where the morphine was stored. Benjamin wanted to protest against this solution as well, but when he saw the look of desperation in her eyes he could not continue.

"All right," he said in a soft, steady voice. "All right."

He went to the cabinet and took down one of the squat glass bottles. Then he carried it to the bed and handed it to Cassandra Nutt.

"Guess we'll have to settle for the metaphor," she said, then she raised the dagger up high above her head and brought it down swiftly so that it pierced the top of the bottle. "Benjamin honey," she whispered. "I do believe I got me some immortal longings."

She let the dagger drop to the bed as she handed the bottle of sweet venom to Benjamin, who proceeded to draw its contents up into a syringe and inject them into the solution that was flowing like a steadfast tributary into her veins. When he was finished, he placed the syringe and the empty bottle in the drawer of the night table. Then he picked up the dagger and returned to the edge of the bed.

"Better than a sloe gin fizz," murmured Cassandra Nutt.

Benjamin sat there as her eyes slowly closed and her breathing became even. Then he watched in silence as the physic took effect and the sweet goddess Nut journeyed back to her starry realm.

27/Time Flies

"ROP UP MY PILLOWS," said Jean Pierre Michel, "and raise the damned volume."

"If you make it any louder," said Charlene, "you're gonna bust an eardrum."

"Besides," said Petrie, "there's nothing to hear apart from this endless speculating. I don't think they'll ever come out."

Benjamin moved closer to Jean Pierre Michel and raised his frail body up as Charlene whacked the pillows behind him. Then he lowered him back down so that he had an unobstructed view of the television.

"It may not happen for hours," said Benjamin. "Why don't you try and sleep for a little while and we'll wake you when it comes."

"When you reach my age," said Jean Pierre Michel, "sleep is a risky business. I'm not taking any chances."

Despite the swarm of timepieces that now filled the mansion, time, that old conjurer, was still up to his old tricks—for thirteen long years had passed since Cassandra Nutt's death and Jean Pierre Michel was still alive. He was no longer able to leave his bed, but he could still talk, he could still see, and he could still, with the same great vigor as ever, make demands. At the overripe age of one hundred and eleven there was little left for him to yearn for. When he yearned for something, however, he did so with the intensity of a five-year-old child.

"Bring me a cup of tea," he said. "That'll keep me up for days."

"One cup of tea," said Benjamin, "coming right up."

"Bring me a glass of milk, Daddy!"

"Me too! Me too!"

"Bring me a Heineken," said Petrie.

A great deal had happened in the thirteen years that had gone by. Benjamin had opened a restaurant called Cassandra's Place next door to Lazy Joe's, and as the turbulence of the sixties had brought chaos to Harlem he'd become a strong white voice in the protests that characterized the decade. Charlene had focused her energy on the fight for equal rights and had lobbied in Washington against the atmospheric testing of nuclear weapons. Petrie had continued his experiments with technology, his latest enthusiasm being for something called a "pocket calculator," which he swore would soon make everyone a veritable math whiz. Most significant of all, however, was that Benjamin and Charlene had finally married and had children: a girl named Cassie and a boy called, for short, JPM. Despite the rude taunts of some of their classmates, they were neither striped nor polka-dotted, but a gorgeous mocha color with hazel eyes and hair like caramel cotton candy. And though their parents adored them, no one loved them more than Jean Pierre Michel. As long as he could watch television with them curled up at his feet—dressed in the white robes that he'd put on for his hundredth birthday and had never taken off—he seemed content to go on living forever.

"Nobody wants any food?"

"Oreos!" cried Cassie.

"Chips!" cried JPM.

"Sara Lee fresh banana cake," said Jean Pierre Michel, "with butter cream frosting."

"Nothing for you, Charlie?"

"Some Grand Marnier," said Charlene, "and something crunchy."

Benjamin toted up the various requests and then headed down to the kitchen to fill them. He was enjoying the feeling of excitement in the air—the anticipation, the suspense—and he could not help feeling that his gift was at least partly responsible. A great many things had been made possible over the past thirteen years as a result of the technology that Benjamin had sparked into being: communication satellites, X-ray crystallography, heart transplants, fiber-optic networks, the synthesization of DNA. Perhaps most remarkable, however, was how this superfast device had made possible man's journey into space. Each year some fantastic new feat had been attempted, and each time Benjamin's gift had helped make that feat a success. Now, as the decade was hurtling to a close, his powers were in charge of the subtle calculations that were about to put a man on the moon.

Benjamin placed a slice of banana cake on a dessert plate and lowered the flame beneath the kettle. It was forty years now since he'd transferred himself to the back of the

Hispano-Suiza, and he'd spent a good deal of that time trying to figure out Jean Pierre Michel. He'd wanted so
much from him for such a long, long time—his attention,
his affection, the loving concern of a father. Over the past
few years, however, as the old man began to slip into his
second century, Benjamin had begun to think less of what
he could get from him than what he could give him. A dish
of ice cream. A digital watch. And that one thing he'd
yearned for, but had never been able to possess—the
moon.

Benjamin had learned a lot about the moon over the
years: that it orbits at a distance of over a quarter of a million miles from the earth, that it has no atmosphere or any
global magnetic field, that the thickness of its crust is
about equal to the distance between Trenton and Newark.
He learned that it was called Luna by the Romans and
Artemis by the Greeks and something different in each cy-
cle by the American Indians, such as Moon of the Falling
Leaves or Moon of the Shedding Ponies or Moon When
the Cherries Turn Black. It was only now, however, on a
warm summer's night as the entire world sat watching,
that Benjamin was finally able to give that elusive, incon-
stant object to Jean Pierre Michel.

"You'd better hurry. They're about to do it."

The voice jolted Benjamin back to the room, and he
turned to find Petrie leaning against the frame of the doorway. For a split second an awareness of both the wonder
and the absurdity of what their efforts had wrought went
ricocheting between them. Then Benjamin instructed his
friend to grab the smaller of the two trays that sat on the
counter, while he grabbed the other, and they made their

way back through the mansion to Jean Pierre Michel's suite.

When they entered the bedroom Jean Pierre Michel, Charlene, Cassie, and JPM were all glued to the grainy image on the television screen. At first Benjamin was unable to interpret what it was, but then his eyes adjusted and he could discern the contours of a ghostly leg as it stepped down upon a barren wasteland.

"That's one small step for man," came a voice, "one giant leap for mankind."

There was a quivering in the air as Jean Pierre Michel leaned forward and squinted at the screen. "Armstrong," he said. "Doesn't sound very Jewish to me."

"You don't see any black boys floatin' around up there, either," said Charlene, "now, do you?"

Benjamin lowered his tray to the bed and studied the stark, chiaroscuro image being beamed, via satellite, from the moon. Yet rather than make him feel that the heavens were attainable, it only increased his sense of their vastness. He knew that the future held more dazzling advances, more protean leaps into the fathomless unknown, yet he wondered where it was destined to end. Petrie insisted that all sorts of amazements were just around the corner—that by the end of the century the means to save a Cassandra Nutt would have become a reality, that the entire world would be wired. Benjamin did not know if any of this was true, but when he looked at what had been accomplished in only thirteen years, it seemed as if anything were possible.

"Let's open the champagne," said Charlene.

"I want champagne, Mama!" cried JPM.

"Me too, Mama!" cried Cassie.

Benjamin fiddled with the bottle of champagne, and there was a loud *pop!* as the cork flew off and the contents foamed up over the neck.

"To progress!" said Petrie.

"To curiosity!" said Charlene.

"To time," said Jean Pierre Michel, "the cagey old bastard!"

As Benjamin raised his glass to join in the toast, his attention was drawn to the small gold alarm clock that sat, amid a cluster of papers and pills, on the night table beside Jean Pierre Michel's bed. He'd seen it before perhaps a thousand times, yet he'd never been so aware of the sound of its ticking, which suddenly reminded him of Cassandra Nutt's dream of him exploding. Charlene felt that the dream had been fulfilled by the explosion of technological innovations that had followed Benjamin's transfer of his powers. Petrie was not so sure, yet he was soothed by "the Cinderella factor," which had translated itself into the periodic breakdown of nearly everything powered by Benjamin's gift and which he took to be a built-in safeguard against any real danger. Benjamin, however, was convinced that this very quality—combined with the human tendency to use good for ill—only guaranteed that the future was ticking.

"What about you, Benjamin?" said Petrie.

"You have to make a toast, too, Daddy," said Cassie.

Benjamin turned back to the upraised glasses and suddenly saw how the light that passed through them cast splashes of color across an outstretched arm, a tousled head, an eager, upturned face. "To getting this far," he said. "To us."

The glasses chimed and everyone drank and then they

all turned back to the television. A second man had now descended from the spacecraft and was bounding, with the first, across the desolate terrain.

"It looks like pumice," said Jean Pierre Michel. "The damned thing looks exactly like pumice."

Jean Pierre Michel's comment did not mean much to the others, but Benjamin turned to him just in time to see a faint smile trace over his lips and his eyes slowly close. Then, with a wheeze and the slightest of shudders, he gently gave up the ghost. Benjamin could almost see it fly out through the window and up into the sky to frolic with the astronauts on the moon. He could feel his heart fly into his throat, and he thought to himself that, had he still had his gift, he would have gone to join him—but then he suddenly understood that he was not meant to follow, that he had other things to do, that it was time for him to stand on his own.

Benjamin turned to look at Charlene, at Petrie, at Cassie, at JPM. They were each fixed firmly on the television screen, entranced by the miracle that was unfolding before them. Benjamin wanted to tell them that they had just missed a different sort of miracle, but he decided to let it wait. The world, he suddenly realized, was full of miracles. Full of comings and goings, as Cassandra Nutt had said.

You just had to watch for them.

You just had to open your eyes—and breathe in deeply—and concentrate.